SCIENTIFIC
SPRAGUE

SCIENTIFIC SPRAGUE

FRANCIS LYNDE

wildsidepress.com

WILDSIDE PRESS

Originally published in 1912.
Published by Wildside Press LLC.
wildsidepress.com

CHAPTER 1

THE WIRE-DEVIL

Connolly, off-trick division despatcher, doubling on the early night trick for Jenner, whose baby was sick, snapped his key-switch at the close of a rapid fire of orders sent to straighten out a freight-train tangle on the Magdalene district, sat back in his chair, and reached for his corn-cob pipe with a fat man's sigh of relief.

Over in the corner of the bare, dingy office, Bolton, night man on the car-record wire, was rattling away at his type-writer; and on the wall opposite the despatcher's table the electrically timed standard clock was ticking off the minutes between eight-fifty-five and nine. While Connolly was striking a match to light his pipe, Bolton tore the type-written sheet out of his machine and twisted himself in his chair to ask a question.

"What's the good word from the Apache Limited?" he inquired, his evil little eyes blinking indecently. And then, before Connolly could reply: "It's up to me to 'buy' for the boys tonight. My little girl-doll is comin' on the Apache. Whadda you know about that: chasin' me all the way from little old New York."

The fat despatcher knew precisely where the Limited was, but he glanced at his train-sheet from sheer force of habit.

"On time at Angels, double-heading with the Nine-thirteen, and the Six-five," he said. Then he shifted over to the car-record man's cause for jubilation. "I didn't know you were a married man, Bolton. If I ever get out of the woods and make good on the job, I'm going to do it myself."

Bolton's mouth widened like a split in a parchment mask, and his laugh was a dry cackle.

"Married—that's a bully good joke. I'll have to tell it to the little doll-girl, when she comes."

Connolly was Irish chiefly by virtue of his name. He entirely missed the pointing of the car-record man's remark, but the apparent gibe touched his vanity and his round and naturally ruddy face grew a shade darker.

"Meaning that no girl with half a chance at other fellows would look twice at a fat slouch like me? That's where you're off your trolley. There is one, Barry, and she's pretty enough to make a wooden-Indian cigar-sign get down from his block and chase her up the street for another look-in. But I've got to make good and pull down a wad, first."

The car-record man's laugh this time was an unchaste sneer.

"Aw, chuck it!" he derided. "Whadda you want to tie yourself up for when there's plenty of—"

"Say, that'll do," Connolly broke in, with a frown of cleanly disgust, taking Bolton's meaning at last. Then he changed the subject abruptly. "Mr. Maxwell's got him a new chum: seen him?"

Bolton nodded.

"Sure, I have; couldn't help seein' him if you happened to look his way. What is he?—champion All-America heavy-weight?"

The despatcher shook his head. "College professor, somebody said; one of Mr. Maxwell's classmates. Specializes in something or other; I didn't hear what."

Again the tag-wire operator's laugh crackled like a snapping of dry twigs. He had risen from his chair and was half-sitting, half-leaning, upon his table-desk, his hands resting palms down, with the fingers curled under the table edge—his characteristic loafing attitude.

"He might specialize in any old thing," he jeered, with a small man's bickering hostility for a big one in his tone. "All he's got to do is to reach out and take it; nobody but a fellow in the Joe Gans class'd have the nerve to tell him not to. I saw him sittin' on the Topaz porch with the super as I came over. He's so big it made me sick at my stomach to look at him."

Connolly's pipe had gone out, burned out, and he was feeling in his pockets for the tobacco sack. While he was doing it the corridor door opened and Calmaine, the superintendent's chief clerk, came in, let himself briskly through the gate in the counter railing, and leaned over Connolly's shoulder to glance at the train-sheet.

"Everything moving along all right, Dan?" he asked.

"Is now," said the despatcher, still feeling absently for the missing tobacco sack. "Twenty-one and Twenty-eight got balled up on their orders over on the other side of the range, but I guess I've got 'em straightened out, after so long a time…. Now what the dickens did I do with that tobacco of mine, I wonder?"

"Have a cigar," said the chief clerk, laying one on the glass-topped wire-table. Calmaine, eastern trunk-line bred, had been inclined to cockiness when he came West, but a year with Maxwell, whose standing was that of the Short Line's best-beloved tyrant, had taken a good deal of it out of him.

"Thanks," returned Connolly, with a fat man's grin, "not for me when I'm despatching trains. The corn-cob goes with the job. Sit in here on the wire for a minute while I go up to the bunk-room and look in my other coat."

Calmaine took the vacated chair and ran his eye along the latest additions to the many columns of figures on the train-sheet. Bolton in his far corner was still loafing, though his night's work of taking and typing the wire car reports from the various stations on the double division was scarcely begun. "You think you're a little tin god on wheels, don't you?" he muttered under his breath, blinking and scowling across at the well-groomed young man sitting in Connolly's chair. "You can let down with Dan Connolly all right, but when it comes to throwin' a bone to the other new dog, you ain't it. One o' these times I'm goin' to jump up and bite you."

The object of this splenetic outburst was still bending over the train-sheet, abstractedly unconscious of Bolton's presence. From the conductors' room beyond the wire office three or four trainmen drifted in to look over the bulletin-board notices; and still Connolly did not return.

Suddenly the sounder in front of the substitute set up a furious chatter, clicking out a monotonous repetition of the "G.S." call, breaking at intervals with the signature "Ag," the code letters for Angels, the desert-edge town from which the Apache Limited had been last reported. Calmaine flicked his key-switch and cut in quickly with the answering signal. Then, reaching for pad and pen, he wrote out the message that came boiling over the wire.

> G.S.
>
> Apache Limited in ditch at Lobo Cut four miles west. Both engines crumpled up. Two enginemen, one route agent, under wreck. Everything off but rear Pullman. Train on fire and lot of passengers pinned down. Hurry help quick.
>
> Ag.

Calmaine was an alert young man, well abreast of his job and altogether capable. But before he could yelp twice Connolly had come in, and it was the fat despatcher who gave the alarm.

"My Lord, Bolton—see here!" he shouted, pushing Calmaine aside as an incumbrance. And then, when the car-record man came over to stare vacantly at the fateful message: "Get a move! Send somebody after Mr. Maxwell, quick! Then get busy on that yard wire and turn out the wrecking crew. Get Dawson on the 'phone and tell him I'll have a clear track for him by the time his wreck-wagons are ready! Jump at it, man! Your wife isn't the only one that's needing help! *Wake up!*"

Over on the sidewalk loggia porch of the Hotel Topaz fronting the electric-lighted railroad plaza, Maxwell, the division superintendent, was sitting out the evening with a broad-shouldered, solidly built young man whose big frame, clear gray eyes, and fighting jaw were the outward presentments of a foot-ball "back" rather than those of the traditional college professor.

"I don't mind piping myself off to you, Dick, though the full size of my job isn't generally known," the athletic-looking stop-over guest was saying. "You got the first part of it right; I'm down on the Department of Agriculture pay-rolls as a chemistry sharp. But outside of that I've half a dozen little hobbies which they let me ride now and then. You'll guess what one of them is when I tell you that I was the man who fried out the evidence in the post-office cases last winter."

"What!" exclaimed Maxwell. "But your name didn't appear."

The big man with the smooth-shaven, boyish face smiled contentedly.

"My name never appears. That is the high card in the game. So far as that goes, I never mess or meddle in the police details. My part of the job is always and only the theoretical stunt. They come to me and I tell 'em what to do. And just about half the time they haven't the least idea why they are doing it."

"Say, Calvin; that interests me a lot more than you know," was the young superintendent's eager comment. "I wish you didn't have to go on to the coast tomorrow morning. We've developed an original little Chinese puzzle of our own here in the Timanyoni that is pretty nearly driving the last one of us wild-eyed. If you could stop over—"

The interruption came in the shape of a one-armed man with a lantern, sprinting like a base-runner across from the railroad building to the hotel. It was the night watchman summoned by the despatcher, and ten seconds later he had delivered his message.

"The Lord have mercy!" gasped the superintendent, bounding out of his chair, "the Limited?—in the ditch and on fire, you say? For Heaven's sake, where?"

"'Tis at Lobo Cut; 'tis Angels reporting it, sorr, so Misther Connolly did be saying. He's clearing f'r the wreck-train now, and he axed would you be coming over."

"Tell him I'll be over in a minute or two: as soon as I've called up the hospital and turned out the doctors."

"Yis, sorr; but Misther Bolton's doing that same now. They do be saying his wife's on the train, and he's *that* near crazy."

Maxwell turned to his guest.

"You see how it is with us poor railroad devils, Calvin. It's a bad case of 'have to,' and I know you'll excuse me. Just the same, it's an infernal outrage—when we haven't been able to get together for a dog's age."

The chemistry sharp, as he had called himself, was standing up and stretching his arms over his head like a pole-vaulter hardening his muscles for the jump.

"I'll trot over to your shop with you, Dick, if you don't object," he said good-naturedly. "I want to see what happens when you get a hurry call like this."

In the despatcher's office Connolly was hammering at his key like a madman, with the sweat running down his full-moon face and the hand which was not in use shaking as if the left half of him had been ague-smitten. Trainmen were coming and going, and the alarm whistle at the shops was bellowing the wreck call at ten-second intervals. Everybody made way for Maxwell when he pushed through the counter gate with his big guest at his heels.

"Any more news, Dan?"

The despatcher flicked his closing switch, and immediately the ague spread to the hand which was no longer steadied on the key.

"Nothing. I've been clearing, and everything is getting out of the way. I've tried twice to get Angels, but I can't raise anybody. I guess Garner, the operator, has set his signals at block and gone to gather up what help he can find."

Just then more men came crowding in from the corridor, and one of them, a small man with hot eyes and a harsh voice, barked at Connolly.

"Orders for the wreck-wagons, Dan; we're ready to go."

Out of the throng behind the counter barrier Bolton, yellow-faced and ghastly, fought his way to the gate and besought the superintendent.

"Let me go, too, Mr. Maxwell!" he panted. "My God! I've got to go!"

"Of course, you shall go, Barry," said the superintendent with quick kindliness, remembering what the watchman had said about Bolton's wife being on the ditched train. "Dan, send the caller after Catherton and let him take Bolton's wire." Then he turned to his guest, who had been standing aside and looking on with a level-eyed gaze that lost no detail. "It's hello and good-bye for us, Sprague, old man; that is, unless you'd care to go along?"

The guest decided instantly. "I was just about to ask you if you couldn't count me in," he returned; and together they followed the rough-tongued little conductor in a hurried dash for the platform.

The wrecking-train had been backed down to the station spur to take on the hospital car, and it was standing ready for the eastward flight; two flat-cars loaded with blocking and tackle, a desert tank-car filled with water, two work-train boxes crowded to the doors with men, and, next to the engine, which was one of the big "Pacific types" used on the fast mail runs, a heavy steam crane powerful enough to lift a locomotive and swing it clear at a single hitch.

"Who's pulling us, Blacklock?" Maxwell asked, overtaking the little man with the hot eyes.

"Young Cargill."

Maxwell turned to Sprague.

"I'm going on the engine, Calvin. There's room for you if you care to try it. If you don't, I'll turn you over to Dawson, our master mechanic, and he'll make you at home in the doctors' car."

"I guess I'm in for all of it," was the even-toned reply, and they ran forward to climb to the cab of the big mail flyer.

"My friend, Mr. Sprague, Cargill," snapped Maxwell, introducing the stranger to the handsome young fellow in overalls and jumper perched upon the high right-hand seat, and Cargill pulled off his glove to shake hands.

"You'll find the Ten-sixteen a pretty hard rider," he began; but Maxwell cut him short.

"You have a clear track, and Blacklock's got your orders. Open her up and see what you can do. It's a plain case of 'get there' tonight, Billy. The minutes may mean just so many lives saved or lost."

"'*Right!*'" yelled the fireman, leaning from the gangway to get Black-lock's signal; and at the word the engineer's hand shot to the lever, the great engine shook itself free, and the rescue race was begun.

For the first few miles of the race the track was measurably straight. Maxwell stood on the raised step at Sprague's elbow, steadying himself with a grip on the sill of the opened side window. When he saw that the ex-fullback was making hard work of it he shouted in the big man's ear.

"Loosen up a bit and take the roll with her," he advised, and Sprague nodded and tried it.

"That's much better," he called back. "What are we making now?"

"Forty, or a little more. She's good for sixty, and so is Cargill, but the tangents are too short to let us hit the limit."

"And the wreck—how far away is it?"

"An hour and forty-five minutes from Brewster, on a passenger sched-ule. We'll better that by ten or fifteen minutes, though."

Evidently young Cargill meant to better it if he could. At Tabor Mine, ten miles out, the big engine's exhaust had become a continuous roaring blast, and the tiny station at the mine siding flashed through the beam of the electric headlight like some living thing in full flight to the rear. At Kensett, where the line skirts the reservoir lake of the Timanyoni High Line Irriga-tion Company, they passed a long freight on the siding; the caboose was only a few yards inside of the clear post, and Sprague winced involuntarily when the engine cab shot past the freight's rear end with what seemed only an inch or two to spare.

Corona was the next night telegraph station, and here the wrecking special met the two following sections of the freight drawn out upon the sidings to right and left. Cargill's grip closed upon the throttle when the switch and station lights swept into view; but the station semaphore was wigwagging the "clear" signal, and once more the big man on the fireman's box sat tight while the flying special roared through the narrow main line alley left by the two side-tracked freights.

Maxwell was holding his watch in his hand when the special cleared the switches at Corona and the great beam of the headlight began to flick to right and left in the dodging race among the foot-hills.

"Well make Timanyoni, at the mouth of the canyon, in ten minutes' better time than our fast mail makes it," he said to Sprague; and the Government man nodded grimly.

"It's all right, Dick," he shouted back. "Just the same, I'd like to know how a man ever acquires the nerve to send a train around the hill corners this way when he hasn't the slightest notion of what may be waiting for him five hundred yards in the future."

Apparently the stalwart young fellow on the opposite side of the cab owned the necessary nerve. Easing the huge flyer skilfully around the sharpest of the turnings, he drove it to the limit on the tangents in spurts that seemed to promise certain destruction at the next crooking of the track. But the wheels of the train were still shrilling safely on the steel when the headlight beam, playing steadily for the moment, brought the lonely station at the canyon's mouth into its field.

Cargill was whistling peremptorily for the signal before the short train had fully straightened itself on the tangent below the station. But for some reason the red light on the station semaphore remained inert. Instantly the sweating fireman jerked his fire-door open, and the four pairs of eyes in the flyer's cab were all fixed upon the motionless red dot over the track when Cargill sounded his second call.

While the whistle echoes were still yelling in the surrounding hills the climax came. Out of the station door darted a man with a red lantern. Cargill pounced upon the throttle, and in the same second the brakes went into the emergency notch with a jerk that flung the superintendent and the fireman against the boiler-head and slammed the guest unceremoniously into the cab corner.

At the shriek of the brakes, the man with the red lantern turned and ran in the opposite direction, waving his signal light frantically; and the wrecking special was still only shrilling and skidding to its stop when a long passenger-train drawn by two engines slid smoothly out of the canyon portal and came grinding down the grade with fire spurting from every suddenly clipped wheel-rim.

Thanks to the man with the red lantern, there were half a dozen car-lengths to spare between the two trains when the double stop was made. But Maxwell was swearing hotly when, with Sprague for a close second, he dropped from the step of the panting 1016 and ran to meet the conductor of the passenger-train in the middle of the scant safety distance. Like the superintendent, the conductor was also boiling over with profanity, but he swallowed the cursing portion of his wrath hastily when he recognized the "big boss."

"Oh, it's you, is it, Mr. Maxwell?" he blurted out. "By hen! I was getting ready to cuss somebody out, red-hot! What's the trouble?"

"There doesn't seem to be any," snapped Maxwell shortly. "Is this the Limited?"

"Sure it is," replied the conductor. "Hadn't it ought to be?"

"And you haven't been in the ditch?"

The big red-faced train captain grinned.

"Not that anybody's heard of. Is that what's the matter? Was you coming to pick us up?"

Maxwell's answer was a barked-out string of orders.

"Let these wreck-wagons in on the siding. Find Blacklock and tell him to get orders to follow you to Brewster as second section. Pull out as quick as you can. You're ten minutes off time, right now!"

In the drawing-room of the rear sleeper of the limited, Maxwell closed the door on his guest and himself, passed his cigar-case, lighted a fresh cigar in his own behalf, and said nothing until after the short shifting stunt had been worked out and the Apache Limited was once more racing on its way westward. Then he opened up.

"You've got it now, Calvin; the thing that has been smashing more nerves for us than we can afford to lose. Of course, you understand what has happened. That blood-curdling report of an accident was a fake wire; God only knows where it came from, or who sent it."

"And there have been others?" queried Sprague.

"A dozen of them, first and last. It began about a month ago. Sometimes it's merely foolish; at other times it's like this—a thing to bring your heart into your mouth."

"And you mean to say you haven't been able to run it down?"

"Run it down? If there is anything we haven't done it's some little item that has been merely overlooked. We've had about all of the company detectives here, first and last, and the best of them have had to give it up. There is nothing to work on; absolutely nothing. This wire tonight purported to come from Angels; as a matter of fact, it may have come from anywhere east of Brewster and this side of Copah. When we come to examine the Angels operator, we'll probably find that he doesn't know a thing about it—not a thing in the wide world."

"Yet it was a real wire?"

"Calmaine, my own chief clerk, took it from the sounder and wrote it down. It seems that Connolly, the night despatcher, had gone out for a moment and Calmaine was holding down the wires for him. I saw the message before we left. The call and signature were all right, and the exact time, nine-thirteen, was given."

"Wire-tappers?" suggested the listener, who had grown shrewdly sympathetic.

"That is what we've all thought. But to tap a wire, you have to cut in on it somewhere. Of course, it could be done in any one of a thousand isolated places, but hardly without leaving some trace. Wickert, our wire-chief, has been over the lines east and west with a magnifying-glass, you might say."

For the measuring of a few other miles of the westward flight of the train the big man in the opposite seat said nothing. Then he began again.

"Have you tried to figure out a motive, Dick?"

"That is precisely what is driving every one of us stark, staring mad, Calvin," was the sober confession. "There isn't any motive—there can't be!"

"No trouble with the labor unions?"

"Not a bit in the world. More than that, the men have spent good money of their own trying to help us find out—as a measure of self-protection. You can see what they're afraid of; what we are all afraid of. Everybody is losing nerve, and if the scare keeps up, we'll have real trouble—plenty of it."

"And you say the source of the thing can't be localized?"

"No. We have a double division, with Brewster as the common headquarters. Sometimes the yelp comes from the east, and sometimes from the west."

Again the big-bodied chemistry expert sank back in his seat and fell into the thoughtful trance. When he came out of it, it was to say:

"You've probably settled it for yourself that it isn't a plant for a train robbery—the kind of robbery which would be made easier by a wreck."

Maxwell shook his head.

"A pile of cross-ties would be much simpler."

"Doubtless. We'll cancel that and come to the next hypothesis. Could it be the work of some crazy telegraph operator?"

"We've threshed out the crazy guess. It doesn't prove up. A madman would slip up now and then—trip himself. I have a file of the fake messages. They were not sent by a lunatic."

"Call it another cancellation," said the guest. "You are convinced that some sane person is doing it. Very good. What is the object? You say you can't find out; which merely means that you've been attacking it from the wrong angle. Or, rather, you've let the professional detectives give you their angle. What you need is a bit of first-class amateur work."

The superintendent laughed mirthlessly. "If I could only find the amateur I'd hire him, Calvin—if it took a year's salary. I don't know what the wire-devil's object is, but I can catalogue the results. These periodical scares are demoralizing the entire Short Line. The service is on the ragged edge of a chaotic blow-up. Half the men in the train crews are running on their bare nerves, and the operators who have to handle train-orders are not much better."

"Yes," said the guest quietly. "I've been noticing. I saw only one man in your office who wasn't scared stiff; and the conductor of this train we're riding on had a pretty bad attack of the tremolos when you told him what the wrecking-train was out for."

"Who, Garrighan? No, you're mistaken there. He's one of the cold-blooded ones," said the superintendent confidently.

"Excuse me, Dick; I'm never mistaken on that side of the fence. There were signs, plenty of them. Ninety-eight men in every hundred will duck and put up one or both arms if you strike at them suddenly. Garrighan did neither, you'll say; but if you had been watching him as closely as I was, you would have seen that he started to do both."

Maxwell was regarding his former classmate curiously.

"Is that how you do it? Is that the way you caught the post-office thieves, Calvin?"

The chemistry expert laughed.

"It's only a little pointer on methods," he averred. "When my attention was first called to such things—it was on a case in the Department of Justice in which I was required to give expert testimony—I was very strongly impressed with the crudities of the ordinary detective methods. I said to myself that what was needed was some one who could apply good, careful laboratory practice; a habit of observation which counts nothing too small to be weighed and measured."

"Go on," said Maxwell.

"The idea came to me that I'd like to try it on, and I did. My theory is correct. Human beings react under certain given conditions just as readily, and just as inevitably, as the inorganic substances react in a laboratory experiment."

Maxwell reached for the box of safety matches and passed it to Sprague, whose cigar had gone out.

"I wish you could stay and put this railroad of ours into your test-tube, Calvin. We're teetering along on the edge of an earthquake—oh, yes—I know you'll say it's only a scare; but the worst panic that has ever gone into history was only a scare in the beginning. One of these fine nights some engineer or some operator with the bare nerves will lose his grip. You know about what that will mean. We've escaped alive, so far; but the first real wreck that hits us will be just about the same as dropping a lighted match into a barrel of gunpowder; I thought it had come tonight; I'm glad it hasn't, but I know it's only postponed."

The chemistry man nodded.

"Somebody is reaching for you with a big stick; that is very evident, Maxwell. And there are brains behind it, too, when you come to think of it. If you wanted to kill a man without getting hanged for murder, one way to do it would be to persuade him to commit suicide. Has it ever occurred to you that somebody may be trying the same experiment on your railroad?"

"Good Lord, no!"

"Stranger things have happened. But that is beside the mark. You say you are needing help. I've half a mind to stop off and give you a bit of a lift."

"By Jove, Calvin!—if you would—"

"Call it a go," interrupted the guest. "I'll take a chance and say that my business in San Francisco can wait a few days. The fellow I'm after out there won't run away; it's the one thing he doesn't dare to do."

"Say, old man! But that's bully of you!" exclaimed the host, reaching across to grip the hand of helping. "You shall have everything in sight; I'll put every man on the two divisions under your orders, and you can have a special train and my private car. If you don't see what you want, just ask—"

The chemistry sharp was holding up his hand and laughing.

"No, no; hold on, Dick. You'll have to let me tackle the thing in my own way, and there won't be any grand-stand plays in it—in fact, I don't mean to appear personally in it at all. Let's see where we stand. You have a division detective of some sort, haven't you?—a fellow who does the gun-play act when it becomes necessary?"

"We have; a young fellow named Archer Tarbell, who got his experience chasing cattle thieves in Montana. He's a fine fellow, and it's breaking his heart because he can't get the nippers on our wire-devil."

"All right. I may want to use him. Now another matter. You have a live newspaper in Brewster; I bought a copy of it on the train this morning. If I remember right, it's called *The Tribune*. Is it friendly to your railroad?"

"Ordinarily, yes; though Treadwell, the owner, is independent enough to print anything that he thinks is news."

"Know him pretty well?"

"Very well, indeed."

"Good. When we get in, make it your first care to see the newspaper people and to persuade them not to make any mention of this little miss-go of tonight. That's the first move and it's an important one. Can you work it?"

"Sure. But I don't see the point."

"Never mind about that; I probably sha'n't do anything that you think I ought to do. Now about this man Tarbell; is he known as a company detective?"

"No, not generally known; he's on the pay-roll as a spare operator—relief man, you know."

"That's better. When I meet him I'll see if I can't get him interested in chemistry. That's how you're going to account for me, you know. I'm an old friend of yours, a Government man out of the Department of Agriculture off on a vacation. Incidentally, I might be wanting to buy a mine, or something of that sort—anything to start the town gossip on a harmless chase and to keep it as far as possible from the real reason for my stopover."

"Everything goes," said Maxwell. "I'll start the gossip. What else?"

"Nothing out of the ordinary. I shall ask you to give me the run of your railroad office, and I'd like to meet anybody and everybody, when it falls in naturally—but always as the chemistry sharp; get that well ground into your cosmos. But here—what's this? Are we already back in Brewster?"

"We are," said the superintendent, with a glance out of the window. Then he became the regretful host again. "I hate to have you go back to the hotel, Calvin. It's just my crooked luck to have you come along when the house is shut up and Mrs. Maxwell and the babies are out of town. They're due to come home in a day or two, and I'm selfish enough to hope that we can keep you over. Let's drop off here at the crossing. It's nearer to the hotel, and it'll give me a chance to reach *The Tribune* office before Treadwell's young men come in with their scare stuff."

It was a half-hour after the arrival of the unwrecked Limited, and the story of the curious false alarm was just getting itself passed from lip to ear among the loungers in the Hotel Topaz lobby, when the Government man came down from his room to file a rather lengthy New York message with the hotel telegraph operator.

"Cipher?—holy smoke!" exclaimed the young man at the lobby wire desk; but a liberal tip made it look easier, and he added: "All right, I'm good for it, I guess, and I'll get it through as quick as I can. Answer to your room?"

"If you please," said the guest; and, as it was by this time well on toward midnight, he went to bed.

By noon of the day following the false alarm run of the wrecking-train to Timanyoni Canyon, all Brewster, or at least the railroad part of it, knew that Superintendent Maxwell was entertaining an old college classmate at the Hotel Topaz. For the town portion of the gossip there was some little disagreement as to Mr. Calvin Sprague's state and standing. Some had it that the big, handsome athlete was a foot-ball coach taking his vacation between seasons. Others said that he was a capitalist in disguise, looking for a ground-floor investment in Timanyoni mines.

These were Mr. Sprague's placings for the man in the street. But to the rank and file in the railroad head-quarters building Sprague figured in his proper character as a Government drug-mixer on a holiday; a royal good fellow who fraternized instantly with everybody, whose naïve ignorance about railroading was a joke, and whose vast unknowledge was nicely balanced by a keen and comradely curiosity to learn all that anybody could tell him about the complex workings of a railroad head-quarters in action.

Naturally, and possibly because Davis, the chief despatcher, was willing to be hospitable, he spent an hour of the forenoon in the wire office, ingenuously absorbing detail and evincing an interest in the day's work that made Davis, ordinarily a rather reticent man, transform himself into a lecturer on the theory and practice of railway telegraphy.

It was in Davis's office that he met Tarbell; and the keen-eyed, sober-faced young fellow who was carried on the division pay-rolls as a relief operator became his guide on a walking tour of the shops and the yards. Tarbell saw in Mr. Maxwell's guest nothing more than an exceedingly affable gentleman with an immense capacity for interesting himself in the workaday details of a railroad outfit; but at one o'clock, when Maxwell joined Sprague at a quiet corner table for two in the hotel café, there were several surprises awaiting the superintendent.

"Getting it shaken down a little so that you'll know where to begin?" was Maxwell's opening question; and the ex-fullback laughed.

"You must take me for a sleuth of the common or garden variety," he retorted. "Did you suppose I had thrown away an entire forenoon scoring for a start? Not so, Richard; not even remotely so. I've been finding out a lot of things. I am even able to suggest an improvement or two in your telegraph installation."

"For example?" said Maxwell.

"Both of your yard offices are cut in on the working wire. If this were my railroad I'd put them on a pony circuit and cut them out of the main line."

"Why would you?"

"We'll have to go back a little for the specific answer in the present case; back to last night, and to the young man who chased out with a red lantern to keep us from running into the passenger train which wasn't wrecked. Why do you suppose he did that?"

"That's easy; he heard the passenger coming down the canyon."

"That was the inference, of course. But when you have taken the thirty-third degree in the exact science of observation, Dick, you'll learn to distrust inferences and to accept only conclusions. He didn't hear the passenger; he didn't know it was coming. If you had been observing him as closely as I was, you would have seen him write this down in his actions as plain as print. He had a much better reason for stopping us—and the passenger. It was a wire order from somebody. If you don't believe it, have Davis call him up and ask him, when you go back to your office."

Notwithstanding the criticism just passed upon him by his table-mate, Maxwell again caught at an inference.

"You've found the wire-devil, Calvin? You've got to the bottom of the thing in a single forenoon?"

"No; not quite to the bottom. But some few things I have learned, beyond any question of doubt. In the first place, this trouble of yours is pretty serious; far more serious than you suspect. In fact, it is designed to remove your railroad from the map, not by murder outright, but by what you might call incited suicide. The condition which you described last night is painfully apparent, even to an outsider like myself. Half of your men are potential powder-mines, ready to blow up if the spark is applied."

"Go on," said Maxwell eagerly. "What else did you find out?"

"I learned that a stop-all-trains order was sent to your young man at the canyon station last night, and that, in all probability, it was sent from Brewster. The ultimate question fines itself down to this: did your night despatcher, Connolly, send that order through his own instrument in his own office? or did he, or some other, send it from the upper yard office?— which, as I have remarked, is rather injudiciously cut in on the regular working wire. I'll venture to make the answer positive; the order was sent from the yard office."

"Connolly!" said the superintendent under his breath. "I can't believe it, Calvin. Who ever heard of a fat villain?"

"Go a little easy on the inferences," laughed the chemistry expert. "I didn't say it was Connolly, though it looks rather bad for him at the present stage of the game. He is in debt, and he wants to get married."

"But, good Lord! What has that got to do with—"

"Hold on," interposed the expert calmly. "We haven't come to that part of it yet. As I say, this stop-order was sent from the yard office. How do I know? Because the sender left his trail behind him in the shape of a wire recently cut and recoupled—the cutout being made to keep the message from repeating itself in the head-quarters office where it might be heard by anybody who happened to be standing around."

"But Connolly couldn't leave his wire to go to the yard office."

"Unfortunately for him, he did leave it. About half an hour after the wrecking-train left he called Davis, who was sleeping in one of the bunk-rooms in your wickiup attic. His excuse was that he was so rattled that he couldn't hold himself down at the train-desk. Davis relieved him for an hour or so, and then he came back."

"Still I can't believe it of Connolly," Maxwell persisted. "If he sent that message to Timanyoni last night, that makes him responsible for all the others—the devil-messages, as the men are calling them. Some of these have come in the night, while he was on duty. How could he have worked it in that case?"

Again the chemistry expert laughed. "A suspicious person might draw a bunch of inferences," he said, "throwing out a dark hint or so about a concealed cut-in on the wires after they enter the attic of the railroad build-ing and a hidden set of instruments. Also, the same person would probably point to the fact that Connolly wasn't at his desk when the fake wreck no-tice came last night. It was your chief clerk, Calmaine, who took it from the wire, and he tells me he was subbing for Connolly for a few minutes while Connolly went upstairs for his smoking-tobacco."

"My Lord!" said Maxwell; "you've put it upon Connolly, fair and square, Calvin; it's all over but the hanging!"

"There you go again," joked the Government man, with his good-na-tured grin. "I haven't said it is Connolly. But I will say this: with another half-day at it, I'll probably be able to turn the case over to Tarbell—and the newspapers."

"The newspapers?"

"Yes. That will be a part of the cure for the crazy sickness among your men. Sit tight and say nothing, and by this evening I'll be ready to put you next."

It was late in the afternoon, and the man from Washington had spent much of the intervening time loafing in the different offices sheltered by the head-quarters roof, when young Tarbell got a telephone summons from the hotel. In the writing-room, which was otherwise deserted, he found the superintendent's guest waiting for him. Sprague waved him to a chair and began at once.

"What did you find out, Mr. Tarbell?"

"Nothing to hurt. The fellow you was askin' about went out on the wreck-train and came back on it."

"You're sure of that?"

"Sure of the first part, and not so sure of the last. I've found half a dozen o' the men who saw him get on the train here, and saw him after he was on. They're a little hazy about the back trip, but he must've come back that way, because he didn't come on the Limited."

"And his wife?"

Tarbell's lip curled in honest cleanliness.

"He ain't got any wife. It was his girl he was expectin', and she didn't come."

"And afterward?" suggested the questioner.

"After he got back he showed up in the office and took his job again, lettin' Catherton go home."

The Government man's eyes narrowed and after a moment he began again.

"How near can you come to keeping your own counsel, Mr. Tarbell?" he demanded abruptly.

"I reckon I can talk a few without sayin' much," said the ex-cowboy. And then, after a pause: "You mean that you don't want to be mixed up in this thing by name, Mr. Sprague?"

"You've hit it exactly. You've got your start and I want you to work it out yourself. You have the line. Somebody—somebody who is not a thousand miles from your head-quarters building over yonder—is working this scare, working it for a purpose which he wishes to accomplish without making himself actually and legally responsible. Had you got that far in your own reasoning, Mr. Tarbell?"

"No, indeedy," was the prompt reply. "I reckon I'm only a plug when it comes down to the sure-enough, fine-haired part of it."

"You'll learn, after a bit," said the chemistry expert shortly. "But let that go. You have the facts now, and they are driven pretty well into a corner. Can you go and get your man?"

Tarbell got up and shoved his hands into his pockets.

"I reckon I can," he admitted slowly, and started to move away. But at the door the big man at the writing-desk recalled him.

"Don't go on supposition, Tarbell. Ask yourself, when you get outside, if you've got the evidence that the court will demand. Ask yourself, also, if you know of your own knowledge, or if you've only allowed yourself to be hypnotized into your belief. If you can get satisfactory answers to these questions, go to it and bring back the money, as they say up in Seattle."

For what remained of the afternoon after Tarbell went away, Sprague sat in the writing-room and wrote letters, sealing and addressing the last one just as Maxwell came over to go to dinner with him. At table there were plenty of uncut back-numbers in the way of college reminiscences to be threshed over, and Sprague carefully kept the talk in this innocuous field until after they had left the dining-room to go for a smoke on the loggia porch. When the cigars were alight, Maxwell would no longer be choked off.

"Anything new in the wire-devil business, Calvin?" he asked.

"I've turned the case over to Tarbell, as I promised. I'm through with my part of it."

"What's that!" ejaculated the superintendent. "You've got your man?"

"Tarbell will get him—most probably before we go to bed tonight. He's a fine young fellow, that reformed cowboy of yours, Dick. I like him."

Maxwell was still gasping. "You're a wonder, Calvin—a latter-day wizard! Good Heavens! Do you realize that we've been working on this thing for a month? And you've cleaned it up in a day!"

The chemistry expert was smiling good-naturedly.

"Perhaps I came at a fortuitous moment, and had exceptional advantages," he demurred.

"But are you sure?" demanded Maxwell soberly.

"So sure that if your 'devil' had caused any loss of life in his monkeyings, I could go into court and hang him."

"Thank God!" said the superintendent; and then again, as if an enormous weight had been lifted from his shoulders, "Thank God!"

Sprague looked up quickly.

"You've been taking it pretty hard, haven't you, Dick? Any special reason?"

"Yes. You know Ford, our president: he has made the Pacific Southwestern System—made it out of whole cloth; and, incidentally, he has made a good few of us fellows who have fought with him shoulder to shoulder from the first. When I was last in New York, a couple of months ago, he rode from the club to the station in the taxi with me. He was in trouble of some sort—he didn't tell me what it was; but the last thing he said as I was boarding the train gave me some notion of it. 'Run that jerk-water Short Line of yours, Dick, as if you were carrying all your eggs to market and had them all in one basket,' he said, and then he added: 'No wrecks, Dick, if you have to sit up nights to head them off.'"

Sprague was smoking peacefully. It was perhaps too much to expect that a man whose problems were chiefly in the field of laboratory science should be very deeply interested in one in which the elements were merely human. When he spoke again it was to recur to his favorable impression of Tarbell. "I like that young fellow," he said in conclusion. "He'll pull you out of the hole—with a little timely help from the newspapers. When he gets the ball into his hands and starts down the field with it, you'd best be prepared for some pretty sensational developments. They're due."

For a little while Maxwell said nothing, and the fine lines between his eyes deepened slowly into a frown of anxiety. Finally he said: "I've got 'em, too, Calvin—the 'jimmies,' I mean. My wife and the two kiddies are coming home on the 'Apache' tonight, and don't you know, I had half a mind to wire her to stop over in Copah until I could go after her? That's a pretty pass for things to come to, isn't it?—when a man's afraid to have the members of his family ride over his own particular piece of railroad?"

Sprague flipped the ash from his cigar.

"That's one of the bridges you don't have to cross until you come to it."

Maxwell got out of his chair and refused Sprague's offer of a fresh cigar.

"No," he said; "this has been one of the days when I've smoked too much. I'm going over to the office to keep my finger on the pulse of things. When it gets too dull for you over here, come across and break in. If I'm not in my own office, you'll find me in room eleven—the despatcher's—keeping tab on the movements of the Apache Limited."

Fully two hours beyond the time when the superintendent had crossed the railroad plaza to climb the stair of the head-quarters building, Tarbell, strolling along the plaza-fronting street, swung himself over the railing of the loggia porch and took the chair next to the man from Washington, who was still sitting as Maxwell had left him and still smoking.

"I've been waiting for you," said the patient smoker, without taking his eyes from the row of lighted windows in the railroad building opposite.

"I allowed you would be," rejoined Tarbell in his gentle Tennessee-mountain drawl. And then, quite as calmly: "I reckon I've found the answers to all them questions you 'lotted to me. I reckon I've got him."

"I've been betting on you, Tarbell," was the word of approval. Then: "It comes pretty near home, doesn't it?"

"It sure does. It's goin' to hurt Mr. Maxwell good and plenty. He counts all the men in the home office as his fam'ly, and there's never been one o' them to go back on him till now."

"What is your evidence?" queried Sprague.

"I reckon you'd call it circumstantial—and so will the judge. But it hobbles him all right. There's a cut-in on the despatcher's wires over yonder, 'way up under the roof where nobody'd find it, with four little fine lead wires goin' down in the wall. I couldn't find where they come out at, but I reckon that don't make any difference: they're *there*."

"Anything else?"

"Yes. I've got a letter that I hooked out of his coat pocket not ten minutes ago; a letter from some gang boss o' his'n in New York, givin' him goss for not showin' up results, and allowin' to pull some sort of a gun on him if the papers don't begin to print scare heads about a certain railroad management, *pronto*."

The chemistry expert smiled shrewdly.

"You are not the young man I took you for, Tarbell, if you are not wringing your brain like a wet towel to make it tell you why anybody in New York should wish to see Nevada Short Line wreck bulletins in the newspapers."

"That ain't no joke, neither," Tarbell admitted gravely, adding, "I been hopin' maybe it would come out in the round-up."

"Yes," said Sprague, half-absently. "It will come out in the round-up." And then, after a thoughtful pause, "Perhaps we'd better go over and relieve Mr. Maxwell's mind. But first it wouldn't be a bad idea to telephone the editor of *The Tribune* and ask him to send his railroad reporter down to Mr. Maxwell's office. If you say that Mr. Maxwell will probably have a bit of first-page stuff for him, it won't be necessary to go into details."

Tarbell went into the hotel lobby to telephone, and afterward they crossed the plaza to the working head-quarters of the double division. Finding the superintendent's office open and lighted but unoccupied, they went on to the despatcher's room. In the public space outside of the counter railing three or four trainmen were grouped in front of the bulletin-board looking for their assignments on the night trains and thumbing the file of posted "General Orders."

Behind the railing Connolly was sitting at his glass-topped wire-table with the train-sheet under his hand and the superintendent at his elbow. Over in the corner under his green-shaded electric bulb, Bolton, the sallow-faced car-record man, was fingering the keys of his type-writer.

Tarbell opened the gate in the railing to admit Sprague and himself. Maxwell looked up and nodded a welcome to his guest.

"Got tired of sitting it out alone, did you?" he said; and then, "I'll be with you in a minute and we'll go over to my office. I'm waiting to get Timanyoni's report of the Limited."

"Mrs. Maxwell is on the train?"

Maxwell nodded, and a moment later Connolly's sounder clicked out Timanyoni's report of the passing train. The fat despatcher was nervous. It showed in his rattling of the key as he O K'd the canyon station's report, and again in a small disaster when, in reaching for his pen to make the train-sheet entry, he overset his ink-well.

"Well, I'm damned!" he grunted, snatching at the train-sheet and pushing the ink flood back with his free hand. Maxwell came to the rescue, and so did Tarbell; and a liberal application of blotters stopped the flood. But at the close of the incident Connolly's hands were well blackened.

It was at this conjuncture that Davis, the chief despatcher, came in on the way up to his room in the attic half-story above. Connolly appealed to him at once.

"If you'll sit in here, just for a minute, Davis, while I go wash my hands?" he said, adding: "I'd ought to be kicked all the way downstairs!"

When Davis had taken the chair and Connolly had gone out, Tarbell whispered to the superintendent. Maxwell nodded, and made a sign to Sprague. When he had closed the door of the despatcher's room behind himself and his guest, he explained:

"Tarbell says he is ready, and we may as well have it over with. Do you want to be present?"

"As a spectator, yes," said the expert.

"All right; we'll go to my office and wait for Archer."

The waiting interval proved to be short. Maxwell had just thrown his roll-top desk open, and the Government man had planted his big bulk solidly in the half-shadowed window-seat, when the door opened and Connolly came in, his full-moon face a frightened blank and his hands still ink-blackened. Tarbell was only a step behind the despatcher, and the reporter from *The Tribune* office was at Tarbell's heels. When the three were inside, Tarbell shut the door and put his back against it.

"Here's your man, Mr. Maxwell," he said briefly; and Sprague, who had started to his feet at the door opening, sat down again in the shadow and said nothing.

Maxwell pointed brusquely to a chair at the desk end. "Sit down, Dan," he snapped. And then: "I suppose you know what you're here for?"

Connolly fell into the chair as if the sharp command had been a blow.

"Know what I'm here for?" he stammered.

"Yes. Nothing will be gained by dodging. You may as well make a clean breast of it. You've been faking these scare wreck reports—don't lie about it; we've got the evidence. I want to know who is behind you. Who bribed you to do this thing?"

"Before God, Mr. Maxwell!" the culprit began, with the sweat rolling down his face; but Maxwell stopped him with a quick gesture.

"I've told you it was no use to try to lie out of it. I have here on my desk a letter which was taken from your coat pocket tonight, since you came on duty; a letter from which you were careful enough to tear the signature, but on which you were not careful enough to destroy the date line. In that letter the writer threatens to give you away to the New York police if you don't get busy and give the newspapers a string of Nevada Short Line wrecks to write about. That is enough to send you over the road, but there's more. The working wires east and west have been cut under the roof of this building, and leads taken off. The leads disappear in the wall back of your bunk-room. I don't ask you what you have to say for yourself; I want you to tell us, right here and now, who planned the thing, and what it was intended to accomplish."

Connolly had been slowly collapsing in his chair under the merciless fire of accusation, and a pasty pallor was driving the pink out of his round face.

"My God!" he gasped thickly; and then he repeated, "My God!" A silence crammed with threatenings settled down upon the small office-room. Suddenly it was broken by the sound of hurried footfalls in the corridor, and Tarbell was hurled half-way across the room when the door was flung open from without.

It was young Cargill, the engineer, who burst into the private office, and his lips were white.

"The Limited!" he broke out. "She's overrun her orders at Corona and she's due to meet Second Eighteen on the single track!"

It was the Government man who led the rush to the despatcher's room, a rush in which even the fat culprit joined. In the wire office Davis had the key; his jaw was set and the perspiration was standing thickly on his forehead, but he had not lost his nerve. Calmaine, the chief clerk, was hanging over his shoulder, and outside of the railing the group of trainmen had grown to a breathless crowd, pressing to hear the latest word.

When Maxwell's party pushed through the gate, Sprague was still in the lead, and his quick glance took in every detail of the scene. Like a flash he turned upon Tarbell, who was fumbling a pair of handcuffs in his pocket, and pinioned him in a grip that was like the nip of a vice.

"Not yet!" he whispered in Tarbell's ear; and then Davis snapped his switch and spoke.

"It's no use," he said, and his harsh tone was only a thin mask for the break in his voice. "It's the real thing this time. First Eighteen was ready to pull out of Corona when the Limited went by. Corringer left his wire and chased the freight, hoping to get its engine to cut loose and run after the passenger. He couldn't catch it."

A low murmur ran through the crowd packed against the counter railing and somebody whispered, "It's got the boss; his wife and babies are on that train. Look at him!"

Maxwell had gripped the back of a chair and he was staring hot-eyed at the despatcher.

"Do something, Davis," he pleaded. "Don't sit there and let those trains come together! For Christ's sake, think of something!"

The chief despatcher ducked his head as if he were dodging a blow and swallowed hard.

"There isn't anything to do, Mr. Maxwell—you know there isn't anything," he began in low tones. "If there was—"

It was Connolly who made the break. Twisting away from Tarbell's grip on his arm he flung himself upon Davis.

"Get out o' that chair and let me have the key," he wheezed; and when Davis did not move quickly enough he pounced upon the key standing. Davis got up and quietly slid the chair under the night man who sank heavily into it without missing a letter in the call he was insistently clicking out, over and over again in endless repetition.

"What is it?" whispered the newspaper man, who was standing aside with Tarbell and Sprague; and Tarbell answered:

"It's the Corcoran coal mine—about half-way between Corona and the first station this side, and a half-mile up the gulch. They've got a private wire, but they ain't got any night operator."

Davis overheard the whisper and shook his head.

"Dan's got his wits with him," he said, in open admiration. "There's a young time-keeper that sleeps in the coal company's office shack, and he's learning to plug in on the wire a little. If Dan can only wake him—" And then, in sudden sharp self-accusation: "God forgive me! Why didn't I think of it and save all the time that's been wasted?" Then, as Connolly closed the circuit and a halting reply clicked through the receiving instrument: "He's got him! Thank the Lord, he's got him! If he can only make him understand what's wanted, there's a chance—just one chance in a thousand!"

With the very seconds now freighted with disaster, and with only the crudest of amateur telegraphers at the other end of the wire, nine men out of ten would have blown up and lost the thousandth part of a chance remaining. But Connolly was the tenth man. With his left hand shaking until it was beating a tattoo on the glass table top he hitched his chair closer and began to spell out, letter by letter, the brief call for help upon which so much depended. Tarbell translated for Sprague, word by word. "Hurry—down—to—main-line—and—throw—your—switch—to—red. Then—run—west—and—flag—passenger."

The key-switch clicked on the final word, and for five long, dragging seconds the silence was a keen agony. Then the sounder began hesitantly: dot—pause—dot; dash—dot—dash, it spelled; and Tarbell translated under his breath, "He says 'O K'. Now, if he can only chase his feet fast enough—"

How Maxwell managed to live and not die through the interminable twenty minutes that followed; how Davis and Tarbell and Connolly hung breathless over the wire-table, while the throng outside of the railing, augmented now to a jammed crowd of sympathetic watchers, rustled and moved and whispered in awed undertones—are themes upon which the rank and file of the Nevada Short Line still enlarge in the roundhouse tool-rooms and in the switch shanties when the crews are waiting for a delayed train.

The dreadful interval seemed as if it would never be outworn, but the end came at last when the hesitant clicking of the sounder was resumed.

"Call it out, Dan," shouted somebody among the waiting trainmen, and Connolly pronounced the words slowly as the amateur at the end of the private wire ticked them off.

"Both—trains—safe—freight—backing—to—blind—siding—at—Quentin—switch—passenger—following—under—flag."

A shout went up that drowned the feeble patter of the telegraph instruments and made the windows rattle. "Bully for the kid at the coal mine!" "Bully for Danny Connolly!" "Come out here, Danny, till we get a chanst at you!"

Maxwell fought his way stubbornly through the crowd, with the news-paper man, Sprague, Tarbell, and Connolly following in his wake. When the five were once more behind the closed door of the private office across the hall, the superintendent turned morosely upon the night despatcher, and he was so full of the thing he was about to do that he did not notice that his guest had taken Tarbell aside for a whispered conference.

"You've drawn the teeth of the law, this time, Connolly," he said sharp-ly. "After what you've just done I'm not going to send you to jail. But the least you can do is to tell me who hired you and sent you out here to make trouble for us. If you'll do that—"

It was Sprague's hand on his shoulder that stopped him, and then he no-ticed that Tarbell had disappeared. "Just a minute—until Tarbell gets back," said the guest, in low tones; and while he was saying it, the door opened suddenly and the ex-cowboy returned, thrusting a sallow-faced young fel-low, shirt-sleeved and livid with fear, into the office ahead of him. Then the Government man went on in the same low tone, "You can say to this young man all the things you were going to say to Mr. Connolly. There was a little miscue on Tarbell's part, and I was just going to tell you about it when the train trouble butted in." Then to the fat despatcher, "Mr. Connolly, sit down. You've jolly well earned the right to look on and listen."

Connolly sat down heavily, and so did the superintendent. Thereupon the man from Washington slipped easily into the breach, turning briskly upon the yellow-faced car-record operator.

"Step up here, Bolton, and make a clean sweep of it to Mr. Maxwell. Tell him how a certain firm of New York brokers—you needn't give the names now—sent you, a convicted bucket-shop wire-tapper, out here to disarrange things on this railroad for stock-jobbing purposes. Then tell him how you tapped the despatcher's wires and put a set of concealed keys under your car-record table in the other room. Tell him how, after you'd faked that wreck message last night, you ran a bluff for sympathy, and how, when it had worked, your nerve flickered and you dropped from the wrecking-train in the yard and sent a stop-order from the yard office. Come to the front and loosen up!"

Bolton was shuffling forward and was beginning a tremulous confession when Maxwell stopped him harshly.

"You can keep all that to tell in court!" he snapped. And then to Tarbell: "Take him away, Archer. And you go back to your job, Dan, and let Davis go to bed. What I've got to say to you will keep." Then to the young man from the *Tribune*, who had his note-book out and was scribbling down his story at breakneck speed: "Write out what you please, Scanlan, but tell Mr. Kendall that I'll be up to the office presently, and that I'd like to see the story before it goes to the linotypes."

When the room was cleared, the snappy little superintendent spun his chair around to face his guest.

"Calvin," he said solemnly, "you'll never know how near you came to making me break my heart tonight. If I'd had to send Dan Connolly to jail after what he did in the other room a little while ago—"

The chemistry expert was grinning joyously.

"It was a curious little slip," he commented. "I thought Tarbell was on; never suspected for a moment that he wasn't until he butted Connolly in here and shot him at you."

"But you knew Connolly wasn't the man? How on top of earth did you run it down, in a single day? I can't surround it, even yet."

"It wasn't much of a nut to crack," laughed the expert easily. "I hope you'll have a harder one for me the next time I happen along. I got my pointer last night—before I knew anything at all about the nature of your trouble. You see, Bolton was the only man in the outfit who wasn't sincerely jarred and horrified by that fake message. I saw it the minute I'd had a look into his eyes. From that on it was easy enough."

"I don't see it," objected Maxwell.

"Don't you? I merely argued backward from the results your wire-devil was trying to obtain and sent a cipher message to a friend of mine in New York. He put me next to a nice little plot in the Street to hamper Ford and break down your company credit. Then I loafed around your shack here until I found Bolton's wire machinery. Bolton didn't catch on, but he was suspicious enough of a stranger like me to take a little measure of precaution by slipping that incriminating letter into Connolly's coat pocket. I supposed Tarbell knew that, or I'd have told him."

Maxwell had been listening in appreciative admiration, but gratitude came quickly to the fore when Sprague paused.

"Calvin, there's no telling how many lives you've saved by this little stop-over of yours here in Timanyoni Park!" he broke out. "You've done it. When that story, properly trimmed down, comes out in the *Tribune* tomorrow morning, the bare-nerves strain will go off like that"—snapping his fingers. "I wish I could show you…. By George! There's the Limited pulling in. I've got to go down and meet the wife and kiddies!"

The big-bodied man who called himself a chemistry sharp and confessed to the riding of many hobbies rose up with a laugh.

"You want to show me? All right: take me downstairs with you and show me Mrs. Maxwell and the babies. As for the other, you know as well as I do that it's all in the day's work. Pitch out or we'll miss the folks—and that would be worse than getting another message from the wire-devil."

CHAPTER 2

HIGH FINANCE IN CROMARTY GULCH

It was a warm night for altitude five thousand feet, and the last few lingerers in the dining-car on the eastbound "Flying Plainsman" had their windows open. Midway of the car a quartette of light-hearted young people were exchanging guesses as to the proper classification of a big man with laughing eyes and a fighting jaw who was dining alone at one of the end tables.

"He looks like money—nice, large, ready money—to me," commented the prettiest of the three young women; but her seat-mate, a handsome young fellow with the badge of his college athletic association worn conspicuously in his button-hole, thought differently. "You've fumbled the ball this time, Kitty," he dissented. "If he isn't the champion of all the amateur heavy-weights, you can put him down as a 'varsity coach out scouting for talent. Jehu! What a 'back' he'd make under the new rules!"

"Vaudeville is my guess," chimed in the next-to-the-prettiest girl mockingly; "the strong man who puts up the dumb-bells, and all that, you know. If you could break into his luggage, I'd wager a box of chocolates that you'd find a perfectly beautiful suit of pink tights with spangled trunks and resined slippers."

A little later the big man in the far corner took his change from the waiter and left the car. As he passed the joyous party at the double table there was a good-natured twinkle in his gray eyes and he dropped a neatly engraved card at the collegian's plate.

"Heavens and earth!—he heard us!" gasped the prettiest girl. And then, feminine curiosity overcoming shame, "What does it say, Tommy?"

The young man held the card so that all could see, and admitted himself a loser in the classification game.

Calvin W. Sprague,
Washington, D. C.
Chemist, Dept. of Agriculture

was what they read; and the fourth member of the group, a young woman with fine eyes and an adorable chin, who was neither pretty nor prettier, but something far more transcendent, took the card and studied it thoughtfully.

"You've all missed the most astonishing thing—how he contrived to overhear us at this distance," she commented musingly. And then, addressing the vanished card-owner through his bit of pasteboard: "So you're a chemist, are you, Mr. Sprague? You don't look it, not the least little bit, and I'm sure you'll forgive me if I say that I doubt it; doubt it very much indeed."

While the young people were debating among themselves as to whether or no there might not be an apology due, the big man who had dined alone passed quite through the string of vestibuled Pullmans and went to light his cigar on the rear platform of the combination buffet and observation car.

Shortly after he had seated himself in one of the platform camp-chairs, the train, which had been rocketing down a wide valley with an isolated ridge on one hand and a huge mountain range on the other, came to a stand at one of the few-and-far-between stations. The pause, one would say, should have been only momentary; but after it had lasted for a full minute or more the solitary smoker on the rear platform left his chair and went to lean over the platform railing for a forward glance.

Looking down the length of the long train, he saw the lights of the small station, with other lights beyond it which seemed to mark a railroad crossing or junction. On the station platform there were a number of lanterns held high to light a group of men who were struggling to lift a long, ominous-looking box into the express-car.

A little later the wheels of the train began to trundle again, and as his car-end passed the station the smoker on the observation platform had a fleeting glimpse of the funeral party, and of the heavy four-mule mountain-wagon which had apparently served as its single equipage. Also, he remarked what a less observant person might have missed: that the lantern-bearers were roughly clothed, and that they were armed.

A hundred yards beyond the station the train stopped again; and when it presently began to back slowly the platform watcher understood that it was preparing to take on a lighted coach standing on a siding belonging to the junction railroad. When the coupling was made and the "Flying Plainsman," with the picked-up car in tow, was once more gathering headway in its eastward flight up the valley of a torrenting mountain river, the big man read the number "04" over the door of the newly added coach. After he had made out the number he coolly put a leg over the barrier railing, brushed the guarding porter aside, and pushed his way through the narrow side corridor of the trailer.

In the rear half of the car the corridor opened into a comfortable working-room fitted with easy-chairs, lounges, and a desk; otherwise, the office in transit of the Nevada Short Line's general superintendent, Mr. Richard Maxwell. Maxwell was at his desk when the big-bodied intruder shouldered himself into the open compartment, but he sprang up joyfully when he recognized his unannounced visitor.

"Why, Calvin, old man! Where in thunder did you drop from?" he demanded, wringing the hand of greeting in a vain endeavor to match the big man's crushing grip. "Sit down and tell it out. I thought you'd gone back east over the Transcontinental a full month ago."

The man whose card named him as a Government chemist picked out the easiest of the lounging-chairs and planted himself comfortably in it.

"Jarred you, did I? That's nothing; I've jarred worse men than you are in my time. Your thinking machinery is all right; I was due to go back a month ago, but I got interested in a little laboratory experiment on the coast and couldn't tear myself away. How are Mrs. Maxwell and the kiddies?"

"Fine! And I'm hurrying to get home to them. I've been out for a week and had begun to think I was never going to get back to the Brewster office again. I've been having the busiest little ghost dance you ever heard of during the past few days."

The big man settled himself still more comfortably in his chair and relighted the cigar, which, being of the dining-car brand, had sulked for a time and then gone dejectedly out.

"Will the busy story bear telling?" he asked.

"Yes—to you," was the half-guarded reply. "You'll be interested when I tell you that I'm inclined to believe that it's 'a little more of the same'—a continuation of our round-up with the 'wire-devil' that you straightened out for us a few weeks ago."

The listener nodded. "Begin back a bit," he suggested; and Maxwell did it.

"After you went west, we put our wire-devil through the courts, and President Ford served notice on the New York high-finance pirates; told them he had their numbers, and that they'd better let up on us. That was the end of it for the time. But a week ago Thursday I got a hot wire from Ford, telling me to secure voting proxies on every possible share of Short Line stock held locally, firing the proxies to him in New York by special messenger, who should reach him, he said, not later than the night of the fifteenth."

"Um," commented the smoker thoughtfully. "Is there much of the stock held out here in your Timanyoni wilderness?"

"A good bit of it, first and last. When the Pacific Southwestern, with Ford at its head, took over the Red Butte Western, the R. B. W. was strictly a local line, and the reorganization plan was based upon an exchange of stock—the new for the old. Then, when we built the extension and issued more stock, quite a block of it was taken up by local capitalists, bankers, mineowners, and ranchmen; not a majority, of course, but a good, healthy balance of power."

Again the giant in the lounging-chair nodded. "I see," he cut in. "There is doubtless a stockholders' meeting looming up in the near future—say on the day after the all-important fifteenth—and the Wall Street people are going after Ford's scalp again, this time in a strictly legal way. He will probably need your Western proxies, and need them bad."

"I've got them right here," said Maxwell, tapping a thick bunch of papers on his desk. "And believe me, I've had a sweet time rounding them up. Every moneyed man in this country is a friend of Ford's, and yet I've had to wrestle with every individual one of them for these proxies as if I'd been asking them to shed their good red blood."

"Of course," was the quiet comment. "The fellows on the other side would stack the cards on you—or try to. What's in the wind this time? Just a stock-breaking raid for speculation, or is it something bigger than that?"

The young superintendent shook his head doubtfully.

"I don't know, certainly; I haven't had a chance to talk with Ford since early in the summer. But I have my own guess. If the Transcontinental could control this five-hundred-mile stretch of ours from Copah to Lorchi, it would have the short line to southern California."

"Therefore and wherefore, if Mr. Ford doesn't happen to have the votes in the coming stockholders' meeting, you'll be out of a job. Is that about the size of it?"

"Probably," admitted Maxwell. "Not that it makes any special difference to me, personally. As you know, I have a mine up on the Gloria that beats railroading out of sight. But I'd fight like a dog for Ford, and for my own rank and file here on the Short Line. Of course, Transcontinental control would mean a clean sweep of everybody: there wouldn't be baskets enough this side of the main range to hold the heads that would be cut off."

"I suppose not. But, as you say, you have the 'come-back' right there under your hand in those proxies. How will you get them to New York?"

"My chief clerk, Calmaine, will deliver them in person. He'll meet us at Brewster and go right along on this train, which, by the way, is the next to the last one he could take and make New York on time. It's all arranged."

The guest smoked on in silence for a little time and when he spoke again it was to ask the name of the junction station at which the late stop had been made.

"It's Little Butte—where our Red Butte branch comes in from the north."

"You'd been stopping over there?" Sprague asked.

"No; I had my car brought down from Red Butte on the local, which doubles back on the branch."

"Um; Little Butte; good name. You people out here run pretty persistently to 'Buttes,' don't you? Did I, or didn't I, see a funeral at this particular Butte as we came along?"

"You did. It's Murtrie; a mining engineer who has been doing a sort of weigh-master's stunt at the Molly Baldwin mine. Died pretty suddenly last night, they say."

"Large man?" queried the Government chemist, half-absently; and Maxwell looked up quickly.

"Beefy rather than big, yes. How could you tell?"

Sprague waved his cigar as if the question were childish and the answer obvious. "It took a dozen of them, more or less, to put him into the express-car."

Maxwell turned back to his desk. "Metallic casket, probably," he suggested. "They had our agent wire Brewster for the best that could be had. Said they were going to ship the body to some little town in Kentucky. They're a rather queer lot."

"Who?—the Kentuckians?"

"No; the Molly Baldwin outfit. The mine was opened by a syndicate of New York people four years ago, and after the New Yorkers had put two or three hundred thousand into it without taking anything out, they gave up in disgust. Then a couple of young fellows from Cripple Creek came along and leased the property. There was a crooked deal somewhere, for the young fellows began to take out pay—big pay—right from the start. Then the New York people wanted to 'renig' on the lease, and dragged the thing into the courts."

"And the courts said no?"

"The courts straddled. I didn't follow the fight in detail, but the final decision was that the lessees were to keep all they could take out each month up to a certain amount. If they exceeded that amount, the excess was to be shared equally with the New Yorkers."

"Lots of room for shenanigan in that," was the big man's passing comment. "Unless these young Cripple Creekers are more honest than the average, they'll stand a good bit of watching, you'd say."

Maxwell laughed. "That was what the New Yorkers seemed to think. They secured a court order allowing them to put an expert of their own on the job. And nobody seems to enjoy the watch-dog stunt. They've had to send in a new man every few weeks."

"Do the Cripple Creekers kill them off?"

"No; they buy 'em off, I guess. Anyway, they don't stay. Murtrie was the last."

"And apparently he hasn't stayed," said Sprague reflectively; and just then a long-drawn wail of the locomotive whistle announced the approach of the train to Brewster. At the signal the guest rose and tossed the remains of the bad cigar out of the window. "Here's where I have to quit you, Dick," he was beginning; but Maxwell would not have it that way.

"Not much, you don't, Calvin, old man," he protested. "You're going to stop over one day with me, at least. No; I won't listen to any excuses. Give me your berth check and I'll send my boy up ahead to get your traps out of the sleeper. Sit down right where you are and take it easy. You'll find a box of cigars—real cigars—in this lower drawer. I'll be back as soon as I've seen Calmaine."

Apparently, the man from Washington did not require much urging. He sat down in Maxwell's chair as the train was slowing into the division station, and was rummaging in the desk drawer for the box of cigars when an alert, carefully groomed young man came in through the forward corridor and met the superintendent as he was going out. There was a hurried conference, a passing of papers, and the two, Maxwell and his chief clerk, went out together, leaving the big man to go on with his rummaging alone.

Shortly afterward came the bump of a coupling touch, and the office-car, in the grip of a switching-engine, raced backward through the yards; backward and forward again, and when it came to rest it was standing on the short station spur at the end of the railroad head-quarters building. From the open windows Sprague could see the long through train, with its two big mountain-pulling locomotives coupled on, drawn up for its farther flight. It was after it had steamed away into the night that Maxwell returned to his side-tracked car to find his guest, half-asleep, as it seemed, in the depths of the big wicker easy-chair.

"I hope you didn't think I'd deserted you," he said, drawing up another of the wicker chairs. "I took time to telephone home. Mrs. Maxwell's dining out at her sister's, and, if you don't mind, we'll sit here a while and go out to the house later."

There was enough to talk about. The two, who had been college classmates, had seen little of each other for a number of years. Maxwell told how he had gone into railroading under Ford, and how in his first summer in the Timanyoni he had acquired a gold mine and a wife. Sprague's recounting was less romantic. After leaving college he had coached the 'varsity foot-ball team for two years and had afterward gone in for original research in chemistry, which had been his "major" in college. Later he had drifted into the Washington bureau as an expert, taking the job, as he explained, because it gave him time and frequent leisurely intervals for the pursuit of his principal hobby, which was the lifting of detective work to the plane of pure theory, treating each case as a mathematical problem to be demonstrated by logical reasoning.

"You ought to drop everything else and take up the man-hunting business as a profession," laughed Maxwell, when the hour-long talk had come around to the big man's pet among the hobbies.

"No," was the instant objection. "That is where you're wrong. A man does his best work as an amateur—in any line. As long as the man-hunting comes in the way of a recreation, I enjoy it keenly. But if I had to make a business of it, it would be different." Then he changed the subject by asking about Tarbell, Maxwell's ex-cowboy division detective, who had served as his understudy in the "wire-devil" case a few weeks earlier.

"Archer is all right," was the reply; "only he'd like to break away from me and go with you. He thinks you are about the one only top-notcher; says he'd like to take lessons of you for a year or so."

Sprague was gazing absently out of the near-by window. "Speaking of angels," he broke in, "there is Tarbell, right now; coming down your office stair three steps at a jump," and a moment later the young man in question had dashed across to the service-car and was thrusting his face in at the open window.

"Trouble, Mr. Maxwell!" he blurted out. "The 'Plainsman's' just been held up and robbed at Cromarty Gulch! Connolly's getting the wire from Corona, and he started me out to see if I could find you."

The superintendent leaped up as if his easy-chair had been suddenly electrified.

"What's that you say?" he demanded; "a hold-up?" Then he went into action promptly, as a trained emergency captain should. "Call Sheriff Harding on the 'phone, and tell him to rustle up a posse and report here, quick! Then get the yard office and turn me out an engine and a coach for Harding's men. Hustle it!"

While he was closing his desk he made hurried explanation to Sprague. "It's probably the Scott Weber gang. They held up a train on the main line over in Utah ten days ago. Come on upstairs with me and we'll get the facts."

When the superintendent, accompanied by his broad-shouldered guest, climbed the stair and entered the despatched office, fat, round-faced Daniel Connolly was rattling the key at the train-sheet table. He glanced up at the door opening.

"I'm mighty glad Tarbell found you," he broke out, with a gasp of relief. "I was afraid you'd gone home." And then he recognized the square-shouldered one: "How are you, Mr. Sprague? Glad to see you again."

Maxwell went quickly around to the wire-table.

"Whom have you got?" he asked.

"Allen, night operator at Corona. The train is there, and I've been holding it to give you a chance to talk with McCarty, the conductor."

"Tell me the story as you've got it; then I'll tell you what to say to Mac," was the brisk command.

"It was in Cromarty Gulch, just at the elbow where the track makes the 'U' curve. Cruger's on the pilot-engine, and Jenkins is running the train puller. Cruger saw somebody throwing a red light at him. They stopped, and four of the hold-ups climbed on the engines and made them cut off the postal- and express-cars and pull on around the curve. Then a bunch of 'em broke in the end door of the express-car and scragged little Johnny Galt, the messenger. While they were doing that, another bunch went through the train and held up the passengers. After they'd gone through Galt's car and taken what they wanted, they made Cruger and Jenkins couple up again and go on."

"What did they take?" Maxwell asked.

"Some little money and jewelry from the passengers, McCarty says; not very much."

"But from the express-car?"

The fat despatcher made a queer face and wiped the sweat from his forehead.

"That's the part of it that's hard to believe. Galt was carrying considerable money, but they didn't try to blow his safe. They—they smashed up a coffin and took the dead man out of it."

"What!" ejaculated the superintendent; "Murtrie's body?"

"I don't know who it was—Mac didn't say. But that's what they did. When the boys got together and pulled Galt out from under the express stuff where they'd buried him, they found the coffin open and the body gone."

Sprague had been listening intently.

"This seems to be something worth while, Maxwell," he cut in. "How much time do we have to waste here?"

"Just a minute. Go on, Connolly."

"That's all," said the fat despatcher. "The train's at Corona now, and they've put Johnny Galt off; and—and the coffin. Mac's asking for orders."

"Give them their orders and let them go, and then clear for my special. I've sent for Harding and a posse, and we'll chase out after this thing while the trail is warm. You'll go along, won't you, Calvin?" turning to the stop-over guest.

The man from Washington laughed genially.

"You couldn't scare me off with a fire-hose—not until I have seen this little mystery of yours cleared up. Let's be doing."

Five minutes farther along the two-car special train had been made up and was clanking out over the switches in the eastern yard. As the last of the switch-lights were flicking past the windows, a big bearded man came in from the car ahead and Maxwell introduced him.

"Sprague, this is Sheriff Harding. Harding, shake hands with my friend, Mr. Sprague, of the Department of Agriculture, Washington, and then sit down and we'll thrash this thing out. You've heard the story?"

The sheriff nodded. "I've heard what Tarbell could tell me. He says the biggest part of the haul was a dead man. Is that right?"

"It seems to be. The dead man is Murtrie, who was supposed to be representing the New York owners of the Molly Baldwin mine. The report goes that he died last night, and his body was put on the train at Little Butte to be taken east to some little town in Kentucky. What's your guess?"

"I'd guess that the whole blamed outfit was locoed—plumb locoed," said Harding. "You couldn't carve it out any other way, could you?"

It was Sprague who broke in with a quiet suggestion. "Try once more, Mr. Harding," he said.

The big sheriff put his head in his hands and made the effort. When he looked up again there was the light of a new discovery in his eye.

"Say!" he exploded. "Murtrie's the last of a string of five or six 'watchers' they've had up at that cussed hole-in-the-ground gold mine—and he's dead. By gravy! I believe they killed him!"

Maxwell's smile was grim.

"It seems to me we're just about as far off as ever," he commented; "unless you can carry it along to the body-snatching in some way. Why should they—"

"Hold on," Harding cut in; "I wasn't through. It's one thing to kill a man, and another to get rid of the body so it won't show up and get somebody hanged. Murtrie was sick; that much I know, because Doc Strader went out to the mine to see him day before yesterday. I was talking with Strader about it, and he said it looked like a case of ptomaine poisoning."

"Well?" said Maxwell.

"Supposin' it wasn't natural; supposin' it was the other kind o' poison: they'd have to get rid o' the body, some way or other, wouldn't they—or run the risk of havin' it dug up and looked into, after Murtrie's friends took hold?"

"Go on."

"That bein' the case, they'd have to call in some sort of outside help; they couldn't handle it alone. Two or three of Scott Weber's gang've been seen hanging around in Brewster within the last few days. Supposin' these fellows at the Molly Baldwin put up a job with Scott to make this play with Murtrie's body?"

"By Jove, Harding—I half believe you've got it!" Maxwell exclaimed; but the chemistry expert said nothing.

"We can tell better after we get on the ground, maybe," the sheriff went on. "I had Follansbee bring his dogs along. There's a trail up through the head of Cromarty Gulch leadin' out to the old Reservation road on the mesa. If they had anything as heavy as Murtrie's body to tote, that's about the way they went with it."

Maxwell had been absently marking little squares on his desk blotter as Harding talked. The sheriff's theory was ingenious, but it failed to account for all the facts.

"There's more to it than that," he said, at length. And then he appealed to the silent guest. "Don't you think so, Sprague?"

"I'm waiting to hear how Mr. Harding accounts for the raid on the passengers," said the big man modestly. "One would think that a gang of body-snatchers would have been willing to do one thing at a time."

"By George! That's so," the sheriff acknowledged. "I hadn't thought of that. But then," he added, after a second thought, "a gang that was tryin' to cover up a killin' wouldn't be any too good to throw in a little hold-up business on the side."

"No," said Sprague; but he made no further comment. So far from it, he sat back in his chair and smoked patiently while Maxwell and the sheriff went on with the theory-building, a process which continued in some desultory fashion until Maxwell, glancing out of a window, said:

"We're coming to it; this is the gulch."

A few minutes later the two-car train slowed down and came to a stand on a sharp curve at the head of a densely wooded ravine in the foot-hills. Harding ran forward to get his posse out, and by the time Maxwell and Sprague had debarked the ground at the track-side was black with men. Sprague laughed softly.

"It's lucky we're not depending upon the old Indian method of 'reading the sign,'" he said. "Whatever the ground might have told us is a story spoiled by this time." Then he laughed again when a man broke out of the crowd, with a couple of dogs towing him furiously at the end of their leashes. "We gabble a good bit about our civilization and the advances we've made," he went on. "Yet, in the relatively simple matter of running down a criminal, we haven't got very far beyond the methods of the Stone Age. The idea of an intelligent being, with a human brain to rely upon, falling back upon the instincts of a couple of brute beasts!"

"Oh, hold on," Maxwell protested. "Those dogs have run down a good many crooks, first and last. Follansbee will take any bet you want to make, right now."

"And he would lose," was the confident answer. "But come on; let's see what's going to happen."

The chase, with the dogs running upon a comparatively fresh scent, led up through the pine wood at the head of the gulch. Beyond the wood was a bare, high-lying mesa table-land, with its summer-baked soil dried out to almost rocky hardness. A hundred yards from the gulch head an indistinct road skirted the mesa edge, and here the dogs began to run in circles.

Sprague was chuckling again, but Maxwell counselled patience.

"Wait a minute," he suggested. "The body-snatchers probably had a team here. The dogs will get the scent of the horses presently."

"Think so?" queried the expert. Then he drew his companion aside. "Do you know anything about this road, Dick?"

"Yes, it's the old wagon road from the Reservation into the park."

"Which way would you go toward Brewster?"

"That way," said the superintendent, pointing.

"All right; let's go a little way toward Brewster, and perhaps I can show you why Mr. Follansbee would lose his bet on his dogs."

When they were well out of the dog-circling area, the chemistry expert stooped and struck a match. "See here," he said; and Maxwell, squatting beside him, saw the broad track of an automobile tire. Sprague gurgled softly. "Do you think the dogs will get the scent of that?" he inquired.

Maxwell stood up and shoved his hands into his pockets.

"Calvin, the way you hop across and light upon the one only sure thing, comes mighty near being uncanny, at times. How the devil did you find out that those fellows came in an auto?"

"If I should tell you that it was pure reasoning, you'd doubt it. But never mind the whys and wherefores just now; they can come later. Tell me how long we're going to stay here losing time on Follansbee and his dogs."

"Not a minute longer than you care to stay. What do you want to do?"

"I want to see that crippled express messenger who was put off the train at Corona. Also, I'd like to have a look at the dead man's coffin."

"You shall do both. If you're taking the case, you are very pointedly the only doctor there is in it," Maxwell asserted. Then he called to the sheriff: "O Harding!" and when the county officer came up: "I'm going to take the train and run on to Corona after Galt. We'll stop here for your orders when we come back."

During the short run around the hills to the small mining-town station, Sprague sat quietly in his chair, puffing steadily at his cigar, and saying nothing. When Maxwell announced their arrival he got up and followed the superintendent into the Corona office.

Galt, the express messenger, was lying on the night operator's cot in the telegraph office. Some physician passenger on the held-up train had dressed his wounds, and he had fully recovered consciousness. His story was a mere amplification of the wire report which had gone to Brewster. He had marked, and wondered at, the unscheduled stop on the gulch curve, but before he could open his door to look out, the postal- and express-cars had been pulled on ahead, his end door had been battered in, and he had found himself trying to fight back a couple of masked men who were forcing an entrance. Then somebody hit him on the head and that was the end of it, so far as he was concerned.

Following this, the Corona night operator was put upon the question rack. He knew only what the trainmen had told him. No; there was nothing missing out of the express-car save the dead man's body. While the train was waiting, he, the operator, and the conductor had made a careful check of the contents of the car from Galt's waybills, and, with the single exception noted, everything was undisturbed. No, there was no panic; the scare was pretty well quieted down by the time the train reached Corona. Of course, a good many of the passengers had got out at the station stop, and everybody was curious to see the coffin.

"You took the coffin off?" Maxwell questioned.

"Yes, it's in the freight-room."

Sprague had taken no part in the examination of the man, and had listened only cursorily to Galt's story. But now he became as curious as any of the morbid passengers had been. Allen, the operator, lighted a lantern and led the way to the freight-room. The coffin was lying upon a baggage-truck. It was encased in an ordinary shipping-box, half of the cover of which had been torn off. The lid of the coffin had been broken, split into three pieces; and one of the pieces was missing. It was a rather expensive affair, wooden and not metallic, of the kind known as a "casket," silk-lined, and with a sliding glass face-plate. The glass had been broken, and the fragments were lying inside on the small silken pillow.

Sprague bent to examine the silent witness of the mysterious robbery and the operator offered his lantern. But the Government man took a small electric flash-light from his pocket and made it serve a better purpose. Only once, while he was flashing the tiny beam of the electric into the coffin's interior, did he speak, and then it was to say to Maxwell: "I thought you said this was a metallic coffin."

"That was the inference, when you spoke of the weight and the number of men required to handle it. Of course, I didn't know anything definite about it."

Once more Sprague peered into the silk-lined interior, stooping to send the light ray to the foot of the casket, which was still hidden under the undestroyed half of the outer case. Then, snapping the switch of the flash-light and carefully replacing the broken box cover, he nodded briskly to Maxwell.

"That's all, for the present. If I were you, I'd have this coffin nailed up in its box, just as it is, without disturbing anything. You can manage that, can't you, young man?" turning short upon the operator.

Allen said he could and proceeded to do it; after which, under Sprague's direction, the case was trundled out to the platform, and the three of them, with Maxwell's private-car porter to help, loaded the coffin upon the front platform of Maxwell's car.

"We'll take it back with us," said the Government man, with a sober twinkle in his eyes. "It's a passably good coffin, you know, and with a little repairing it will do to use again—say, when we have found the man it belongs to."

While the night operator, the porter, and the two enginemen were carrying the wounded express messenger to the private car and making him comfortable in Maxwell's own state-room, the superintendent's curiosity got the better of him.

"You're not saying much, Calvin," he offered. "Have you found any clew to the mystery?"

"Clews?—yes; I've found plenty of them. They're slightly tangled as yet, but we'll get hold of the proper thread in a little while. When do we start back?"

"Any time, if you've seen all you want to. I'll have Allen get orders for us right now, if you say so."

The big-bodied Government man stood aside while the Corona operator called the despatcher and obtained the order for the return of the two-car special to Brewster. But after the bit of routine was finished he made another suggestion.

"I'd like to know, in so many words, exactly what was taken from the passengers on the train, Dick," he said. "Can't you have this young man catch the train somewhere and instruct the conductor to find out for us?"

Maxwell nodded and gave Allen the necessary directions. "Tell Mc-Carty to wire his answer direct to me at Brewster," he added; and then, as the train was ready, the start was made for the return.

At the curve in Cromarty Gulch they found only Tarbell awaiting them. When the ex-cowboy had climbed aboard and the homeward run was resumed, Tarbell made his report. Harding and his posse were following the automobile tracks on foot. It was the sheriff's theory that, sooner or later, the men in the machine would have to stop somewhere, whereupon the dogs would once more be able to take up the trail. Harding was convinced now that he was trailing the Weber gang, and he believed that the start toward Brewster was only a blind.

Sprague smiled again at the mention of the dogs.

"How far is it to Brewster?" he asked.

"About thirty miles, by the wagon road," Maxwell guessed.

"Good; we're safely rid of Mr. Harding and his people, and of Follansbee and his dogs, for some little time, I take it. Now we are free to do a little business on our own account. I want to know everything you can tell me about this man Murtrie; what he looked like, what he did, and all the rest."

"It's a sort of thankless job to backcap a dead man," Maxwell demurred. "Just the same, Murtrie always looked to me like a hired assassin—the kind you see on the vaudeville stage, you know. He was a big, beefy fellow, with a puffy face and a bad eye."

"Light or dark?"

"Dark; black eyes and a heavy, drooping mustache. To tell the truth, he looked as little like an expert mining engineer as anything you can imagine. Wouldn't you say so, Tarbell?"

The sober-faced young man who had made his record running down cattle thieves in Montana nodded gravely.

"What time he put in up at the Molly Baldwin wouldn't count for much," was Tarbell's comment. "Mighty near any hour o' the day or night you could find him tryin' out his 'system' at Bart Holladay's faro game; leastways, when he wasn't hangin' round the railroad depot."

"Yet you say, Maxwell, that he was sent out here by the New York mineowners to keep cases on the gold output?" questioned Sprague.

"Why, yes; that is what everybody said."

"It's what he said himself," Tarbell put in.

"But you didn't believe it?" queried Sprague, turning upon the ex-cowboy.

"I didn't know just what to believe," was the frank admission. "He was mighty thick with Calthrop and Higgins, the two fellows that are operatin' the Molly Baldwin under the lease; but, as I say, he didn't stay there none to speak of. And as for his bein' a minin' sharp—I don't know about that, but I do know that he was a brass-pounder."

"A telegraph operator, you mean?" said Sprague quickly. "How do you happen to know that, Archer?"

"'Cause I caught him more than once 'listenin' in' at the commercial office downstairs in the depot."

"How could you tell?" demanded the chemist shrewdly.

"If you was an operator yourself, you'd know, Mr. Sprague. You can take my word for it, all right."

The man whose recreative hobby was the application of scientific principles to the detection of crime, smoked in reflective silence for a minute or two. Finally he said: "You are a much better spotter than you think you are, Archer. It is a pity that this man Murtrie is dead. If he wasn't, I'd like to have you shadow him a bit more for us. Where did you say he kept himself chiefly—in Brewster, I mean?"

"At Bart Holladay's road-house, on the Little Butte pike. It's a tough joint, with faro and roulette runnin' continuous in the back rooms, and half a dozen poker games workin' overtime upstairs."

"I see," said Sprague thoughtfully; "or rather, I'd like to see. Maybe, before I go home, you'll take a little time off some evening, Archer, and drive me out to this road-house. It's a free-for-all, isn't it?"

Tarbell grinned. "All you got to do is to give the barkeep' the high sign and go in and blow yourself. Anybody's money's as good as anybody else's, to Bart."

"All right; we'll put that down as one of our small recreations, after this dead-man muddle is straightened out for Mr. Maxwell. Is this Brewster we're coming to?"

It was; and when the train shrilled to a stand at the station the company ambulance was waiting to take the wounded express messenger out to the hospital. Also, there was a young man from *The Tribune* office, who was anxious to get the latest story of the sensational hold-up of the "Flying Plainsman." Tarbell was detailed to give the reporter the facts in the case, so far as they had developed, and Maxwell and his guest climbed the stair to the despatcher's room in the second story. Connolly was rattling his key in the sending of a train-order when they entered, but he "broke" long enough to hand the superintendent a freshly written telegram.

It was from McCarty, the "Plainsman" conductor, and it was dated from Angels.

To R. Maxwell, G. S.,

Brewster:

"Can't find that anybody lost anything. Hold-up in Pullmans was probably meant to keep passengers bluffed while the others went through express-car.

McCarty.

Sprague nodded slowly when the telegram was handed him. "That is what I suspected; in fact, I was morally certain of it, but I thought it would do no harm to make sure." Then he turned to the chubby despatcher who had finished sending his train-order. "Mr. Connolly, has any one been here to ask questions about this hold-up—since we left, I mean?"

Connolly looked his astonishment and nodded an affirmative.

"Two men from out of town, weren't they?" Sprague suggested.

Again the despatcher nodded, and it was only his respect for the big man that kept him from asking how the incident could possibly be known to one who had been thirty miles away at the moment of its happening.

"Go on and tell us about it," Sprague directed; and at this Connolly found his tongue.

"It was them two fellows that are operating the Molly Baldwin mine, Calthrop and Higgins. They'd heard of the hold-up through the operator at Little Butte, they said, and they drove down in their auto. They seemed to be a whole lot stirred up about the taking of Murtrie's body; said they felt responsible to his friends in the East. They wanted to know particularly what we were doing about it, and if there was any chance of our catching up with the body-snatchers."

Sprague waved his cigar in token of his complete satisfaction. Then he went abruptly to something else.

"Mr. Connolly, where can you catch that eastbound train again for us by wire?"

Connolly glanced at his train-sheet.

"She's due at Arroyo in eight minutes. It ain't a stop, but I can have the operator flag her down."

"Good. Do it, and send this message to McCarty, conductor. Are you ready?" And when the despatcher, quickly calling the station in question, signalled his readiness, Sprague went on, dictating slowly: "'Hold your train and have Calmaine, chief clerk, come to the wire.' Sign Mr. Maxwell's name—that's all right, isn't it, Maxwell?"

"Anything you say is all right," was the quick response.

"It won't ball things up—holding your train a few minutes at Arroyo?"

"Connolly will see to that. It's off time now and running on orders, anyway."

"Then we can sit down quietly and wait to hear from the exceedingly capable-looking young man who has the honor to be your chief clerk," said the Government man, and he calmly planted himself in the nearest chair.

"Calmaine will probably be abed and asleep in the Pullman," Maxwell suggested. "I suppose your call is important enough to warrant his getting up and dressing?"

"It is—fully important enough; as I think you will be ready to admit when we hear from Arroyo." Then he extended a handful of cigars. "Have a fresh smoke; oh, you needn't look cross-eyed at them; they're your own, you know. I swiped them out of your private box in the car when you weren't looking."

Maxwell took a cigar half-absently. His mind was dwelling upon the mystery surrounding the unexplainable hold-up, with the surface current of thought directed toward Connolly's sounder, through which would presently come the expected message from Arroyo.

It was while he was holding the lighted match to the cigar that the sounder began to click. He translated for Sprague: "Train here. McCarty gone to wake Mr. Calmaine." After that there was a trying wait of perhaps five minutes. Then the sounder began to chatter rapidly, and Maxwell bounded from his chair.

"Good God!" he ejaculated, "he says Calmaine isn't on the train!"

"Ah!" breathed the big-bodied expert, rising and stretching his huge arms over his head. "Again we get the expected precipitation in the test-tube. Mr. Connolly, suppose you ask McCarty if Mr. Calmaine has been on the train at all."

Connolly hastily tapped out the question, and a moment afterward vocalized the answer.

"He was on the train when it left Brewster. Nobody seems to remember seeing him after that."

Sprague turned to his host.

"I think we can let Mr. McCarty go in peace now, with a promise that we sha'n't bother him again tonight. Tarbell is the man we shall need from this on. Where has he gone?"

Tarbell was at that moment opening the corridor door, having but now got rid of the newspaper reporter. Sprague began on him briskly.

"Archer, the muddle is cleared up, and I'm minded to take that bit of recreation we spoke of a while back—at this Mr. Bart Holladay's show place, you know. How far did you say it is?"

The ex-cowboy looked dazed, but he made shift to answer the direct question.

"About two mile, I reckon."

"Outside of the city limits?"

"Yep."

"Then we can't take a policeman along for protection—I'm a tenderfoot, and all tenderfoots are nervous, you know. That's too bad. And Mr. Harding isn't here to let us have the backing of the county officers. Dear, dear! Are they *very* bad men out there, Archer?"

Tarbell grinned sheepishly, feeling sure that the big man was in some way making game of him.

"They'd eat you alive if they thought you was an officer headin' a raid on 'em. Otherwise, I reckon they wouldn't bite you none."

"Well, I suppose we shall have to risk it—without the policeman," said the expert with a good-natured laugh. "Perhaps we can persuade them that we are just 'lookers,'" he suggested. And then: "I suppose you have your artillery with you?"

Tarbell nodded. "A couple o' forty-fives. I'd hardly go huntin' train-robbers without 'em."

"Of course not. Suppose you divide up with Mr. Maxwell here, and then go and find us an auto; just the bare car; we'll manage to drive it ourselves. And, Archer, get a good big one, with easy springs. If there is any one thing I dislike more than another it is to be jammed up in a little, hard-riding car. I need plenty of room. I guess I grew too much when I was a boy."

The young man with the sober face went away, still more or less dazed; and Maxwell dropped the weapon that Tarbell had given him into the outside pocket of his top-coat.

"I am completely and totally in the dark as yet, Calvin," he ventured. "Did you mean what you said when you told Tarbell just now that the muddle was cleared up?"

"I did, indeed. And it is as pretty a piece of off-hand plotting as I have ever come across, Dick. Don't you see daylight by this time?"

"Not a ray. It may be just natural stupidity; or it may be only a bad case of rattle. I blew up and went to pieces when that wire came about Calmaine. Why, good heavens, think of it, Calvin! If the boy's gone, those proxies are gone, too!"

"Quite so. And you are wondering why a good, steady, well-balanced young fellow like your chief clerk should get himself lost in the shuffle when his mission was so vitally important. What do you suppose has become of him?"

"I can't begin to guess. That is what is driving me mad. Of course, the supposition is that he got mixed up in this body-snatching business in some way. But why should he? Why the devil should he, Calvin, when he had every possible reason for dodging and keeping out of it?"

"I don't know," rejoined the big man, with a head-wagging of doubt, real or simulated. "One of the most difficult things to prefigure—you might say the only one which refuses to come under the test-tube formulas—is just what a given man will do under certain suddenly sprung conditions. It is the only problematical element which ever enters into these puzzle-solvings of mine. I haven't the pleasure of an intimate acquaintance with your chief clerk, but from the little I've seen of him I should say unhesitatingly that he is a young man for an emergency, quick to think, and fully as quick to act. I'm banking on that impression and hoping that he hasn't disappointed me."

"Then you know what has become of him?"

Sprague smiled impassively. "I shouldn't be able to convince you that it is knowledge," he admitted. "You'd call it nothing more than a wild guess. Isn't that our auto that I hear?"

Maxwell stepped to a window and looked down upon the plaza.

"It's somebody's auto," he said. "There are two men in it." And a moment later—"They are coming up here."

The demonstrator of scientific principles hooked his elbows on the counter railing and laughed gently. "Our two nervous friends from the Molly Baldwin," he predicted. "They are still worrying about the loss of their corpse." And even as he spoke the two young lessees of the mine came tramping in, their faces sufficiently advertising their anxiety.

Maxwell nodded to the file-leader of the pair.

"Hello, Calthrop," he said. "What do you know?"

"Nothing more than we did. We heard that you'd got back from Cromarty and thought maybe you could tell us something."

"Not anything definite," was the superintendent's brief rejoinder. "You know the facts; Murtrie's body was taken out of its coffin and carried off. There were auto tracks on the mesa at the head of Cromarty Gulch, and Harding and his posse are following them. That's all."

"Wh-where is that coffin, now?" It was the younger of the two who wanted to know.

Without looking around, Maxwell felt that Sprague's eyes were signalling him, but he could hardly determine why he was moved to tell only part of the truth.

"It was taken off at Corona."

The one who answered to the name of Calthrop swore morosely. "It's the Scott Weber gang, ain't it, Mr. Maxwell?" he asked.

"I think so; and Harding thinks so. But why they should steal only a dead body is beyond me—or any of us."

The two young men exchanged a whispered word or two and went out, with the anxiety in their faces thickly shot with fresh perplexity. At the door Higgins turned for another asking.

"If we pay the freight on it, can we have that coffin back, Mr. Maxwell? We bought it and paid for it."

This time Maxwell caught Sprague's eye and read the warning in it. "We'll see about that later," he said.

When the door slammed at the outgoing of the pair, Sprague was laughing again.

"After those two young fellows have turned a few more sharp corners in the rather crooked course they're steering, they'll learn to take their medicine without making faces over it," he remarked. "Any signs of Archer yet?"

Maxwell turned back to the window.

"Yes; he's coming. He's pulling up on the other side of the plaza—doesn't want to run afoul of these mining friends of ours, I suppose."

"Archer has a head on him, all right, and I like him. You want to swing onto that young fellow, Dick. He'll make a good man for you some day. Let's go down and join him."

Tarbell waited when he saw the boss and his guest coming across the plaza, and when his two fares were stowed in the roomy tonneau of the big car he let the clutch in for the short run to the western suburb. The night was clear and starlit, but there was no moon. Since the hour was well past midnight, the streets were practically deserted. Beyond the last of the street-crossing arc-lamps the western road led away through a forest of dwarf pine, a broad white pathway winding among the trees and roughly paralleling the railroad.

At one of the shorter turns in the pike they came upon the brilliantly lighted road-house. In appearance it was a modern roadside tavern, one of the many which owe their sudden recrudescence to the automobile. It was withdrawn a little from the highway, and was surrounded by ample stables and shelter sheds opening upon a great square yard with wide carriage gates. Tarbell backed the auto to a stand among a number of others in the yard, and a man with a lantern came, ostensibly to offer help, but probably to make sure that the new-comers were harmless.

"It's all right, Jerry," said Tarbell, hopping out. "Mr. Maxwell and a friend o' his from the East. Games goin'?"

The man nodded and held his lantern so that Maxwell and his guest could see to get out of the tonneau. Then he turned away and left them.

Tarbell led the way to the porch entrance and on the step explained the sight-seeing process to the one who was supposed to be inexperienced.

"It's an open game, as I let on to you," he told Sprague. "You go into the bar and buy. After that you do as you please."

Sprague paused for a single question.

"What do we find?" he asked.

"A lot of young bloods from town, mostly," was Tarbell's reply. "Holladay's got sense enough to keep his own gang in the quiet and take his rake-off as it comes—from the bank and the tables and the roulette wheels."

Sprague made the single question a little more comprehensive.

"I didn't mean the people, so much as the place; if we should want to get out in a hurry—how about that?"

Tarbell indicated a hall door at the side of the main entrance, adding the information, however, that it was usually kept locked.

"Good. After we get to going, inside, you make it your job to unlock that door, Archer, and to put the key in your pocket. Now I'm ready, and I want to see it all." And they went in.

The bar-room proved to be typical of its kind: plainly furnished, with a wide country-house fireplace and a sanded floor. As the night was close and warm, the card-tables were ranged beneath the open windows; only two or three of them were occupied, and the bar itself was empty. Maxwell and his guest sat down at one of the unoccupied tables, and Tarbell ordered for the three. When the liquor was served, he said: "You don't need to sop it up inside of you if you don't want to; it's none too good."

With this for a caution the two who were warned carefully spilled their portions on the sanded door, and Sprague ordered cigars, skilfully juggling them when they came and substituting three of his own—or rather of Maxwell's. Then he made a sign to Tarbell and they began to make a slow tour of the open game-rooms.

The first-floor rooms, where a pair of roulette wheels were spinning and a faro game was running, were well filled. Brewster had lately passed an anti-gambling ordinance, and the vice had been temporarily driven beyond the corporation limits. Maxwell saw a few men whom he knew, and many who were well known to the Brewster police. Under the archway dividing the red-and-black wheels from the faro table Sprague whispered in his ear.

"I'm looking for a man whose New York name is 'Tapper' Givens," he said. "He has a red face, black hair and eyes, and weighs about one hundred and eighty pounds. He may, or may not, be wearing a heavy black mustache, and—"

Maxwell looked up with a puzzled frown. "Say, Calvin; you're describing the dead man," he broke in.

"Am I? Never mind if I am. If you should happen to see any one filling the requirements, just point him out to me. I might overlook him in such a crowd as this, you know." And then to Tarbell, who had just found them again: "Got that key, Archer?"

The ex-cowboy showed the hall door key cautiously in his palm and returned it to his pocket. Sprague smiled and whispered again.

"How about the rooms upstairs? Are they open to inspection, too?"

Tarbell shook his head. "No; private poker games, most of 'em."

"Nevertheless, I think we shall have to have a look-in," said the big man quietly. "Can't you arrange it?"

"Not without riskin' a scrap."

"We don't want to start anything, but we've just naturally got to have that look-in, Archer," persisted the guest.

The grave-faced young Tennessean thrust out his jaw. "What you say goes as she lays," he returned, and thereupon he showed them the way upstairs.

At the stair-head there was a guard, a bullet-headed ring-fighter posing as a waiter, with a square patch of an apron and a napkin thrown over one arm.

"Mr. Maxwell's lookin' for one of his men," said Tarbell, realizing that some sort of an excuse must be offered; and the ring-fighter, who knew the railroad superintendent by sight, nodded and said:

"That's aw right; who is ut?"

"Harvey Calmaine," said Tarbell, giving the first name that came into his head.

To the astoundment of at least two of the three, the bullet-headed guard stood aside and pointed to a door at the farther end of the upper hall.

"He's in there," he grunted. "Somebody's been givin' him th' knock-out drops, an' they're workin' over him." Then he spun around and put a ham-like hand flat against Maxwell's chest. "Ye'll gimme yer wor-rd, Mis-ther Maxwell, that ye haven't got the sheriff's posse at yer back?"

"No," said Maxwell, and he managed to say it with a degree of cool-ness which he was very far from feeling. "We're all here; all there are of us."

"Aw right; gwan in. But there'll be no scrappin', mind ye. If there does be anny, I'll be takin' a hand, meself."

Sprague took the lead in the silent march to the indicated door, his big bulk looming colossal in the narrow, low-studded hallway. Reaching the door, he turned the knob noiselessly. "Locked," he muttered, and then he drew back and put his shoulder to it.

The lock gave way with a report like a muffled pistol shot and the door flew open. The room was lighted by a single incandescent bulb swinging on its cord from the ceiling. On a cot which had been dragged out from its place beside the wall lay the chief clerk, bare-footed, gagged, and securely bound with many wrappings of cotton clothes-line. Standing over him, one of them with the lighted match he had been holding to the bare foot-soles still blazing, were two others; a red-headed, yellow-faced man with one eye missing, and a thick-shouldered athlete aptly answering to Sprague's description whispered to the superintendent in the room below.

Maxwell sprang forward with an oath when he recognized the man with the burning match. "*Murtrie!*" he exploded; and the torturer with the black eyes and puffy face dropped the match-end and grabbed for his weap-on. He was a fraction of a second too slow. Tarbell had covered him with a movement which was too quick for the eye to follow and was reaching backward for the other gun—which Maxwell gave him—while Sprague closed the door and set his back against it.

"The jig is up—definitely up, Givens," said the Government man pleas-antly. And then to Tarbell: "Herd those two into a corner, Archer, while we take some of these impediments off of Mr. Calmaine."

When the chief clerk was freed he tried to sit up; tried and would have fallen if Maxwell had not caught him. "They've burked me," he mumbled; "but—they didn't make me tell, and they didn't get—the papers."

"Take it easy," said Maxwell soothingly; "You'll be all right in a minute or so." Then, in a fresh access of rage: "They'll pay for this, Harvey, if it takes every dollar I've got in the world!"

Calmaine tried sitting up again, found that he could compass it, and reached feebly for his shoes and socks.

"The—the proxies are safe—if it doesn't rain," he quavered, his mind still running on the precious papers of which he had been the bearer. "Get—get me out of this and into an auto and I'll find them for you. We might—might catch Number Six, if we hurry."

Tarbell, with Sprague's help, had deftly handcuffed the two men whom he had backed into a corner. It was the one-eyed man who first found speech in an outpouring of profanity venomous and horrible. "You ain't got us out o' here yet," he spat, trailing the defiance out in more of the cursings.

"But we're going to get you out if we have to throw you through the window," said Sprague quietly. Then to Maxwell: "Help the boy with his shoes, Dick. We're due to have a jail delivery here, any minute."

It took some little time to get the maltreated chief clerk shod and afoot, and even then he was well-nigh crippled. But he was game to the last. "They took my gun away from me," he complained. "If I only had something to fight with—Archer, give me that black devil's pistol."

Sprague's warning had not been baseless. The stair-head guard had doubtless seen Sprague shoulder the locked door open, and had sprung a still alarm. There was a hurrying of many feet in the hall, marking the gathering of the gambling-house fighting force. While Calmaine was asking for a weapon, the crowd in the hall began to batter at the door, against which Sprague had once more put his huge bulk, and were calling to Murtrie to open to them.

Sprague gave his directions snappily, as if he were signalling his football squad. "Draw that cot a little this way—that's right. Now then, Archer, stand here against the wall with your two jail-birds, and when I give the word, rush 'em for the yard by the stairway entrance. If they don't obey, plug 'em, and plug 'em quick. Maxwell, you and the boy get over on this side. When you're ready, turn off that light. Quick! They're going to charge us!"

The simple programme was carried out precisely and to the letter. When the rush came the room was in darkness, and Sprague stepped lightly aside. Thereupon a dozen charging men, finding no resistance in the suddenly released door, piled themselves in cursing confusion over the barricading cot.

"Now!" shouted Sprague, and the dash for liberty was made, with the big man in the lead clearing the hall of its stragglers, brushing them aside with his mighty weight or driving them before him like chaff in the fury of his onset. At the stair-head there were more coming up from below: Sprague caught the bullet-headed ring-fighter around the waist, and using him as a missile, cleared the stairway at a single throw. "Come on!" he yelled to those who were behind; and a moment later the unlocked door at the stair-foot gave them egress to the open air and to the yard where the automobiles were parked.

Quite naturally, the din of the battle had precipitated a panic in the unlicensed road-house, and the building was disgorging, through doors and windows, and even over the roofs of the shelter sheds. Tarbell drove his two prisoners into the tonneau of the hired car, while Maxwell promptly cranked the motor and Sprague lifted Calmaine bodily to the front seat. Ten seconds beyond this, while the panic was still at its height, the hired car, leading all others in the townward rush, was leaving a dense dust trail to befog its followers, and the capture and rescue were facts accomplished.

With Tarbell at the steering-wheel, the car sped silently through the western suburb and came into the deserted, echoing streets of the city. Without asking any questions, the ex-cowboy drove straight to the county jail and pulled up at the curb in front of the grim building, with its heavily grilled windows showing their steel barrings in the street light. Sprague passed the two prisoners out to him, jerking even the bigger of the two clear of the auto step as if he had been a feather-weight. But when Tarbell would have marched the pair across the sidewalk, Sprague called out.

"Just one question, Givens," he said brusquely. "You know what you're in for; you know that you are still wanted in Cleveland on that charge of counterfeiting. But if you'll answer one question straight, we'll forget the Ohio indictment for the present. What did you do with the swag that you lifted a few hours ago?"

For five full seconds the black-haired man kept silence. Then he spoke as the spirit moved him.

"It's where you won't get it—you n'r them make-believe crooks up at the Molly Baldwin!" he rasped.

"Oho!" Sprague laughed. "So you planned it to give your side partners in this little game the double-cross, did you? It's like you. Take them away, Archer."

"And—and hurry back!" whispered Calmaine hoarsely. "We've simply *got* to catch Number Six, I tell you!"

Thus urged, Tarbell expedited matters with the night jailer and came running back to take his place behind the steering-wheel.

"Where now?" he asked, dropping the clutch in; and it was Calmaine who gave the direction.

"The Reservation Road east; it's the one we came in over."

Tarbell easily broke all the speed records, to say nothing of speed limits, in the race to the eastward over the dry mesa country. Twenty-odd miles from town they met the sheriff's party, and there was a momentary halt for explanations. "Camp down right where you are, and we'll go back pretty soon and send a bunch of autos out after you," was Maxwell's word of encouragement; and then the big car sped on its way toward Cromarty Gulch.

Calmaine seemed to have preserved his sense of locality marvellously. A few hundred yards short of the spot at the gulch head where Follansbee's dogs had begun their aimless circlings, he told Tarbell to pull up.

"They are right along here, somewhere," he said, getting out to hobble painfully ahead of the others when Tarbell took off a side-lamp to serve for a lantern. "They had me blindfolded, at first, and I didn't know what they were trying to do with me. When they chucked me into the auto, I tried to make a get-away. While they were knocking me silly again, I managed to get the papers out of my pocket and fire them into the sagebrush. It was right along here, somewhere."

It was Sprague who discovered the thick packet upon which so much depended. It was lying cleverly chance-hidden under a clump of the greasewood bushes. "Found!" he announced. And then he gave the young chief clerk his due meed of commendation. "You're a young man to bet on, Mr. Calmaine. What we've been able to do, thus far, wouldn't amount to much if you hadn't kept your head." Then he turned quickly to the superintendent. "How do we stand for time, now, Maxwell?"

Maxwell held his watch to the light and shook his head dejectedly.

"Number Six, the Fast Mail, is due at Corona in five minutes. We can never make it in this world!"

"You bet we can!" shouted Tarbell. "Help Mr. Calmaine, and pile into the car—quick!"

The short race to the near-by mining-camp was a sheer breakneck dash, but Tarbell made good. When the four of them leaped from the car and stormed into Allen's office, the Fast Mail had already whistled for the "clear" signal, and the operator was reaching for the cord of his semaphore to give the "go-by" wigwag. They yelled at him as one man; and a few seconds later the fast train slid to a shrieking stop at the station.

Maxwell would have sent Tarbell on to New York with the precious proxies, but Calmaine pleaded pathetically for his chance to finish that which he had begun.

"I'll be all right as soon as I can get into the sleeper and get these infernal shoes off," he protested. "It's my job, Mr. Maxwell; for pity's sake don't make me a quitter!"

"Let him go," said Sprague; "he's earned his chance to stay in the game—and this time he'll make a touch-down." And so it was decided.

When the Fast Mail, with its lately added passenger, had slid away among the hills to the eastward, the three who remained at Corona climbed into the hired auto and Tarbell drove another record race to town, pausing only once, when they reached the sheriff's roadside camp, to take on Harding and as many of his deputies as the car would hold.

By Maxwell's direction, Tarbell drove first to the railroad head-quarters, where the superintendent and his guest got out. At the office entrance another dusty car was drawn up; and in the upper corridor they found the two young men from the Molly Baldwin mine, still seeking for information. Sprague disposed of them, and he did it with business-like brevity.

"Your dead man has been found," he told them crisply. "He is at present in the county jail, with one of his accomplices; and when he is given the third degree, he will probably tell all he knows. It's a weakness he has—not to be able to hold out against a bit of rough handling. If you two fellows will make a clean breast of your part in the swindle to the prosecuting attorney, and promise to play fair with your lessors in future, it is likely that you'll be let off with a fine, and you'll probably be able to bag the remainder of the gang and to recover your lost gold."

The two young men heard, gasped, and backed away. When they were gone, Maxwell unlocked the door of his business office, snapped on the lights, opened his desk, and pressed the electric button which summoned Connolly, the night despatcher.

"I thought you'd like to know that we've caught up with the dead man, Dan," he said, when the fat despatcher came in; and then he briefed the story of the chase, winding up with a peremptory order to be sent to the division despatcher at the Copah end of the line not to let the eastbound connection get away from the Fast Mail at the main line junction.

When Connolly had gone back to his key, Maxwell wheeled upon his guest.

"It's late, Calvin, and by all the laws of hospitality I ought to take you home and put you to bed. But I'll be hanged if you shall close an eye until you've told me how you did all this!"

The expert chemist ex-foot-ball coach planted himself in the easiest of the office chairs and chuckled joyously.

"Gets you, does it?" he said; and then: "I'm not sure that I can explain it so that you will understand, but I'll try. In the first place, it is necessary to go at these little problems with a perfectly open mind—the laboratory mind, which is neither prejudiced nor prepossessed nor in any way concerned with anything but the bare facts. Reason, and the proper emphasis to be placed upon each fact as it comes to bat, are the two needful qualities in any problem-solving—and about the only two."

"You are soaring around about a mile over my head; but go on," said Maxwell.

"All right; I'll set out the facts in the order in which they came to me. First, I see a dozen men loading a coffin into an express-car. I note the extreme weight, and wonder how a dead man, any dead man who doesn't have to have his coffin built to order, can be so infernally heavy. Next, you tell me about your proxy fact—which doesn't have any bearing at the moment—and then you tell me about the dead man, and how his friends were shipping him to Kentucky. Then comes the news of the bizarre hold-up in Cromarty Gulch. Instantly the reasoning mind, the laboratory mind, if you prefer, goes to work, with the two foreknown facts—the heavy-dead-man fact, and the fact that your chief clerk is on that train with his valuable papers—clamoring each for its hearing. Don't let me bore you."

"Heavens—you're not boring me! What next?"

"Reason, the laboratory brand of it, tells me immediately that your proxy fact has the emphasis. You had told me that your Wall Street opponents had been throwing stumbling-blocks in your way in the obtaining of the proxies. Here, said I, is the last desperate resort. Nevertheless, there were complications. I was pretty sure that the hold-ups had taken Calmaine and his papers; that this was what the hold-up was for. But in order to get track of them—and of Calmaine—other facts must be added. We added them on the trip with the special train; all we needed, and a few more thrown in for good measure."

"I don't see it," Maxwell objected.

"Don't you? When we reached the scene of the hold-up, I was already doubting the heavy-dead-man theory; doubting it extremely. Also, my reason told me that the robbers, carrying some weight which was heavier than any dead person, would not trust to a team which could be overtaken, if need be, by pursuers on foot. Hence the automobile track that we found. Then we came to the coffin, and half of the mystery vanished at once. If you hadn't been excited and—well, let us say, prepossessed, you would have noticed that there was no smell of disinfectants, that the coffin pillow wasn't dented with the print of a head, that the broken glass was lying on the pillow, as it wouldn't have been if the man's head had been there when the plate was smashed, that—"

"Great Scott," Maxwell broke in, in honest self-depreciation, "what blind bats we are—most of us!"

"Oh, no; I was bringing the specially trained mind to bear, you must remember; the scientifically trained mind. You couldn't afford to cultivate it; it wouldn't leave room for your business of railroad managing. But I'll cut it short. I saw that there had been no corpse in the coffin, and that there had been something else in it—something heavy enough to leave its marks on the silk lining, which was torn and soiled. Also, I saw, away down in the foot end of the thing, an ingot-shaped chunk of something that looked like a bar of gold bullion; one piece of the heavy coffin load that had been overlooked in the hurried emptying. That's why I advised you to bring the coffin back on your train. There's a ten-thousand-dollar gold brick in it, right now!"

"Heavens and earth!" gasped the listener; but Sprague went on rapidly.

"Just here is where your machine-made detective would have missed the emphasis. But the scientist, having once for good and sufficient reasons placed his emphasis, never has occasion to change it. The main thing yet was the stopping of your messenger to Ford. I was convinced that the gold robbery, in which, of course, not only the two young lessees, but the man Murtrie as well, must be implicated, was only a side-issue, intended either to divert attention from the main thing, or as a double-cross theft on the part of Murtrie. When you and Tarbell described Murtrie for me on the way back to town, I had it all, simply because I happened to know the man. He is a counterfeiter, whom I have twice run down for the Department of Justice; but who, both times, contrived to break jail and get away."

"But how were you able to strike so sure and hard at Holladay's?"

"Just a bit more reasoning; as you'll see presently. After we had established the fact that Calmaine wasn't on the train—but argue it out for yourself. They'd take him somewhere where he could be kept safe and out of the way until the criminals concerned were all securely out of the country. And where would they take him if not to the unlawful den out yonder on the pike where Murtrie was best known, and from which, no doubt, he secured his helpers for the hold-up job?"

"But hold on," Maxwell interrupted. "I haven't got it entirely clear yet. If Murtrie put up this job with Calthrop and Higgins—"

Sprague shook his head.

"You have no imagination, Dick. Murtrie came here to do you up in the proxy business—as the Wall Street crowd's last resort. He got in with Calthrop and Higgins and showed them how to beat their game, meaning to put the double-cross on them—as he did—when the time came. He was merely killing two birds with one stone; but your bird was the big one. I don't know what sort of a dodge he put up with Calthrop and Higgins, but I can suppose that there is a trusty confederate at the Kentucky end of the string who is doubtless waiting now for a corpse that will never come."

"Of course!" said the unimaginative one disgustedly. "Just the same, it's all mighty miraculous to me, Calvin—how you can reason out these things hot off the bat, as you do. Why, Great Jonah! I had all the opportunities you had, and then some; and I didn't see an inch ahead of my nose at any stage of the game!"

The big man rose and yawned good-naturedly.

"It's my hobby—not yours," he laughed; and then, as the telephone buzzer went off with a purring noise under Maxwell's desk: "That will be Mrs. Maxwell, calling up to ask why in the world you don't come home. Tell her all right, and let's go. It will be the biggest miracle of all if you succeed in getting me up in time for breakfast tomorrow—or rather, I should say, today, since it's three o'clock, and worse, right now."

Maxwell put the receiver to his ear and exchanged a few words with some one at the other end of the wire. When he closed his desk and made ready to go, a little frown of reflective puzzlement was gathering between his eyes.

"You know too much—too thundering much, Calvin. As I said a while back, it's uncanny. It was Alice; and she said the very words you said she would: 'Why in the world don't you come home, Dick?' If you weren't so blooming big and beefy and good-natured—but, pshaw! Who ever heard of a fat wizard? Come on; let's go and hunt a taxi. It's too far to walk."

CHAPTER 3

THE ELECTROCUTION OF
TUNNEL NUMBER THREE

At ten o'clock on the second Tuesday after the return of the lately promoted chief night despatcher, Dan Connolly, from his wedding trip, the business of the Brewster wire office had settled down, momentarily at least, into the comfortable rut of routine. Everything was moving smoothly on the double division, and between the leisurely inscribing of the figured entries on the train-sheet, the fat, jolly-looking night chief had a chance to fill his corn-cob pipe and to swap a word of gossip now and then with Johnson, the car-record operator who, as "Wire-Devil" Bolton's successor, was clattering at his type-writer in the far corner of the bare room.

It was after he had finished typing the long "record" report from Red Butte that Johnson twisted himself in his chair to say: "Who is that fellow 'Scientific Sprague' that I've been hearing so much about since I came on the job, Dan?"

The fat despatcher chuckled reminiscently and sat back in his tilting chair.

"Mr. Sprague? He's a whole team, and an extra horse hitched on behind, Shorty; that's about what he is. Don't you ever go around advertising your freshness in the Timanyoni by giving it out that you don't know Mr. Calvin Sprague."

"I reckon I've already done done it, haven't I?" laughed the car-record man. "What if you fix me so I won't have to do it again?"

Connolly held a lighted match to the blackened bowl of the corn-cob, and then put both match and pipe aside to take the "train-passing" report of the incoming westbound "Quick-step" as it was clicked through the sounder from the first telegraph station east of Brewster.

"Mr. Sprague is about the biggest man that ever walked into this office, Shorty," he averred, after he had made the proper train-sheet entry for the approaching train. "Big up and down, big through the middle, big sideways, and biggest of all in his think-tank. He can look you over twice and tell you the exact size of the yellow spot on your liver; and if that won't do, he'll look you over again and tell you how all-fired near you came to breaking your bond record one night up at that little shack station you've been running in the mining country."

The newly appointed car-record man bounded out of his chair as if he had been shot.

"I—I didn't, Dan!" he protested, dry-lipped; "so help me God, I didn't!" And then, curiosity getting the better of the sudden shock: "How in Sam Hill did you know?"

Connolly grinned good-naturedly and made a motion with the flat of his hand as if he would reach across the room and push Johnson back into his chair.

"Take it plumb easy, kid," he laughed. "I was only talking through my hat—just hitting out in the dark to show you how Mr. Sprague could size you up if he wanted to. But you asked who he is: he's a friend of Mr. Maxwell's, and he lives in Washington when he's at home—does chemical stunts in one of the Government offices. He's happened to soak in here a couple of times when we were needing a bushel or two more brains than we could make out to rustle up among ourselves, and—"

The break came in an importunate chattering of the west-line sounder on Connolly's table, and the despatcher righted his tilted chair with a thump and fell upon his key. The car-record man sat back with his hands locked at the nape of his neck and looked on absently. Out of the din and clatter of the several sounders he could easily have picked the story that was coming from the west over Connolly's wire, but the trained operator's habit of ignoring the irrelevant wire chatter was upon him, and his first intimation of the nature of the story came in the fading of the ruddy flush in Connolly's full-moon cheeks and the uncontrollable trembling of the despatcher's left and unbusied hand.

Instantly the short-legged car-record operator left his chair and crossed the room to hang over Connolly's shoulder.

"What's the trouble, Dan?" he asked.

"It's just a little more of the same," breathed the fat one vindictively. "I don't know what in the devil has got into the trainmen lately; this dog-blasted railroad's getting so it runs itself! Here's Seventeen overrunning her orders and trying to make the west end of Tunnel Number Three against the Fast Mail. Nophi says he argued with 'em, but they said they had plenty of time and went on. By grabs! If I was Mr. Maxwell I'd make a sizzlin' red-hot example of some of these crazy chance-takers!"

Johnson was running his eye down the columns of figures in the time-table.

"I wouldn't worry till I had to," he put in. "The Mail's twenty minutes off her schedule, and that gives Seventeen thirty minutes to make the six miles from Nophi to the tunnel and the mile and a quarter more to take her through to the west end siding. She'll make it all right."

"I know. But by Jasher! That ain't railroading," insisted Connolly. "Two months ago you wouldn't find a single train crew on the Short Line that'd take chances stealing sidings this way, and now they're all doing it. Besides, the tunnel's all tore up, with that electric-wiring gang working in it, and every crew on the west end knows it."

As he fumed, the despatcher rattled his key in the call for Junico, the only night station west of the tunnel at which there would be any chance of communicating with the off time eastbound Fast Mail. He knew it was only a chance. If the Mail had made up no more than five of the twenty minutes, it would already have passed Junico.

At the close of the impatient call the circuit broke and Junico "signed in." Connolly asked his question in clipped abbreviations, and got his answer shot-like. "Number Six passing now."

"*Hold Six*," snapped the despatcher hurriedly. For a full minute the sounder was silent. Then it began again. "Chased out quick as I could, but couldn't catch 'em," was Junico's incident-closing reply.

Connolly pounded with a fat fist upon the plate-glass top of his table in impotent wrath.

"There it is!" he gritted. "Now if anything happens to get in the way of them cussed chance-takers on Seventeen, there you are!"

Apparently there was nothing to be done but to await the event and to hope for an auspicious outcome. As Connolly had said, it wasn't railroading; and yet he knew well enough that on many railroads the stealing of sidings, the crawling up upon meeting-points by train crews hard pressed to make their schedules, is a violation of rules which is constantly winked at, and punished only when trouble ensues.

In the present case there should have been no trouble. With a clear thirty minutes in which to make less than eight miles, the time freight should be safely in on the siding at the west end of Tunnel Number Three some minutes before the Fast Mail could possibly cover its own intervening distance.

But on this particular Tuesday night the fates were inauspicious. Fifteen minutes farther along, after Johnson had gone back to his table in the corner, Connolly's west-wire sounder began to chatter furiously. The fat despatcher broke in promptly, and again the trembling fit seized upon the unbusied half of him.

"Oh, good Lord!" he groaned; and again: "Oh, good *Lord*!" Then the corridor door opened and Maxwell, the superintendent, came in, looking as he always did, the square-shouldered, square-jawed fighter of transportation battles, with a few streaks of youthful gray beginning to show in his tightly curled mustaches—a militant figure of a man giving a truthful impression of the fit and purposeful railroad field officer.

"What's the matter, Dan?" he demanded, making a quick push through the gate in the counter railing.

Connolly explained hastily.

"Seventeen tried to steal a siding on Six. Gallagher, the work-line operator at the electric gang's camp, has just called up to say that the freight's stuck in the tunnel—something off the track. A flagman has come back to the camp with the news, and he says the tunnel is blocked so they can't get through with a flag for Six."

"Good God, Dan—they've *got* to get through!" Maxwell exploded; and pushing the despatcher aside he cut in on the wire himself. There was a brief and brittle colloquy in which the emphatic word was made to do duty for entire sentences, a wait, and when the clicking began again the superintendent translated audibly, quite as if Connolly, listening with all of his five senses concentrated in the single one of hearing, were not taking the hopeful information as it came from the sounder.

"Stribling's there, and every sprinter in the camp is turning out to do a Marathon over the hill to the west end. Just the same, it will be touch and go if they make it in time to warn the Mail. How much late is Six?"

Connolly gave the time, making the proper deduction for the few minutes made up west of Junico. Maxwell glanced up at the time-standard clock on the wall.

"There is an even chance," he asserted hopefully. "There ought to be somebody in that mob of wire-stringers who can run the two miles in time to head off the Mail. How did you come to let things get into such a snarl as this, Dan?"

Again Connolly explained, and he did not try to make it easy for the offending crew of Number Seventeen. "Jasper didn't ask for orders at Nophi. He simply took snap judgment and went along, leaving the Nophi man to tell me after the thing was done."

"Jasper and his engineer will get thirty days on this, no matter how it turns out!" snapped the boss. "There is a good deal too much of this rule-breaking lately, and it's got to stop short. I won't have it.... Suffering cats! I wish those sprinters would hurry up and get word to us! My God, Dan, if that fast train gets into the tunnel before they catch it—"

A thunderous clangor in the station yard below the office windows cut into the sentence, and again the superintendent looked up at the clock.

"That's the 'Quick-step,' isn't it?" he said. "She's bringing an old friend of ours from the East, Dan—Mr. Sprague."

For a moment Connolly was able to take his mind off of the tragedy or near-tragedy which was working itself out to some kind of a climax in the far-away Hophra Mountains to the westward.

"You asked him to come and tell us why we're having this fit of extra cussedness all over the line?" he asked.

"Oh, no; the Department of Agriculture is sending him to make some soil tests in the Timanyoni. He writes that he is likely to be with us for a month or two."

"I'm glad," said Connolly simply. "Somehow, you feel as if you'd got a good solid mountain at your back when Mr. Sprague's around. I wonder if he'll come up here before he goes over to the hotel?"

Even as he spoke the door opened, and the man who looked like the elder brother of all the foot-ball "backs" in the intercollegiate try-out came in.

"Hello, hello, hello," he said jovially; "same old shop—same old worries, eh? How are you, Maxwell? And you, Mr. Connolly? Glad to see you both. What's the trouble this time? Anything a journeyman chemist can help you out on?"

Maxwell's mustaches took a sharper uptilt. "How did you know there was any trouble, Calvin?" he demanded quickly.

The big man leaned across the counter rail and laughed softly.

"There is nothing very occult about that," he rejoined. "You have it written all over your faces, both of you; and it is also written in the face of that young man over in the corner, who would like to hear what we're saying and can't quite compass it."

Maxwell explained briefly.

"Two of our trains are trying to get together on a single track up at Tunnel Number Three in the Hophras. There is a break-down in the tunnel, and half a hundred men are sprinting over the mountain to try to head off the other train."

"What? half a hundred? There ought to be at least one or two good sprinters among that many—somebody who can make your touch-down for you. How does it come that you happened to have as big a crowd as that on the side-lines—at this time of night?"

The superintendent went into details far enough to account for the crowd of volunteer rescuers.

"We are electrifying Tunnel Number Three, and the contractors' camp is at this end of the tunnel. It was the contractors' operator who sent in the alarm, and his chief engineer turned out the entire camp for us when I told him what to do."

"And you are waiting to get word?"

"Yes; waiting and hoping. By great good luck the Fast Mail is behind time. If it hasn't made up—"

A fierce clattering of the sounder on Connolly's table tore into the sentence, and in the midst of it Maxwell shot out his arms and drew a deep breath.

"Thank God!" he ejaculated, "they've caught the Mail! Now I'll go with you, Calvin." And then to Connolly: "Straighten things out for those fellows at the tunnel as quickly as you can, Dan, and get the wheels in motion again. Order up the engine from Second Seventeen if they need power to get that raffle out of the tunnel, and have somebody send over to Lopez Canyon for Benson to take charge. If you want to reach me, I'll be over at the hotel."

At the Hotel Topaz, across the plaza from the railroad head-quarters building, Maxwell saw his friend and sometime college classmate properly registered for a comfortable suite, and otherwise hospitably provided for before the pair of them went to smoke their bedtime pipes in the deserted writing-room facing the plaza.

"It's just my luck, Calvin, to be homeless about every other time you happen along," Maxwell apologized, when the pipes were lighted. "Alice's father and mother came through from California a few days ago, and carried her and the children off with them to New York and the Long Island shore. I'm a widower."

"That's all right," laughed the big man. "I'm going to be here in your midst for a month or more, and I wouldn't think of camping down on you for that length of time, anyway. Tomorrow you'll chase out and help me find a couple of office rooms where I can set up a small laboratory; and after that I'll go out in the woods and dig dirt—which it is my official nature so to do. That's enough about me. How are you getting along with the railroad wreckers?"

Maxwell lighted his pipe and answered categorically.

"We have heard nothing more, directly, from the Wall Street people since that break they made a few weeks ago trying to hold up the proxies I was sending to President Ford in New York," was Maxwell's summing up of the current situation. "But Ford assures me from time to time that they haven't quit. The latest competition rate ruling by the Interstate Commerce Commission makes it absolutely necessary for them to own or control a shorter line than their present one to Southern California points—this in order to protect their holdings in the big stock pool. They'd have what they need if they could corral the Nevada Short Line and tie it in with the Transcontinental's branch at Copah. Ford says they seem to consider it only a question of time until they absorb us. The T-C. people are spending a lot of money on their Jack's Canyon branch, putting it in shape for heavy traffic; and they can't hope to get the traffic unless they get us."

"This tunnel trouble tonight had nothing to do with the fight, I suppose?" queried Sprague reflectively.

"Oh, no. That was merely the outgrowth of a curious sort of letting down that comes once in a while on every railroad, no matter how well it may be manned or handled. Our let-down has been coming on gradually ever since we got over the 'Wire-Devil' scare. Men, good men who have been with us for years, take chances that would make your hair stand on end. Like this tonight," and he went on to describe the causes which had led up to the near-tragedy at Tunnel Number Three.

"I see," said Sprague. And then: "You say you are electrifying? I thought that was a luxury in which only the rich Eastern roads could indulge; and then only for their city terminals."

"It isn't exactly a luxury in our case; it's a working necessity. Tunnel Number Three is part of a shortening project carried out two years ago. It dodges under Burnt Mountain and cuts out five and two-tenths miles of the costliest, crookedest track in Tumble-Tree Canyon; track that we were never able to keep open for ten days in succession during the summer season of cloud-bursts and heavy storms. It is a timbered tunnel a mile and a quarter long, and the greater part of it is through loose, dry shale that practically kiln-dries the timber arching. From the time we began using it we've been fighting fire in it almost daily."

"Just so," said the chemistry expert. "So now you are putting in electricity to get rid of the fire-throwing locomotives. Where do you get your juice?"

"In Lopez Canyon, about three miles from the eastern portal, there is an excellent water-power. Eventually we shall use electricity for the entire hill-pull over the Hophras and so make a very handsome reduction in our fuel account."

"Good!" was the approving comment; and then the commentator came back to the details. "Electricity is another of my pet hobbies," he confessed. "What company is installing you—General Electric?"

"No; a New York firm—Grafton Brothers. I never heard of them until they came here."

Only the keenest of observers would have noted Sprague's accession of interest at the mention of the brotherly firm name.

"The Graftons, eh?" he said slowly. "How did you come to give them the job?"

"We had nothing to do with it out here. The deal was made in New York, with the Pacific Southwestern officials."

Sprague was nodding absently as if in answer to some unspoken query of his own when he said, "Have you ever met either of the Graftons, Dick?"

"No; they are only a name to me. Their representative on our job is an engineer named Stribling; a fine young fellow and a cracker-jack in his business. He was the man who turned out the crowd of sprinters for us tonight."

"Oho! General favorite all around, is he?"

Maxwell laughed dryly. "He has captured everybody except the one man who has had the most to do with him; that's Benson, our chief engineer. Jack is a sort of two-fisted bluffer himself—though it is only fair to say that he usually makes his bluff good—and I think he'd always bet on the field against a favorite. He says Stribling is too smooth; too damned smooth, is the way he generally phrases it."

"I shall have great pleasure in making the acquaintance of this Mr. Benson of yours some day," said the man from Washington. And after that he smoked on in silence until Maxwell was about to bid him good-night and suggest a bell-hop and the elevator—did suggest them, in fact.

"No, I'm not sleepy," was the rejoinder. "I was just thinking about railroads and tunnels and the like. If I were a railroad man, Dick, I believe I should have a crazy horror of a tunnel."

"Why?"

"Oh, I don't know; superstition, perhaps. You know the old saying:

> *Every superstition*
> *Is a foolish superstition*
> *Save the little superstition*
> *Of me.*

A tunnel always seems to me like a man's neck. One little grip and a squeeze, and your man, though he may have a couple of hundred pounds of other organs in perfect working order, is dead."

Maxwell laughed at the quaint conceit, though he was prompt to make the timely application.

"That would be true enough for us if Tunnel Number Three should ever be wiped out," he admitted. "As I have said, it is in dry shale, a good part of it, and it had to be carefully supported by follow-up timbering as we went along in the digging. I wanted Ford to let us keep the roundabout track in commission, against emergencies, but he decided it would be too expensive—as it probably would have been."

"And you have let the roundabout track lapse?"

"Oh, yes; the cloud-bursts of the first summer wiped it out for us completely."

"So this tunnel is really the neck of your five-hundred-mile-long man, is it?"

"It is. If Burnt Mountain should happen to fall in on us one of these fine nights—which it won't—we'd be definitely out of the game as a through line. It would bottle us up for weeks, if not for months."

A slow smile spread itself over Sprague's smooth-shaven, good-natured face.

"If I had as tender a neck as that, Dick, I'd have night sweats thinking about it; I should, for a fact," he averred. And then, after a pause: "Ah; I've been waiting for that. The lights have just gone out in your office over there in the railroad building. Who is so industrious as to stay on the job until nearly midnight?"

"It is Harvey Calmaine, my paragon of a chief clerk. He's a mighty hard-working young fellow—a treasure, as you may remember. He has been getting up some statistics for me, and he won't take the time out of the working day."

"H'm, yes; he is a fine young fellow, Dick, and no mistake." Then, after he had refilled his pipe: "He still limps a little from that foot-scorching episode in Bart Holladay's back room—when they were torturing him to make him tell what he had done with the proxies—doesn't he?"

Maxwell turned upon his companion with a frown of mystification wrinkling between his eyes.

"How did you know that, Calvin?" he demanded.

Sprague chuckled gently.

"Some fine day, Dick, you'll learn to use your eyes and ears. I saw young Calmaine walking across from the railroad building just now—as you did, only you didn't remark it consciously; and at the present moment I hear him coming through the lobby, with the limp very distinctly noticeable in the click of his heels upon the tiled floor. And now I'll venture a guess: he is looking for you, and when he finds you he will give you a telegram."

Almost as he spoke, Calmaine came up behind them. As Sprague had predicted, he had a telegram in his hand, which he gave to his superior with a word in explanation. "That is only a translation. The original is a cipher, and I locked it up in the office safe. It came just as I was getting ready to knock off."

Maxwell read the telegram and passed it on to Sprague.

"It's a little odd that Ford should use the same figure of speech that you did a few minutes ago," he remarked. And then, with a short laugh, "If I were inclined to be superstitious I might wonder if your marvellous second mentality wasn't looking over Calmaine's shoulder as he translated that."

Sprague had glanced at the message. It read:

Big Nine still feeling for a strangle-hold on us. Look sharp that it does not get its fingers on your windpipe.

Ford.

The big man passed the square of paper back to his friend and stood up to stretch his arms over his head, yawning like a sleepy farm-hand.

"I've got to set up my shop and go to work sometime tomorrow," he said. "Let's go upstairs and turn in for a few lines of sleep."

"Not me, just yet," said Maxwell, with a curt disregard for his English. "I'm going over to the shack for a little while."

"What for?" questioned the sleepy one, with half-absent interest.

"To try and get Benson on the wire and have him post guards in that tunnel. There is no reason on earth for it, but between you and Ford you've got me nervous on this choking proposition. Good-night, old man. Breakfast with me in the morning, and afterward I'll take you out and steer you up against some of the real-estate robbers and get them to find you an office."

On the following day the superintendent was as good as his word in the office-finding matter, and by noon the Government soil-tester was comfortably established in a couple of rooms on the second floor of the Kinzie Building, in the same corridor with Mr. Robert Stillings, the local attorney for the railroad company.

The two-room suite gave him an office—which he said was about as necessary as an auxiliary tail to a cat—and a second room in the rear which he speedily transformed into a working laboratory, using the young man named Tarbell, who still figured on the railroad pay-rolls as a "relief operator," for his errand-boy and man-of-all-work in securing the needed furnishings and equipment.

Later in the day Maxwell brought his brother-in-law, "Billy" Starbuck, around to the new office, introducing him as a mine owner and a gentleman of easy leisure, and one who knew every square acre of soil, arable or otherwise, in the entire Timanyoni.

"Billy has nothing on earth to do, and, like me, he is a temporary widower," Maxwell explained. "We married sisters, and his wife has gone with mine and the Fairbairns to dabble in the salt sea waves at Norman Towers. Make use of him as you can, only don't take his word for the gentleness of the horse you're going to ride. He is an absolutely truthful man on any other subject, but he never misses a chance to play a bucking bronc' against a tenderfoot."

Sprague foregathered at once with the clean-cut, rather shabbily clothed young mine owner whose principal affectations were his worn khaki suit, a cowboy Stetson tilted carelessly to the back of his head, and a vocabulary of cow-camp slang which happened to be no measure of his knowledge of grammatical English. Before he left the newly established laboratory in the Kinzie Building, Starbuck had engaged to go with the expert on a soil-collecting trip through the Park, the trip to begin early in the morning of the following day, and to continue indefinitely; or until the chief soil-hunter should be sufficiently saddle-sore to wish to cut it short.

"I like that brother-in-law of yours a whole heap, Dick," was Sprague's verdict when he met the superintendent at dinner in the Topaz café that evening. "He is a man with a history, isn't he?"

The queer look which Sprague seemed to be able to evoke at will in his table-mate crept into Maxwell's eyes.

"Did you ever meet Billy before I took him into your office this afternoon?" he asked.

"No."

"Ever hear of him before?"

"No."

"All right; now I'm going to try you out good and hard. You intimate that he is a man with a history. What is his history?"

The expert sat back, thrust his hands into his pockets, and for a moment seemed to go into a trance, with his gaze fixed upon the ornate decorations of the café ceiling.

"I'll make what you will probably call a series of wild guesses," he said at length, "prefacing them with the assurance, which you must take at its face value, that Mr. Starbuck has told me nothing whatever of himself—at least, not consciously."

"Go on," said Maxwell.

"In the first place, he is an educated man—a college man—and he talks cowboy English only because it suits his fancy to talk it. Also, though he wears khaki and a cowboy hat, he is quite as much at home in evening clothes as you or I. Am I right, so far?"

"Yes."

"Beyond that, he is a man of many accomplishments, most of which he is at some pains to conceal. In his younger youth, if not later, he was a bit wild—too much money to spend, I take it—and the wildness, or some of its consequences, landed him in jail; no, it wasn't a jail—it was a penitentiary."

Maxwell's look of amused half-triumph had changed to one of sober consternation.

"*Calvin!*" he exclaimed, in low tones. "You must know; you must have heard—"

"I pledge you my word, Dick; I am cutting this out of whole cloth, so far as any outside information is concerned. But let me go on. Whatever

Mr. Starbuck was, or whatever he did, he was never a criminal in the true sense of the word. So far from it, I can assure you of what you doubtless know for yourself; that he is a man to tie to—a true man and a loyal friend and kinsman. I'm going to take the field with him tomorrow morning, and we shall come back brothers of the blood. That's a measure of my regard for him."

Maxwell put down his knife and fork and said what clansman relationship demanded.

"Listen," he began, "and see how frightfully near you have shaved the truth in your 'guesses.' In his early manhood Billy was a cowpunch—in the college-graduate class, as you intimate. He discovered a mine, sold it for a fat wad, and went to New York, where he blew in the wad to the final dollar."

Sprague nodded. "That was the wild side-step that I couldn't quite place," he said, and the superintendent went on.

"When his money was gone he went to work as a stenographer for a firm of brokers, and was holding the job down when the safe was tapped and a sum of money stolen. He was arrested, tried, and sentenced to a term in Sing Sing, where he served his time. It was late in the first year of his freedom before a few of us who were his friends here in the West found out that he had voluntarily gone to prison to save a fellow-clerk—a half-dead, broken-down scoundrel with a wife and children, a sick mother, and a crippled sister."

"Fine!" Sprague was beginning to say; but Maxwell interposed.

"No, hold on; you mustn't set him down as an impossible hero. He'd be the first to object to that. I said 'voluntarily,' and it really amounted to that, though when Billy promised not to betray the scoundrel he had no idea that he was going to be made to suffer in his place. Nevertheless, since the promise had been given, Billy made good."

Sprague smiled. "Entirely without prejudice to a hearty and man-sized hatred for the man who let him go in the hole, you'd say?"

"Exactly; entirely without prejudice to that very human passion."

"Well," said the expert; "my summing up was true, anyhow. I was sure he had that kind of stuff in him, and that he had been tried out along some such line as that."

Maxwell nodded, and then he became insistent.

"Now tell me—you've got to tell me, Calvin, how you did it."

Sprague's mellow, booming laugh earned him more than one curious glance from the surrounding tables.

"I can no more tell you, Dick, than I can explain why, to a majority of people, white is white and black is black. For my own satisfaction I define the 'how' as a natural growth, favored by habit and training, of the scientific attitude; the mental slant which, if given free play, almost unconsciously notes, marks, deduces, reasons; deeming nothing too small or too trifling to go toward making up the whole of any conclusion. More than that, in my own case the faculty is able to hold itself workably aloof from the ordinary distractions of conversation and the like. It goes on, using the outward senses when it needs them, to be sure, but only as aids to the developing of its own little film in its own little darkroom. Do you get the idea?"

"Only partly. Even science has to have its raw materials to work on."

"Oh, yes; and the materials lie all around us constantly, if we only know how to weigh and measure them. In Starbuck's case, now, there were little lapses from the cowboy talk to tell me that he was an educated man; also, he has the true modesty of those who can really do things. Then there were gaps in his talk, little loopholes, you might call them, through which I could look back through the years and get glimpses of that period of dissipation. Each glimpse revealed a tiny ear-mark of the man who knows— who can only know—because he has been there."

"Go on," urged Maxwell, still only half-convinced that the deductions were not, in the last analysis, only shrewd guesses. "None of these things told you that he had been in prison."

"No; as to that, I'll admit I set a harmless trap for him. I fancied once, and then again, that I saw the prison look in his eye; the quick side-glance that a long-term prisoner learns to give without turning his head—notice it the next time you happen to be in a penitentiary, if you are ever so unfortunate as to visit one."

"I have noticed it," said Maxwell, and the expert went on.

"When I saw that, the scientific mentality said instantly, 'That look wasn't acquired in a jail term—it took longer.' The next suggestion followed as a matter of course. Every long-term man answers to a number instead of to his name. At the moment I was numbering the bottles of chemicals which Tarbell had been buying for me, and I turned the talk upon my peculiar system of labelling—by numbers. Starbuck himself did the rest. He said, 'I reckon I wouldn't rent even a post-office box if it had to have a number on it.' That was all, but it was enough."

Maxwell was toying with his dessert.

"As I have said several times before, Calvin, you are almost uncanny now and then. You know too much. Some fine day it will strike in on you— sour on you and make you sick."

Sprague's mellow laugh sounded again.

"I haven't begun to tell you all I know. For example, I might say that all through this spell of gossip about your brother-in-law you've been giving the subject no more than a scant half of your mind. The other half has been tussling with your railroad involvement, and you've been wondering where the Big Nine is going to land on you next. What do you hear from Tunnel Number Three?"

"Nothing much; or at least nothing out of the ordinary. They got the tangle straightened out last night after a time. Benson wires that Stribling put the entire electrifying force under his orders, and was all kinds of nice about it."

"'Electrifying,'" repeated Sprague musingly. "A slight change in the spelling would make it 'electrocuting,' wouldn't it? How long will it be before the installation is completed?"

"They are starting the turbines in Lopez Canyon today, for a try-out. The wires are all strung, and Stribling is installing some sort of a safety contrivance in the tunnel as a finishing touch; a switch of some kind that will shunt the current in case any accident should happen to a train in transit. It's all Greek to me—and to Benson, for that matter. Neither of us knows enough about electric installations to keep us from spoiling."

"But the date," said Sprague, with the amiable persistence which was one of his chief characteristics. "When will the current be turned on?"

"Stribling sends word that he will be ready to cut the power in on the tunnel wires tomorrow evening at six o'clock, and asks if I'm going to be on hand to see it done."

Sprague was deftly clipping the tip from one of the cigars which the waiter had brought, preparatory to lighting it.

"Do you happen to have a time-table in your pocket?" he asked.

Maxwell had one, and he passed it across the table. The Government man postponed the lighting of his cigar and began to turn the leaves of the official schedule hand-book. At the pages listing the trains on the Hophra Division he paused and ran his finger slowly down the columns giving the movement of traffic to and through Tunnel Number Three.

"You would have to leave here early in the afternoon to reach the tunnel by six—or rather to be there at six—wouldn't you?" he asked, returning the time-table.

Maxwell shook his head and smiled. "You forget that I'm not tied to regular trains on my own piece of railroad," he suggested. "I couldn't afford to go up on Three and spend two or three hours loafing around. If I go, I shall order out a car and engine and make a quick job of it. It is only sixty-three miles, and I can make it special in an hour and thirty minutes or thereabouts."

"I see," said Sprague reflectively. "Leaving Brewster about three-thirty, say?"

"Yes; that would be plenty early enough."

"But you don't know yet whether you will go at all?"

"No. There is a delegation of ore-shippers coming down from Red Butte tomorrow, and I'll be busy with it a good part of the day."

After that the talk drifted to other things, among them the expert's mission to the Timanyoni, which, he admitted in confidence, was the preliminary to a possible Government reclamation project. And finally, when Maxwell broke away to go back to his office across the plaza, his going or not going to the tunnel to be present at the turning on of the power current on the following day was left undecided.

According to the prearranged programme, Sprague left Brewster at daylight the next morning, riding with Starbuck to the upper valley of the Gloria where the first of the soil specimens were to be collected. But for some reason, saddle-soreness on the part of the tenderfoot, or another, the trip was a short one, ending a little after noon, when the two came jogging back through the Brewster streets.

From their corner table in the Topaz café, where they ate their late luncheon together, they saw Maxwell entertaining a party of the ore-shippers; and later Sprague, whose half-absent gaze seemed to miss nothing, saw a good-looking young fellow in shabby, work-stained brown duck push through the swinging glazed doors opening from the lobby and go around to whisper to Maxwell at the table of entertainment. Sprague called his companion's attention to the new-comer.

"That will be Mr. Benson, chief engineer of the railroad, for a guess," he ventured; and Starbuck nodded.

"Right you are. It's Jack; and to look at him you sure wouldn't think he was a married man, with a nice, tidy little wife at home, would you, now? He always looks as if he had just tumbled out of the dirtiest car in his work-train."

The soil expert smiled leniently. "Possibly he is here on business, and sometimes business won't wait," he suggested. "See; your brother-in-law is excusing himself to the ore people and is going out with Benson. After we finish our luncheon I'll ask you to do me a little favor, Mr. Starbuck. Find Mr. Maxwell and tell him we're back—just on the chance that he didn't see us over here in this dark corner of ours. I'd like to meet Mr. Benson, if it can be managed without too much trouble."

Starbuck's keen gray eyes searched the round, double-chinned face of his newly made acquaintance shrewdly.

"I reckon I'm on," he said slowly. "I was beginning to climb on before you said anything. That New York crowd is after Dick and his railroad with a black-snake whip; I know that much. Is the whip getting ready to pop again?"

"I'm a little afraid it is, Mr. Starbuck, and I am hoping that Mr. Benson will be able to tell us whether it is or isn't," was the even-toned rejoinder.

"At all events, I'd like to meet him and have a talk with him—some time before three o'clock. Bear the hour in mind, will you, please? and try to arrange it for me."

"Sure," said Starbuck; and when they rose from the table he went in search of the superintendent and Benson, leaving his luncheon companion to go around to the Kinzie Building laboratory alone.

It was something less than half an hour after Sprague had stripped his coat and gone to work on the soil specimens of the morning's gathering when Starbuck came in, bringing Maxwell and Benson. As Starbuck made it appear, the visit was merely a neighborly drop-in, with no better excuse than the expressed purpose of introducing Sprague to a possible helper.

"I thought you might be able to use Jack in some way, Mr. Sprague," he said, after the introduction was a fact accomplished. "He sure knows a heap more about Timanyoni dirt than anybody else between the two ranges; carries right smart of it around on his clothes a good deal of the time."

Benson took the joke in good part; and when Sprague had found and opened a box of his irreproachable cigars, the talk, touching lightly at first upon Sprague's business in the West, came around, or was brought around, to Benson's part in the electrification job. The big expert with the fighting jaw and the sympathetic gray eyes had a way of leading even a reticent man to tell of his troubles; and Benson, knowing the part Sprague had taken in defeating the two previous attempts to wreck the Short Line, felt free to unburden himself.

"I can't make Maxwell, here, believe that Stribling is anything but the fine, open-handed young fellow that he seems to be; but I want to tell you three together what I have often told Maxwell: I've got a hunch. I don't *know* a blessed thing. Stribling has always treated me fine, and he is a fellow you can hardly help cottoning to, right from the jump. But some way something inside of me keeps on telling me that he's too smooth—too damned smooth. Last night, for instance, in that derailment muddle—there wasn't anything he wouldn't do, didn't do, to help us out. He packed his men into the tunnel so thick that nobody could get near that derailed car; in fact, he had the car on the rails and the train backing out before I could get any action at all."

"What caused the derailment, Mr. Benson?" Sprague put in quietly.

"That was one of the things that made me hot. Stribling's messing in made it impossible for anybody to tell. There was nothing the matter with the track or with the car, so far as I could see after the thing was over. Bamberg, the engineer who was pulling the train, swears that somebody flagged him down with a red light when he was about half-way through the tunnel, and he stopped. Then the red changed to white and gave him the 'go-ahead.' When he tried to start his train, this box-car, somewhere along in the middle of things, jumped the track and blocked the tunnel. He felt the jerk and stopped again."

Sprague waved a hand in token of his complete satisfaction.

"Suppose we ignore this train tangle for the present and come to other things," he interposed. "I've been wondering if you could describe for me, briefly, the details of this tunnel installation, Mr. Benson?"

"Why, yes; it's simple enough—it's merely a trolley line on a big scale: two heavy copper trolley wires strung through on catenary brackets, with double insulation. That's all, except the safety-switches—cut-outs—one at each end and one in the middle of the tunnel."

"Ah?" said the expert, mildly interested at last; "one in the middle, you say? What is that for?"

"It is the real safety device, Stribling says; the others are merely mechanical cut-outs for the use of the wire repairers. He was explaining it to me this morning when he was connecting it in with the power wires. It's an ordinary oil-protected switch so adjusted that in case an accident happens to a train in the tunnel the circuit will be broken automatically and the live-wire current cut out. It's a good thing, you'd say. It would make your flesh creep to think what it would mean to have those high-power wires short-circuiting into a wreck."

"We won't think of it," said the big man quizzically. "We'll think rather of this Mr. Stribling and your—thus far—unexplained suspicions. How did he contrive to send you down here today?"

Benson looked up quickly.

"How did you know he sent me? I didn't say he did, did I? But I guess that is what it amounts to. He made it a sort of personal matter; urged me to come and bring Mr. Maxwell back with me; said that on a job as big as ours he didn't want to take any chances with his reputation as an electrical engineer or leave any room for a misunderstanding. He'd like to have Maxwell go foot by foot over the installation and see that everything is all right and safe before the power is turned on and the first electric train is sent through."

Sprague put his face in his hands and for a few seconds the silence in the makeshift laboratory was unbroken. Then suddenly he came to life again.

"You were telling us about this internal safety device," he broke out abruptly. "It's an oil-switch, you say?"

"Yes; there is an iron tank to hold the oil, and——"

"Hold on; where do you find room in the tunnel for a tank?"

"In one of the side excavations. When we were driving the tunnel we left side niches every two hundred feet or so; safety-holes for the men in blasting, and places where we could store dynamite and tools out of danger and out of the way."

"Stop. Was this particular dodge-hole where the safety switch is placed ever used for dynamite storing?"

"Yes; there are a lot of empty boxes in it now. In the arching, the timber-setters had covered them in, I suppose, and they were overlooked in the cleaning out."

"You are sure they are empty?"

"Oh, yes; they're empty all right. Stribling called my attention to them this morning, and I kicked over two or three of them, at his suggestion, just to make sure that they were empty."

"I see; he called your attention to them, did he? That is interesting, but not nearly as interesting as this oil-switch you've been trying to describe for me. Go over it again, will you?"

The young chief engineer was evidently disappointed. The scientist of whose gifts he had heard so much seemed to have a brain in which pertinacity, the pertinacity which clings helplessly to trivial and perfectly obvious things, was the over-shadowing faculty.

"I don't know that I can make it any plainer," he said, with a touch of impatience. "It's just an ordinary electric circuit-breaker, the same as they use on street-cars, and it is buried in oil to keep it from arcing—as all switches are when they're under voltages as high as ours will be. The mechanism is suspended in a tank by its own wires, and the tank is filled with oil. I was there when they were filling the tank this morning, and Stribling poured a queer sirupy mess in on top of it—some patent stuff to keep the oil from thickening under exposure, he said."

"A patent mixture, eh? I'm interested in patents," said the listener, going off at another of the blind tangents. "How did it come—in a can?"

"Yes; in four square cans, holding about a gallon or so each, I should say. They were packed in a box—like varnish cans, you know—only they were taller and not so big in section."

"I suppose you weren't near enough to notice any name or advertisement on these cans, were you?"

Benson had by this time lost all hope of finding anything like continuity in the big man's mind, but he answered the query.

"Yes, I was near enough; Stribling was up on the tank and I passed the cans up to him, one at a time—and spilled the stuff all over me doing it. There wasn't any name on them. They were just plain square tin cans; that's all."

Sprague got up and crossed over to Benson's chair.

"Spilled it on you, eh? Is this the stain of it on your coat?" he asked; and when Benson nodded: "It's too bad to spoil a perfectly good working-coat that way. Suppose you let me have it and I'll see if I can't take those spots out of it."

Benson obeyed, half-contemptuously, and, together with the two who had taken no part in the colloquy, looked on curiously while the expert, who had apparently lost all interest in everything save the coat-cleaning, swiftly treated the stained patches with various chemicals, put the resultant washings into a beaker and began to add ingredients from sundry bottles on the laboratory shelves, holding the beaker to the light after each fresh addition to note if there were changing colors in the solution.

At the close of the rapidly conducted experiment he poured a little of the solution into a tiny test-tube, which he proceeded to heat over the flame of a small alcohol lamp. This part of whatever experiment he was attempting appeared to be unsuccessful. Almost immediately the test-tube cracked with a miniature explosion, scattering bits of broken glass and extinguishing the flame of the little lamp.

Sprague tossed the neck of the shattered glass tube aside and returned the brown-duck shooting-coat to its owner. Benson put it on, and was curious enough to say: "Did you think you could find out what Stribling's protective mixture was from those grease-spots?"

"Mere force of habit," laughed the chemist, putting on his own coat. "I'm obliged to analyze everything I get hold of, you know; it's a sort of disease with me, I guess."

"But could you tell what it was, just from those discolored washings?" queried Maxwell.

"Perfectly. Mr. Stribling's 'patent' is a compound in which the chief ingredient is a grease derived from the spent lye of the soap-makers, and one of the principal uses of which in the arts is, as Mr. Stribling says, to keep oils, and other things, from drying out." Then, more pointedly to the superintendent: "I suppose you'll go up to the tunnel and look the job over, making our careful young friend Stribling entirely happy, won't you?"

Maxwell looked at his watch.

"Perhaps I'd better. Benson wants to get back, anyway. Will you two go along?"—to Sprague and Starbuck.

"I don't mind," said the expert, with a barely perceptible nod to Starbuck; and after he had rearranged the chemicals on his newly made shelves the four left the office and had themselves dropped to the ground floor of the building.

It was while they were walking two and two down the street that Sprague dropped a few steps behind with Starbuck and passed him a carefully wrapped package which he took from under his coat.

"I have another little experiment in mind, Mr. Starbuck," he said in low tones. "When we are on our way through the tunnel, watch your opportunity to drop out of the procession long enough to empty the contents of that package into the patent grease, which you will find, not floating on the oil, but in some sort of a receptacle let into the top of the oil-tank of that safety contrivance which Mr. Benson has so accurately described for us. I'm curious enough to want to prove up on my analysis of a few minutes ago—to see if it was correct."

"What will happen if it was correct?"

"Nothing; nothing alarming, I assure you. But be careful not to get any of the stuff in that package on your hands when you break the paraffin seals. And perhaps it might be as well if you don't let our young electrical friend see you do it. He might think we were messing in where we had no business to."

Starbuck made a sign of complete understanding, and a few minutes later, when they reached the main street, made a time-saving suggestion.

"Suppose you folks take a taxi to the roundhouse," he said. "I'll mosey up to the despatcher's office and get your clear-track orders for you."

Maxwell approved the suggestion and they separated, Starbuck catching a passing electric car for the plaza-fronting railroad head-quarters, and Maxwell impressing the first auto hack he could find to take the remaining three of them directly to the western yards. The hackman drove across the city and let them out at the nearest street-crossing, and from thence they walked the final hundred yards over the ties of the shop track.

At the roundhouse door they met a big, bearded man whose carefully creased brown hat and rather vociferous business suit would have marked him elsewhere as a gentleman of elegant, if somewhat precarious, leisure. Judson Bascom was this gentleman's name, and he was comparatively a new-comer in the Short Line service; having been appointed to succeed Fred Dawson, master mechanic, promoted.

Bascom was stooping to pat a stray dog, but he rose to his feet when the three came down upon him.

"You're the man we're looking for, Bascom," said Maxwell shortly. "I want a light engine to go up to Tunnel Number Three. What have you got in?"

The big master mechanic twiddled the bunch of charms on his watch-fob, and the stray dog began to sniff warily at Benson's heels.

"The Nine-fifteen's got fire in her; will she do?"

"Yes. Get me a crew as quickly as you can. I want a man who isn't afraid to run."

The man in the brown hat and the loud plaids dragged out a fat gold watch and shook his head.

"I guess that'll be me. There's nobody 'round, and I suppose you wouldn't want to wait until I can send the caller out after somebody?"

"No; I'm in a hurry," snapped the boss. "Let's get a move. My car is in the shop, so you can couple onto that caboose over there on the split track. There are four of us to go, and we'd crowd you in the cab."

Big and leisurely-looking as he was, the master mechanic made good time. In a minute or two he had the smart, light eight-wheeler on the turntable, with the blower roaring, a red-headed pit-boy to fire, and half a dozen roundhouse men to put their shoulders to the table-levers. The shifting took five minutes more; and by that time a switching-engine, with Starbuck hanging from the step, came racing down the yard from the mile-away head-quarters.

Starbuck swung off before the switcher came to a stop, and joined the three who were waiting at the step of the caboose.

"Hell's a-poppin'," he said laconically. "Davis hasn't got a single west wire that he can use. They all went out, blink, about twenty minutes ago."

"What's that?" demanded Maxwell. "Not all of them, surely!"

"Every blamed one—commercial wires and all. Can't get a whisper out of anything west of Little Butte. He says it acts like a general 'ground,' and then again it don't."

The nattily dressed master mechanic had dropped from his engine-step to come and join the group at the caboose. Maxwell put him in possession of the blockading fact in a brief sentence.

"The wires are dead and we'll have to bluff our way from siding to siding. Are you game for it, Bascom?"

The big man inclined his head. "I guess so," he said.

"All right. Go to Little Butte for the first lap. There is nothing in the way between here and the junction. All aboard, gentlemen."

The start was made briskly enough, but two miles beyond the yard-limits the caboose-car chucked noisily as Bascom slowed for the single-span bridge over the Gloria.

"Good Gad!" raged Maxwell, jumping up and jerking the air-whistle cord for full speed ahead. "If he's going to slow up for every trestle we come to, we'll never get anywhere!"

"We can prod him," said Benson.

For the few miles intervening between the bridge and Little Butte the master mechanic did not need prodding. Taking the air-whistle hint for what it meant, he hurled the wild train around the curves and over the tangents wholly without regard for the comfort of the four men who vainly tried to keep their seats on the bunk benches in the caboose. At Silver Switch the landscape was merely a blur; and in rounding the great side-cut at the Butte bluff the short car shrieked and groaned and seemed to be riding like a toe-balancer on the outer rail.

At the Little Butte stop the four made a dash for the operator's office, where Bascom presently joined them. There was no information to be got out of Wooffert, the station agent. His wires were working north on the Red Butte branch, but there was a dead "ground" somewhere to the westward. Broken snatches were still coming through from Caliger, ten miles up the main line west, and the instruments acted as if somebody had been pouring cold molasses into them.

Maxwell had his pocket time-card out, though he did not need to consult it. "Sixteen and Eighteen are somewhere between here and Nophi," he announced. "We've got to find and pass them as we can. Let her go, Bascom."

A half-minute later the up-valley race was begun. In the lower reaches the tangents were long, giving the volunteer engineer measurably safe sights ahead; and there was no occasion for Maxwell to jerk the whistle cord. Again the big man in the engine cab was hurling the train along with small regard for anything but speed.

At Caliger another stop was made. Like the man at Little Butte, the operator knew nothing save that his wires were dead. At his last report both of the down-coming freight trains had been on time. Maxwell did some quick figuring.

"We're pretty safe to run to Hatcher's," he told Bascom. "That will give us five minutes against Sixteen, provided she's not running ahead of her schedule. Can you make Hatcher's in forty minutes?"

"I'll make it or land this outfit in hell," said the master mechanic grittingly. And once again the wheels began to spin.

It proved to be a close call at Hatcher's, the little "blind" siding in the upper valley. One mile short of the passing track Bascom began to blow his whistle like a madman, and the four on the caboose, leaning far out on the platforms, saw a long freight lumbering down from the west. A short, stabbing puff of steam from the freight locomotive's whistle, soundless because of the din of hammering wheels and shrieking flanges, told them that the freight engineer had seen and heard and was trying to stop. Also, it was apparent to the two who looked on with railroad knowledge that the stop could not be made within the siding's switch limits.

Bascom took a chance and a risky one. Speeding like a fiend, he sent his one-car train onward to what promised to be a smashing head-on collision with the freight. But at the lower switch, with the slowing freight less than three hundred yards away, he made a grinding stop; his fireman leaped from the gangway and ran to turn the switch; and an instant later the wild train was snatched in on the siding and the freight was rolling past in safety over the reset switch.

"Good work!" said Sprague, speaking for the first time since the departure from Little Butte. "This man Bascom may not be the heavy villain that he looks to be, but he is certainly carrying his nerve with him this afternoon."

Maxwell was leaning out and shouting to the volunteer in the cab.

"Easy, Bascom!" he yelled; "they're carrying green!"

Bascom looked back and nodded; and the red-headed fireman strolled on ahead to take his stand at the upper switch.

"Anything significant about the St. Patrick's Day color?" queried Sprague; and Maxwell said there was.

"It means another section following," he explained; and then: "Here it comes!" And as he said it, another freight came into view, plunging around the curves toward the siding.

Unhappily for the speed-making purpose, this train, too, was carrying green, and Maxwell swore impatiently to the universe in general. "Three sections to this; and Eighteen's pretty sure to have two or more. It's three fifty-five, right now, and we've got thirty miles to go!"

Benson laughed.

"Stribling will wait until the last minute for you, never fear. With two hours we could mighty near get out and walk it."

"I reckon we're going to get a chance to walk a piece of the way," said Starbuck in his slow drawl. "That maverick choo-choo wrangler up ahead will have us in the ditch before he hits the Nophi grades, if he keeps up his lick."

"I don't want to call him down," said Maxwell, dubiously. "He's probably got a grouch because I pulled the string on him back yonder at the Gloria bridge."

"There comes the third section!" Benson called out; and a minute afterward the third and last division of the overland freight went hurtling past on the main track.

Bascom's makeshift fireman was promptly on his job. While the tail-end of the third section was clanking over the frogs he jerked the switch, and at the same instant the master mechanic jerked the throttle of the Nine-fifteen. The wild train shot out into position on the main line, halted for the fraction of a minute needed to enable the fireman to run up and scramble to the footboard, and the breakneck race was continued.

By this time none of the four thought of going back into the caboose. They were crowded together upon the front platform, ready to make the leap for life which seemed momentarily imminent as Bascom snatched the short car recklessly around the curves and over the switches at the various stations. Train Number Eighteen, also a through freight, was scheduled one hour behind Sixteen; but in the absence of all wire reports of its progress, nobody knew just where it would be found.

As a matter of fact, it was met between two sidings, ten miles on the hither side of Nophi; and, happily for the safety of all concerned, the meeting with the first section chanced upon a piece of straight track—one of the exceedingly few tangents in the rough, gulch-like valley known as Tumble-Tree Canyon. As before, Bascom held his whistle open, and, thanks to the brakes and a liberal sanding of the rails, a collision was averted.

When the two locomotives were nose to nose, and a flagman was racing frantically back to flag the following section, Maxwell sprang off and fell upon the conductor of the freight.

"How many sections of you?" he demanded explosively.

"Two," said the man, putting up an arm as if he expected to be hit.

"How close are you?" was the next shot-like question.

"That's them, comin' now," said the conductor, as a hoarse whistle bellow answered the racing flagman's stop signal.

Two miles back of the halted freights there was a disused saw-mill spur, not over a hundred feet long, to be sure, but it would serve. Maxwell's decision was made instantly.

"Back up, both of you, until we can get in on Crawford's spur," he ordered; and as the conductor started to run to the rear; "Don't waste time doing that! Whistle for 'em, you blockhead!" and he made impatient motions as of an engineer pulling the whistle-lever.

The first-section engineer, leaning from his cab window, heard, saw, and understood. Three shrieks of his whistle were answered by three of the hoarse bellows from the rear, and the two long freights began to pound heavily in the reverse motion up the grade.

"Push 'em, Bascom!" shouted Maxwell, as his own engine crept up after the retreating first section. "We'll go in at Crawford's and let 'em by."

The two miles to the passing point, worried out slowly at the pace set by the laboring freights, seemed to stretch themselves out into ten. Sprague was looking at his watch.

"Sixteen miles yet, you say, and we have an hour and twenty minutes in which to make them. That looks as if we were still margined well enough to pull through."

"I guess so," said Maxwell. The laboring freights were at last backing around the curve from which the saw-mill spur branched off, and again the red-headed fireman was on hand with his switch-key. Luckily the unused lock did not refuse to work, and presently the light rails of the abandoned spur were buckling and bending ominously under the Nine-fifteen, as Bascom trundled the wild train out upon them.

Almost immediately the whistles screamed again, and the two freights slid away down the grade. "'Right!'" yelled the red-headed one, shifting the rusty switch again; and once more the race was resumed.

When the Nophi smelter stacks came in sight in the vista opened up by the flying swing around the mountain of approach, four watches were out.

"We're nearly an hour to the good yet," cried Benson.

"Yes; and we ain't there yet," said Starbuck, who seemed to have acquired a pessimistic slant.

Maxwell swung far out as they were rounding the great curve and got a clear view of the small smelter-town yard. Straightening up, he pulled the whistle cord to attract Bascom's attention, and then leaned out and made the necessary hand-signal to run through the small town without stopping.

In some inexplicable way the signal, or rather the giving and receiving of it, proved fatal. Bascom looked back to nod his understanding, and when he faced about again he saw, too late, that a box-car, set out by one of the lately passing freights on the smelter-loading track, had "drifted" down the siding to a point at which it would not clear the main line. There was a ripping crash, a roar of steam escaping through a broken cylinder, and the race, so far as Engine Nine-fifteen was concerned, was over.

When the four passengers had picked themselves up out of the heap into which the sudden stop had piled them, they went forward to see what was to be done. There was nothing to be done locomotive-wise; but there was still plenty of time, even if the six remaining miles should have to be covered by a picked-up team borrowed from the smelter folk.

But the team expedient proved unnecessary. At the Nophi station they found a section gang at work, with a hand-car available; and on the "pump special" they made their entry, some thirty minutes past five, into the Grafton Brothers' camp at the eastern tunnel approach.

Stribling, a handsome young fellow with a frank, open face and honest eyes, was on hand to meet them.

"By Jove, Mr. Maxwell!" he said, with what was apparently a most palpable relieving of anxious strain, "I was afraid you weren't coming, and I'd just about made up my mind to 'phone over to Lopez to tell Canby and the rest of them that we'd postpone. I've got my record to make yet, most of it, and I couldn't afford to turn that power on and start an engine through until after you and Benson have gone over the completed installation with me."

"Well," Maxwell rejoined, "that's what we're here to do. You know Starbuck, my brother-in-law? I thought so. Now shake hands with my friend Sprague, of the Department of Agriculture, and we'll go through with you."

Starbuck was watching Stribling's face when the young electrical engineer shook hands with the big man from Washington. There was a query in the younger man's eyes, and Starbuck saw it. Also, he marked the half-second of hesitation which came between the introduction and its acknowledgment. But a moment later they were all on their way to the black-mouthed tunnel, Stribling walking ahead with the superintendent and Sprague, and Starbuck following with Benson.

For convenience in his work Stribling had set up a small steam-driven dynamo at his camp and had strung the tunnel with incandescents, hence there was plenty of light in the long bore for the examination of the power wiring. When they plunged underground the construction man was still walking ahead with Maxwell and Sprague, explaining, for the benefit of the superintendent's guest, the design of the catenary brackets and the double set of insulators.

"I'm betting on every detail in the mile and a quarter," the young engineer was saying, as the two laggards closed up. "It's my first big job, as Mr. Maxwell knows"—this also for the guest—"and I've simply got to make good on it. I could have had that waiting motor-engine out there pulling trains through the mountain this morning, but I made up my mind that we wouldn't turn a wheel until Mr. Maxwell had seen everything for himself."

"That's business," said Sprague, encouragingly. "Old Davy Crockett's maxim, eh? 'Be sure you're right, and then go ahead.' But let me tell you, Mr. Stribling: Mr. Maxwell will look wise and say, 'Yes, yes,' but he'll have to take your word for it, after all. What we average people don't know about modern electrical installations would fill a—" he looked around as if in search of a measure of capacity—"would fill a tank as big as that one across the track—the one you've dipped your wires into over there in that side cave."

"The oil-switch, you mean? Yes, that is a little safety wrinkle we're putting in wherever there's a chance of an accident breaking down the power wires. I'll explain it as we come back."

When the young engineer led the way onward again a glance to the rear would have shown him that only three of the four were at his heels. Starbuck had seen his chance, and in a quick withdrawal he dodged into the side cavern housing the oil-switch. Two of the empty dynamite boxes enabled him to breast the top of the tall iron tank. What he saw was a little puzzling. Oil-switch tanks are usually left open to the air, but this one was fitted with a galvanized-iron cover made in the form of a shallow pan with double sides spaced about six inches apart. The inner compartment of the pan was half-filled with a transparent oily liquid, and the outer annular space around it was closely packed with chopped ice. Hastily breaking the seals of the package he had been carrying under his coat, he dumped the contents into the central receptacle and fled without waiting to prove Sprague's assertion that nothing alarming would happen. When he rejoined the inspection party

Sprague was still holding Stribling in talk, and the young mine owner made sure it was done to cover his own momentary absence.

The remainder of the trip through the tunnel was made without incident, and on the way back Stribling halted the party at the safety switch side cavern which, oddly enough, was charged with a curiously acrid odor that made breathing in it chokingly difficult. Coughing and gasping, Stribling explained the mechanism briefly. An electro-magnet, energized by the power current itself, held the switch in contact. If the current should be interrupted, as in the case of a breakage due to a wreck, the switch would be thrown and all the tunnel wires rendered instantly harmless.

"And these boxes are what your machinery came in?" said Sprague, pointing to a litter of small dust-covered packing-cases scattered about the tank.

"Oh, no; those are dynamite boxes," was the hoarse reply. "They are empty—at least, Mr. Benson says they are, and he ought to know, since they are some of his leavings." And then: "Suppose we move on. The air is frightfully bad in here. The engineer must have stopped the ventilating fans."

Sprague had picked up a rusty bolt left by the timber-framers.

"You've got a good solid oil-tank here," he said, hammering lustily on the iron with the bolt.

Starbuck was watching Stribling, and he would have sworn that the young engineer's jump took him two feet clear into the air.

"Great Scott! Don't do that, Mr. Sprague!" he cried. "You might break some of the—some of the adjustments, you know!"

Sprague's mellow laugh echoed hollowly in the timbered cavern.

"If they're that delicate, perhaps we'd better take your suggestion and move on," he said. "I guess we've seen enough, anyway, eh, Maxwell?"

The superintendent acquiesced and the tunnel-threading was resumed to the portal, and beyond to the little shack where Stribling had his office. Here the young man became the hospitable host.

"Sit down, gentlemen, and I'll call Canby at the power plant and ask him if he is all ready to 'cut in.' If he says yes, you can take the 'phone and give the order, Mr. Maxwell. It's your railroad."

The four disposed themselves as they pleased in the cramped little office fronting the tunnel. Sprague took his stand at the single window to stare absently at the black hole in the mountain side—an unrelieved spot of gloom now that the incandescents had been turned off. Starbuck chose a corner, and did not take his eyes from Stribling, who was sitting at his desk with Maxwell opposite.

With the receiver at his ear the young engineer exchanged a few words with the company's electrician at the power-house three miles away. Then he pushed the 'phone across the desk to Maxwell.

"Canby says he's ready," he announced, in a voice that was strangely sharp and tremulous. "Give him the word, and then watch this volt-meter on the wall behind me. It will tell you when the current comes on."

Maxwell hesitated for a single instant and looked across at Sprague. But the expert's back was turned and he was still staring fixedly at the distant tunnel mouth. The superintendent took the receiver and spoke crisply.

"This is Maxwell: if you're ready, turn on the power."

At the word, Sprague faced about quickly and fixed his gaze upon Stribling. The young man had turned aside in his chair and his face was ghastly. Benson and Maxwell were watching the indicator on the wall; but Starbuck was rising noiselessly from his seat on the cot, with one hand buried in the side-pocket of his coat. For ten dragging seconds the index finger of the volt-meter remained motionless. Stribling was twitching in his chair, and finally he burst out.

"Those dynamite boxes! We ought to have taken them out! What if they shouldn't happen to be empty—all of them?"

As he spoke, the index of the volt-meter began to jump like a thing suddenly endowed with life, and Benson cried out, "There she comes!" Stribling crouched in his chair as if shrinking from a blow and covered his face with his hands. Ten seconds, twenty seconds, ticked themselves off on the little desk clock at Maxwell's elbow, and then Sprague's voice broke into the tense silence.

"It's all over, Stribling. You can sit up now and take your medicine. The end of the world is still safely in the future."

The young man whirled in his chair and his right hand shot toward a half-opened drawer of the desk. It was Starbuck who interposed.

"Nixie," he said sharply; "it isn't time for you to pass out yet. Keep your hands out of that drawer, or I'll put these on," jingling a pair of handcuffs before the culprit's staring eyes.

Stribling leaped from his chair and took one long haggard look through the open door at the tunnel mouth where nothing was happening. Then he dropped back and became the trapped animal fighting for life.

"What have you got on me?—or what is it you think you've got?" he rasped.

It was the man from Washington who replied.

"Don't make it harder for yourself than you have to," he said gently. "We've got it all. We know that you had that train stopped last night so that you could unload those empty dynamite boxes—they are empty, you know—without discovery. We also know that this morning you placed a quantity of nitro-glycerine in that safety switch, and that you have the wiring rigged to fire the stuff and destroy the tunnel."

The young man looked up and his smile showed his teeth.

"But the current is on and the tunnel isn't destroyed," he interrupted.

"No; you overdid it a little in asking Benson to help you handle the nitro-glycerine and in letting him spill it on his clothes; also you skipped a stitch when you thought that by smuggling those dynamite boxes in and calling everybody's attention to them, you'd put the blame of the explosion upon Benson and the railroad people. You forgot that all makers of dynamite nowadays stamp the date on the boxes. The tunnel was completed two years ago; and the date on one of the boxes, at least, is January of the present year. You are down and out, Mr. Stribling, and there is only one way in which you can dodge the stripes. That is by telling us who hired you to do this."

A silence, tense like the silence of the court-room when the judge pronounces the sentence, fell upon the group gathered in the little shack-office, and it lasted for a full minute. At the end of it Stribling jerked his head up and spoke.

"I'm a man again now, Mr. Sprague, if I haven't been for the past two months," he said steadily. "I'll tell you this: you can give me the third degree, if you want to—there are enough of you here to do it—and after that you can send me to the pen if you feel like it. But, so help me God, you'll never make me welsh on the man for whom I did this: never, so long as I have the breath to say no!"

Again the tense silence supervened, and Starbuck held up the handcuffs tentatively. Sprague shook his head, and spoke again.

"You've considered this resolution well, have you, Stribling?"

"I have. I owe that man everything I've got in this world: education, the chance to hold my head up with others and, more than that, he once saved my father from going where you mean to send me—over the road. I'll admit all you have charged. I did set the trap, and I don't know yet why it hasn't gone off. All I ask is that you'll remember that I picked a time when there wouldn't be any lives lost."

"I discovered that last night," said Sprague quietly; adding, with a glance for the superintendent's brother-in-law, "I guess we'll have to turn him over to you, Mr. Starbuck." Then, turning once more upon the culprit: "Why did you find it necessary to cross the power wires with the telegraph lines early this afternoon, and so to destroy the instruments on a hundred miles of railroad, Stribling?"

The young engineer looked up hardily. "It was necessary. I took care to have Canby and the railroad electricians all over at the power plant, and

I couldn't take the chance of leaving them in communication with head-quarters at Brewster."

Maxwell, who had sat as a silent listener, shook his head sadly and got up and went out, followed by Benson. A little later Sprague, standing at the window, saw them trying out the electric locomotive in short runs up and down the tunnel approach. Starbuck came out of his corner and snapped the manacles on Stribling's wrists, and the young man made no resistance. Sprague turned at the click of the handcuffs, standing to frown down thoughtfully upon the self-confessed wrecker.

"I was in hopes we were going to get the men higher up this time; get them so they would stay got," he said, half to himself. "But it seems that a bit of common human gratitude is going to blunder around and get in the way. Stribling, I'm honestly sorry for you. I'm afraid we made a mistake in not letting you get hold of that gun a few minutes ago."

The young man with the honest eyes looked up quickly. "You did, indeed, Mr. Sprague. It's the simplest way out of it for me."

"You are still determined not to do the larger justice by giving us the information we need?"

The young man raised his manacled hands.

"Think of it a minute," he pleaded. "You wouldn't do it yourself; you know you wouldn't."

"I don't know—I don't know; perhaps I shouldn't," admitted the big man thoughtfully. Then he went on with visible reluctance: "I'm afraid we shall have to pinch you, and pinch you hard, my boy. And it's a shame, when you were only a tool in the hands of the men who ought to do time for this thing. I suppose we shall be taking the seven o'clock passenger back to Brewster. Is there anything you'd like to do before it comes along?"

"Yes; I'd like to write a letter or two."

"You shall do it, and you shall have privacy." And then to Starbuck: "Fix him so that he can."

Starbuck unlocked the manacle from Stribling's right wrist and locked it again around the arm of the office chair. "Will that give you room enough?" he asked.

"More than enough," was the quiet reply. And when Starbuck had taken the pistol from the half-opened desk drawer the two who were free went out and closed the door against any possible intrusion upon the captive's privacy.

"I'll stay round," Starbuck volunteered, when they were outside. "You go over and ride the engine with Mr. Maxwell, if you want to."

It was half an hour later when the three who had been trying out the electric locomotive side-tracked the big machine at the sound of the down passenger's whistle signal at the western tunnel approach, and crossed the tracks to where Starbuck was standing guard at the reopened door of the office-shack.

"Still writing?" asked Sprague of the silent guard.

"No; for the last ten minutes he's been sitting there with his head on the table, just as you see him. He asked me to open the door a while ago, so he could see better."

Moved by a common impulse they entered the office-room, stepping softly. But the young man at the desk was far beyond all earthly disturbances. One letter, addressed to a girl in New York, lay on the desk, stamped and sealed. Hanging beside the chair, and ingeniously strung and weighted so that they could touch nothing, were the two heavily insulated power wires which he had somehow managed to disconnect from the volt-meter switchboard at his back; these and a freshly burned shrivel on the hand of the arm that was crooked for a pillow told how it had been done.

"Good God!" Maxwell exclaimed; "we might have thought of that! Poor fellow! He couldn't face it out, after all!"

Starbuck gently released the handcuffs and slipped them into his pocket. Then he helped Benson put the body of the man who could not face it out upon the cot in the corner. The train was coming, and Benson pushed the others toward the door.

"Don't stay here and miss your train," he said. "I'll do what there is to be done. I was going to stay, anyway."

* * * *

The evening train was feeling its way down over the wireless line and was half-way to Brewster before the three men sitting in the otherwise unoccupied smoking-compartment of the sleeper broke the silence which the sudden tragedy had laid upon them. But at the lighting of his third cigar Maxwell could contain himself no longer.

"It's another of your miracles, Calvin," he said. "By this time I'm so well used to them that nothing you do fazes me any more. But I'm sure Billy will sleep better tonight if you tell him how you did it."

The big man grunted softly.

"I think both of you have put the broken bits of the puzzle together before this," he returned. "The motive was the chief thing; what I call the 'nucleus thought,' and we had that all ready-made. We knew that this 'Big Nine,' as Ford names it, was out after your scalp; and as soon as you told me about the tunnel and the Grafton Brothers' contract the probable point of attack was no longer in doubt. You see, I happen to know that the Graftons have always been hand-in-glove with your principal competitor—had installed all the block signals for it, cutting a fine melon for themselves in the process, too."

"Still," said Maxwell, "it's a long way from that to this."

"It was only taking one step after another, and Benson gave me three or four of them. The details of Stribling's exceedingly simple plot became very plain after Benson had told us about the train-stopping, the empty dynamite boxes, the safety switch—which could have been just as easily and effectively placed at either end of the tunnel as in that hole in the middle of it—and finally about the pouring of the sirupy stuff into the oil-tank. There was a bit of fine work on Stribling's part. Benson doubtless knows nitro-glycerine when he sees it; but under the circumstances he would be completely disarmed—as he was."

"But how did you know that there would be a false cover on the tank?" queried Starbuck.

"A bit of pure reasoning. The specific gravity of glycerine is greater than that of the heaviest of the earth oils; hence the explosive would sink to the bottom of the tank and mix with the oil to some extent. I reasoned that Stribling would not take the risk of the mixture."

"He didn't," said the mine owner; "the pan was there and it was packed in ice."

"But the laboratory experiment?" put in Maxwell.

"Was a simple test for nitro-glycerine, of course. You saw it blow up the test-tube, but even then only one of you—Mr. Starbuck here—suspected the truth. You did, didn't you, Mr. Starbuck?"

"I had a guess comin'," said the young mine owner quietly; adding: "That was why I took the trouble to hunt me up a pair of handcuffs when I went to get the train-orders."

"But if there was nitro-glycerine in that tank, why didn't it go off when the current was turned on?" queried Maxwell.

"For the very simple reason that Mr. Starbuck, at my direction, dumped a large dose of neutralizing chemical into it as we passed the tank on our way through the tunnel, and so saponified it. That was why I had the courage to hammer on the tank with my bolt, and why Stribling, not dreaming that his touchy explosive's teeth had been drawn, nearly had a fit."

"One other thing," Maxwell put in. "You asked Stribling why he burned the telegraph wires out; how did you know they had been burned out?"

Sprague chuckled good-naturedly.

"I knew that at Little Butte; you might have known it if you hadn't been so excited as to forget that you had a nose. That office, as well as the next one—I've forgotten its name—fairly reeked with the smell of burnt rubber and insulation, and I said to myself that there were only two torches in these mountains that could heat things hot enough to burn the instruments: namely, lightning and the high-voltage current from your plant in Lopez Canyon."

Again a silence, broken only by the train clamor, settled down upon the three in the Pullman smoking-room. After a time Maxwell drew a long breath and said:

"It was a narrow squeak; a horribly narrow squeak, Calvin. We have a good deal to say nowadays about the lawlessness of the mob and the individual; but big money doesn't seem to know that there are any such things as justice and equity and a square deal."

Sprague sat up and methodically relighted his cigar.

"Oh, I don't know about that," he demurred. "You can't say that all big money is lawless. Of course, there are buccaneers in every chapter of the world's history, and we have ours, neatly labelled with the dollar-mark instead of the skull and cross-bones. Good big money is an undoubted blessing; it is only bad big money that is a curse."

Maxwell's smile was mirthless.

"When a man puts a gun in your face and holds you up, it isn't very consoling to remember that there are a good many other men in the world who wouldn't treat you that way," he commented. And then: "I hope we've seen the last of this fight in the dark with that stock-jobbing gang in New York."

"You haven't," Sprague declared definitely. "They'll come back at you, and keep on coming back, until you get a fair grand-jury underhold on the men at the top. I counted confidently upon being able to give you that underhold today. I thought we had Stribling where he would be obliged to turn state's evidence. It was our misfortune that he happened to be too good a man; that he was only the tool of a villain and not a villain himself. They'll hit you again, Maxwell, and go on hitting you until you can strike back hard enough to put some of the men higher up in the prisoner's dock."

This might have stood for the final word; but the true finality was reached a couple of hours later when the superintendent and the Government expert were smoking their bedtime pipes in the Topaz lobby.

"We haven't fully grasped the real pity of this thing yet, Dick," said Sprague, at the end of the ends. "It is this: that greed, the infernal lust of money that has laid hold upon our day and generation, can take so fine a thing as that poor boy's gratitude, transform it into criminality, and make him pay the price with his life. Isn't that enough to make your blood run cold? Let's turn in and forget it if we can. Good-night. I'm going to bed.

CHAPTER 4

THE MYSTERY OF THE BLACK BLIGHT

The wreck at Lobo Cut, half-way between Angels and the upper portal of Timanyoni Canyon, was a pretty bad one. Train Six, known in the advertising folders as "The Fast Mail," had collided in the early-morning darkness with the first section of a westbound freight which, though it was an hour and fifty minutes off its schedule time, had run past Angels without heeding the "stop for orders" signal plainly displayed.

Ten minutes after the crash, the second section of the freight had shot around the hill curve to hurl itself, a six-thousand-ton, steel-pointed projectile, into the rear end of the first section, and the disaster was complete. Somewhere under the smoking mountain of wreckage marking the spot where the Mail and first-section locomotives had locked themselves together, reared, and fallen over into the ditch, two firemen and an engineer were buried. Out of one of the crushed mail-cars two postal clerks were taken; one of them to die a few minutes after his rescue, and the other bruised and broken, with an arm and a leg dangling, as he was carried out to safety.

At the other point of impact there had been no loss of life, though the material damage was almost as great. The engine of the second section had split its way sheer through the first-section caboose—which, in the nature of things, had no one in it to be killed—and through two of the three merchandise-cars next in its plunging path. With a mixed chaos of groceries, farming implements, and splintered timbers for its monument, the big mogul had burrowed into the soft side bank of the cutting as if in some blind attempt to bury itself out of sight of the havoc it had wrought.

On the Thursday morning of this, the worst of a series of accidents thickly bestudding that fateful month of August, Maxwell, the general superintendent, chanced to be two hundred miles away to the eastward. His service-car was in the Copah yards, and he was asleep in it when the night watchman came down from the despatcher's office to rouse him with the bad news.

What could be done at such long range was done instantly and with good generalship. The wires were working with Brewster, the division head-quarters in Timanyoni Park. With his own hand Maxwell sent the orders to Connolly, the despatcher, to Fordyce, the trainmaster, and to Bascom, the master mechanic. A relief train was to be made up with all haste to take the doctors to the wreck, and to convey the passengers of Number Six back to Brewster. Following the relief train, but giving it precedence, should go the wrecking-train. The superintendent even went so far as to specify the equipment which should be taken: the heavier of the two wrecking-cranes, a car-load of rails for temporary tracking, and two or three water-cars for the extinguishing of the fire.

These things done, and the arrangements made to start his own special immediately for the scene of disaster, the superintendent had the fine courage, in the face of this last and most unnerving of many disheartenments, to return to his car and to go back to bed. He had been up very late in conference with his president, Ford, and he knew that the demands awaiting him at the end of the five-hour run to Lobo Cut would call for all the reserves of strength and energy he could hope to store up during the distance-covering interval.

Much good work had already been accomplished when Maxwell's special, feeling its way past the four long freights and the midnight passenger, all held up at Angels, came upon the scene of destruction among the foothills at an early hour in the forenoon. The relief train had come and gone, bearing away the unhurt, the injured, and the dead. A temporary working-track had been laid through the cut, and the mighty one-hundred-and-fifty-ton steam crane, its movements directed by a big, rather flashily dressed man with an accurately creased brown hat pulled down over his brows, was reaching its steel finger here and there in the débris and plucking the derelict freight-cars out of the way.

Up at the other end Fordyce, the trainmaster, was working with another crew, using a mammoth block-and-tackle, with a detached locomotive for its pulling power. When Maxwell came on the ground, Fordyce, a gnarled little man with a twist in his jaw and a temper like the sparks from an emery wheel, was alternately cajoling and cursing his men in a praiseworthy attempt to make his block-and-tackle outheave the master mechanic's powerful crane.

"Yank 'em—yank 'em, men! Get that rail under there and heave! Wig it—*wig it*! Now get that grab-hook in here—lively! Don't let them fellows at the other end snake two to our ONE!"

Maxwell stopped to exchange a word or two with the sweating trainmaster and then passed on down the wreck-strewn line. At the master mechanic's end of things he came upon Benson, chief of construction, who had accompanied the wrecking-train from Brewster only because he had happened to be on the way to Angels and saw no other probable means of reaching his destination.

"Pretty bad medicine—the worst of the lot," commented the young chief of construction, when, tramping soberly, they came to the place where the two great locomotives, locked in their death grapple, were nuzzling the clay bank of the cutting.

Maxwell's teeth came together with a savage little click.

"A few weeks ago, Jack, we were scared stiff for fear the 'Big Nine' crowd of stock-jobbers would succeed in doing something to put us on the panic-slide. Now we are doing it ourselves, just about as fast as we can. Is it true that there were four killed?"

"Yes; both firemen, and Bamberg, the engineer of the freight. The other man was a postal clerk; and his mate had an arm and a leg broken."

"Many injuries?"

"Astonishingly few, when there was such a good chance for a general massacre. Both men on the second section engine jumped, and both were hurt, though not badly. There was nobody in the split caboose when it was hit. On the Mail, Cargill, who was running, got off with a pretty bad scalp wound. An express messenger had his foot jammed; and the train baggage-man had a lot of trunks shaken down on him. In the coaches there were a few people thrown out of their seats and hurt by the sudden stop; but in the sleepers there were a good many who slept straight through it, incredible as that may sound."

"I know," said Maxwell; "I've seen that happen more than once, when the Pullmans stayed on the rails." Then, with a slight backward nod of his head he changed the subject abruptly. "Bascom—has he been handling it all right?"

"He's a dandy!" said Benson. "Personally, I'd about as soon associate with any one of a dozen Copah tin-horns that I could name as to foregather with Mr. Judson Bascom. But he's onto his job, all right. He laid this temporary track himself; I haven't butted in at all, either here or at Fordyce's end."

"How did you happen to get here? I thought you were up Red Butte way," said the superintendent.

"I was; but I came down to Brewster on Six last night, meaning to go through to Angels. While we were changing engines I ran upstairs to get some maps and papers out of my office, and took too long about it; the train got away from me and I chased out with the wreck-wagons. That's how near I came to being mixed up in this thing myself."

"And you want to go on to Angels now?"

"Yes; when I get a chance. Those irrigation people in Mesquite Valley are howling to have an unloading spur built up from the old copper-mine track, and I thought I'd go and look the ground over."

The superintendent's frown was expressive of impatient dissatisfaction.

"That Mesquite project is another of the grafts that are continually giving this country a black eye, Jack. It's 'bunk,' pure and simple. Everybody who has ever been in the Mesquite knows that you couldn't raise little white beans in that disintegrated sandstone!"

"It'll do for an excuse to rake in a few hundred thousand Eastern shekels," Benson remarked. "There will be plenty of 'come-ons' to buy the land when the dam is built."

Bascom's great crane was poising a crushed and mangled box-car in air, and when the crooking steel finger swung its burden aside and dropped it with a crash out of the way, Maxwell turned upon his heel.

"I have my car here, and I'm going back to Angels to do some wiring," he said. "Come along, if you want to see those irrigation people. But I'll tell you right now, I won't approve any recommendation for more track-laying for them."

They had walked possibly half the length of the long blockade when a noisy automobile, dust-covered and filled with men, drew up on the mesa flat above the wreck. Benson looked up with a scowl.

"There's another gang of those newspaper ghouls!" he commented, as two of the three men in the tonneau got out and began to unlimber their cameras and tripods. "It's no picnic to drive a car from Brewster over the range, to say nothing of the danger; and this is the second squad since daylight. There have been enough pictures taken of this wreck to fill all the newspapers between New York and San Francisco for a week!"

Maxwell's smile was a mere teeth-baring.

"Yes; we're getting the advertising all right," he said. "We've been getting it for a month or more." Then, as they tramped on out of the wreck raffle and headed for the waiting office-car: "I had a talk with Ford last night; that is what took me to Copah. We're in bad, Benson. Ford says they've taken to calling us 'the sick railroad' on the Stock Exchange, and our securities are simply going to the puppies. Another month like this one we've just stumbled through will either wipe us from the map or clean us up definitely and put us into the hands of a receiver."

"Does Ford say that?" gasped the young chief engineer.

"He said a good bit more than that. He still insists that these troubles of ours are helped along from the outside; that they are in reality just so many moves in the game that a certain Wall Street pool is playing to get control of our road. I tried to show him how impossible it was; how the entire slump in discipline which causes all the trouble is merely one of those crazy epidemics that now and then sweep over the length of the best-managed railroads on earth."

"And he wouldn't believe it?" queried Benson.

"No; the last thing he said to me as his train was pulling out proved that he didn't. He intimated that there wasn't any 'act-of-God' verdict to be brought in, in our case, and told me to go back to Brewster and dig until I found the real cause."

By this time they had reached the service-car special, and Maxwell passed the word to his engineer to back up the line to Angels. When the wreck and the wreckers had vanished beyond the hill curves, Benson filled his short pipe and at the lighting of it asked another question.

"I've been wondering if we couldn't get a little expert help on this thing, Maxwell. Have you tried to interest Mr. Sprague in this discipline business?"

The superintendent shook his head.

"Sprague isn't going around doing odd jobs in psychology for anybody and everybody," he deprecated. "He is a Government chemist, and he is out here on the Government's business. Besides, it isn't a case for a detective; even for the best amateur detective in the bunch—which is easily what Sprague might claim to be, you'd say. You see, there isn't anything special to detect. What we need is a doctor; not a plain-clothes man."

Benson's left eye closed itself slowly in qualified dissent.

"What does Mr. Sprague himself have to say about it?" he queried.

"He hasn't said anything. In fact, I haven't seen him for over two weeks. He's been out with Billy Starbuck, gathering soil specimens; they are still out somewhere, I don't know just where."

Neither of the two men riding the rear platform of the backing service-car spoke again until the car stopped with a jerk at the edge-of-the-desert station with the celestial name, which had once been the head-quarters of the original Red Butte Western Railroad. Then Benson summed up the situation in a couple of terse sentences.

"If we don't do something, and do it quick, there is a bunch of us so-called railroad bosses on this high line who may as well pack our duffle-bags and fade away into the landscape. Three wrecks within a week; and this last one will cost a hundred thousand cold iron dollars before we're through with the lawyers; I'll be hanged if I wouldn't call in the doctor—some doctor—any doctor, Maxwell. That's my ante. So long; see you a little later about this Mesquite business, if you're still here." And he put a leg over the platform railing and went away.

Three minutes later, when the superintendent had crossed the station platform and was on his way around to the door opening into the operator's office, two men mounted upon wiry range horses rode down the single remaining street of the dead-alive former railroad town, pointing for the station.

One of them, a good-looking youngish man with a preternaturally grave face and the shrewd thoughtful eyes that tell of days and nights spent afield and alone with the desert immensities, was the superintendent's brother-in-law by courtesy. The other, a gigantic athlete of a man, whose weight fairly bowed the back of the stout horse he rode, was Mr. Calvin Sprague.

Maxwell paused when he saw and recognized the two horsemen. But when they came up, the weight of the recent disaster made his greeting a rather dismal attempt at friendly jocularity.

"Well, well!" he said, gripping hands with the athlete; "Billy certainly had it in for you this time! Rode you over the range, did he? I'll bet you'll never have the nerve to look a horse in the face again, after this. Where on top of earth have you two been keeping yourselves for the last fortnight?"

"Oh, just sashayin' round on the edges," drawled Starbuck, replying for both; "gettin' acquainted with the luminous landscape, and chewin' off chunks of the scenery, and layin' awake nights to soak up some of the good old ozone."

"Ozone!" chuckled the big man; "I'm jammed gullet-full of it, Dick, and I have a hunch that it's going to settle somewhere below the waist line and make me bow-legged for life. King David said that a horse is a vain thing for safety, but I can go him one better and say that it's the vainest possible thing for just plain, ordinary, every-day comfort. I'm a living parenthesis-mark—or a pair of 'em, if you like that better." Then without warning and almost without a break: "Where is the wreck, this time?"

Maxwell's frown was a little brow-wrinkling of curious perplexity.

"You've just ridden down from the hills, haven't you? How do you know there is a wreck?"

"That's too easy," laughed the expert, waving a Samsonic arm toward the five side-tracked trains held up in the Angels yard. "If you didn't have your track cluttered up somewhere, those trains wouldn't be hanging up here, I'm sure. Is it a bad one?—but you needn't answer that; I can see at least one dead man in your eyes."

"There are four of them," said the superintendent soberly, "and some others desperately hurt. We're in a bad way, Sprague. This is the third smash within a week."

Sprague dismounted stiffly and secured his saddle-bags containing the soil specimens gathered at the price of so much discomfort.

"Starbuck," he said whimsically, "I'm willing to pay the price of a hundred-dollar guinea-pig, if necessary, to have this razor-back mustang shipped home in a palace stock-car to his stable in Brewster. Mr. Maxwell's office-car is good enough for me from this on."

Starbuck smiled grimly and took the abandoned horse in charge. "I'll take care of the bronc'," he agreed; and the big man limped around the station to board the service-car while Maxwell went into the office to do his telegraphing.

When the superintendent returned half an hour later he found his self-invited guest lounging luxuriously in the easiest of the big wicker chairs in the open compartment of the car, smoking the fattest of black cigars and reading a two-days-old Denver paper.

"This is something like," he said. "I was never cut out for a pioneer, Richard; Starbuck has proved that to my entire satisfaction in these last two weeks. But that's enough of me and my knockings. Sit down and tell me your troubles. I see the papers are making space-fillers out of your railroad to beat the band. Are you ready to come around to my point of view yet?"

Maxwell sat down like a man who was both worried and wearied.

"The Lord knows, I wish I could come around to your point of view, Calvin. If I could see any possibility of charging these things to outside influences.... But there isn't any. The trouble is purely local and internal— and as unaccountable as the breaking out of an epidemic when the strictest kind of quarantine has been maintained."

Sprague smiled incredulously.

"There never was a case of typhoid yet without its germ to account for it, Dick," he asserted dogmatically.

"I know; but that theory doesn't hold good in the psychological field. We've got a good set of men, Sprague. To a degree which you don't often find in modern railroad consolidations, we've had that precious thing called *esprit de corps*. We've never had any labor troubles since Lidgerwood's time, and there are no grievances in the air to account for the present let-down. Yet the let-down is with us. Almost every day some man who has hitherto proved trustworthy falls down on his job, and there you are."

"You've tried all the usual remedies, I suppose?"

"I should say I had! I've stormed and cursed and pleaded and reasoned until I'm worn out! If I fire a bunch of them, I have to hire a new bunch, and inside of a week the new men have caught the disease for themselves. One bad wreck will make a hundred trainmen uncertain and jumpy, and a second one will turn half of the hundred into irresponsible lunatics. You'd have to mix and mingle with the force as I do to understand the condition things have gotten into. It's horrible, Calvin. It is like the black blight that you have seen spread through a well-kept orchard."

"There is a cause," said the expert, settling himself solidly in his chair. "I tell you, Dick, there's a germ in the air, and that second mentality of mine that you are so fond of poking fun at tells me that in the case of your railroad orchard the germ has been deliberately planted. You say it's impossible: I've a good notion to let the soil-testing rest for a few minutes and show you."

"If I thought there was the least chance in the world that you could show me—"

"Is that a challenge? By Jove! I'll take you. When can you get me back to Brewster?"

"As soon as the track is cleared. We ought to be able to get through by noon."

The expert got up, shook the riding kinks out of his legs, and threw the newspaper aside.

"I'm going out to walk around for a bit, and after a while I'll ask you to take me down to this wreck," he said; and Maxwell, who had a deskful of work awaiting him, nodded.

"Say, in an hour?"

"An hour will do; I'll show up within that time."

Later, the superintendent, wading through the files of business correspondence which always accompanied him in his goings to and fro on the line, had window glimpses of Sprague strolling up and down beside the waiting trains in the yard or standing to chat with some member of the loafing crews.

The glimpses were provocative of good-natured incredulity on the part of the desk-worker. Thrice during the summer of warfare Sprague had been able to step into the breach, each time with signal success. But in each of the three former instances there had been tangible causes with which to grapple; flesh-and-blood criminals to be ferreted out and apprehended. Maxwell, glancing out of the window again, shook his head despondently. What could the keenest intelligence avail in the case of an entire railroad suffering from an acute attack of nervous disintegration and recklessness? Nothing, the superintendent decided; there was nothing for it but to settle down upon a grim determination to outlive and worry through the period of disaster; and he was still grinding away at his desk with that thought in the back part of his mind when Sprague came in and announced his willingness to be taken on to the wreck.

Maxwell gave the necessary order, and in due time the one-car special had repassed the few miles intervening between Angels and Lobo Cut, to come to a stand on the curve of hazard. Sprague was lighting a fresh cigar preparatory to a plunge into the track-clearing activities, and Maxwell looked up from his work.

"Want me to get off with you?" he asked.

"No; it's the very thing I don't want," declared the expert briefly; and therewith he went out to drop from the car-step and to take the plunge alone.

In the two hours which had elapsed since the departure of the superintendent's car the track-clearers at both ends of the wreck had made astonishingly good progress. Step by step the master mechanic had worked his big crane up the line, tossing the derelicts aside or righting them upon the rails, as their condition warranted; and farther along Fordyce, with his huge tackle and its pulling locomotive, had been equally enthusiastic.

It was Sprague's boast that his methods of investigation, in the field of his hobby, as in all others, were purely scientific; and he insisted that the true scientist and the most successful is the one who can best qualify as a shrewd and wholly impartial observer.

Where another man might have asked questions, he stood aside and looked on and listened. In the fierce toil of track-clearing no one seemed to pay any attention to him, and the picture which presented itself was a life-sketch of the railroad force *in petto* and in the raw. The big onlooker took his time and made his mental jottings thoughtfully, strolling from one group to another and lingering longest near the hot boiler-cab of the great crane where a wizened human automaton in dirty overalls and jumper jerked the levers and spun the wheels of the hoist in obedience to the signals given by the flashily dressed master mechanic.

It wanted less than a quarter of an hour of noon when the final obstruction was heaved aside, and the track gang, which had been following the wreckers, trued and spiked the distorted rails of the main line into place. Sprague closed his mental note-book and went back to join Maxwell.

In the office-car the porter-cook had laid the table for the mid-day meal; and the superintendent and his guest ate it in transit, the office-car special being the first of the halted trains to pass westward over the newly cleared line.

"Well?" said Maxwell interrogatively, when the meal had progressed to the meat and vegetables without comment on the part of the one who had lifted the challenge.

"You've got the disease, all right; it's with you, and in the epidemic form, too. Its expression came out emphatically every now and then in that track-clearing hustle. One little snappy, snarly fellow lying under a box-car to make the hoisting-hitch voiced it precisely when his mate yelled at him to come out, that the hitch might slip. He yapped back, 'Who the hell and blinkety-blank blankation cares!' That's one form your disease is taking, and you'd say it would account for a good many of the smashes."

"Well?" queried the superintendent again. "You didn't stop at that?"

"No; I made a few other preliminary observations which may or may not prove up. Give me a little time; and when we get back to Brewster, detail that ex-cowboy 'relief operator' of yours, Tarbell, to run errands for me. If I can't show you good, tangible results within the next forty-eight hours or so, you may discharge me and hire a Pinkerton."

"You'll fail," said Maxwell gloomily. "I've been through a sickness of this kind before. There's no cure for it. It has simply got to run its course and wear itself out."

"That's what they used to say about cholera and the plague and yellow-fever, and all those things," laughed the man from Washington; but he did not go any farther into the matter of theories.

The run of the special train to Brewster was made without incident, and from the station Sprague went directly across to his hotel.

"I'm going over to clean up," he announced. "By and by, when you get around to it, send Tarbell over and tell him to wait in the lobby for me."

It was possibly an hour later when the young man who resembled William Starbuck sufficiently to pass for the mine owner's younger brother, got out of his chair in the quietest corner of the Hotel Topaz lobby and crossed to the elevators to meet the Government chemist.

"How are you, Archer?" was the renovated soil-gatherer's greeting. And then, as he led the way back to the quiet corner from which the young man had been keeping his watch upon the elevators: "We're up against it good and hard, this time, young man. Your boss has stumped us to prove a thing which he says can't be proved. Sit down and let's see if we can't start the thin edge of a wedge. I'll do the hammering and let you hold the wedge, and you can squeal if I strike off and hit you. How long has this case of bad railroading, which is smashing things right and left, been going on?"

The young fellow who was on the railroad pay-rolls as a "relief operator" took time to consider.

"A month or better."

"How did it begin?"

"I don't know. One way 'r another, the boys've just seemed to be gettin' sort o' careless and losin' their grip. After two or three wrecks had happened, it was all off. Half o' the men've taken to runnin' on their nerve, and the other half act like they don't care a durn."

"Is it only in the train service?"

"Lord, no; it's mighty near everywhere. It's sort of a dry rot; cars go without repairin', engines burn out, and twice within the last week the roundhouse has caught fire. You'd think every man on the road had just turned loose all holts and didn't give a cuss whether he ever got 'em again or not."

"What do the men themselves say about it?"

"There's a heap o' kickin' and knockin'. Some say it's Mr. Maxwell. When he gets good and mad and fires a bunch of 'em, they raise a rookus about it; and when he lets the next bunch down easy, they kick the other way."

Sprague sat back in the big leather-upholstered lobby chair and for a time seemed to be absorbed in a study of the rather over-massive beam arrangement of the ceiling. Suddenly he turned to ask: "How much of a prohibition country is this, Archer?"

Tarbell laughed.

"I reckon you don't need to ask that, with three saloons in every block in Brewster. We haven't got the water-wagon bug much out here. They say it don't breed well this side o' the main range."

"Much drinking among the railroad men?"

"Well—m—m—not so you could notice it. There's a rule against it."

"While they're on duty, you mean?"

"Any old time."

"Is that rule enforced?"

"Mr. Maxwell allows it is. He's sure some Ranahan when it comes to buckin' the booze-fighters."

"Still, there is more or less drinking among the men; you know there is, don't you, Archer?"

The young man grinned soberly.

"I ain't tellin' no tales out o' school, Mr. Sprague, not me," he drawled.

"Get rid of that notion," said the big man sharply. "You are working for Mr. Maxwell and his rules are your law and gospel. I'll tell you what I've seen, and then you can tell me what you've seen. I counted sixteen men in one place on this railroad today who, within the half-hour that I was looking on, stopped work either to hit or to pass a pocket-flask. Now go on."

"If you hold me up that-away, I reckon maybe there *is* a good many empty bottles layin' round on the right-o'-way—more'n what the passengers throw out o' the car windows," was the reluctant admission.

"And more than there used to be, say, two or three months ago?"

"Yes; right smart more."

"I thought so. We don't need to look any further, Archer, for the disease itself. Your 'dry rot' is very pointedly a wet rot. Booze and the running of a railroad are two things that won't mix. Now we'll come to the nib of it. Why is there more drinking now than there used to be?"

The younger man took time to think about it before he said: "You got me goin'; I don't know the answer to that."

"I didn't suppose you did," was the curt rejoinder. "But you are going to learn the answer, Archer, my son. It is now four o'clock; by half-past seven this evening I want you to be back here prepared to tell me who has been letting down the fences for the railroad men in this matter of drinking."

"Holy Smoke!" exclaimed the ex-cowboy, jarred for once out of his plainsman calm, "how am I goin' to do that, Mr. Sprague?"

"That is for you to find out, my boy. If you don't use your brain you'll never know whether or no you've got any. That's all—until half-past seven. You'll find me here at the hotel."

It was an even hour before the time appointed for Tarbell's return when Maxwell joined the chemistry expert at the table in the Topaz café where they usually sat when they could dine together.

At the unfolding of the napkins Sprague said: "I've found your germ, Dick, and things are beginning to develop. What do you think of that?"— passing a bit of dingy coarse-fibred paper across the table.

Maxwell opened the paper and read the ill-spelled type-written note it bore.

> Mr. Spraig:
>   Weer onto you with both feet. keep youre fingers out ov the geers or maybe youll git em mashed.
>
>   A well-Wishur.

"Where did that come from?" asked the superintendent, plainly amused.

"It was pushed under the door of my room upstairs about half an hour ago. The man who left it was short, thick-set, smooth-shaven, and he wore a pepper-and-salt suit and a slouch hat. Also, his breath smelled of whiskey."

"You expect me to recognize the description?"

"I didn't know but you might."

"I don't," Maxwell denied. Then his smile of amusement changed to one of amazement. "How could you know all these things about this man if you were on the other side of a closed door, Calvin?"

Sprague laughed. "See how easy it is to jump to conclusions," he derided. "I wasn't on the other side of a closed door; I was in the corridor when the fellow passed me, looking for the number on the door. I saw him leave the note. I'll ask one question, and then we'll dismiss that phase of the case. Is the wrecking-train back from Lobo yet?"

"Yes; it came in about four o'clock with the string of crippled cars. But you say you have found the germ; does that mean that you are going to prove up on your assertion about the epidemic?"

"I can't tell what it means yet; but I can tell you the name of the germ. It's whiskey."

"Drinking among the men?"

"Worse than that; drunkenness among the men. Enough of it, I should say, to account for all of your troubles and then some."

"Oh, you're off—'way off!" objected the harassed one irritably. "I know there is some drinking; in a wide-open country like this it is almost impossible to stamp it out entirely. But to account for the epidemic in that way, you'd have to imagine every other man in the service carrying a pocket-pistol on the job!"

"And you think that couldn't happen without your knowing it, eh? A little farther along I may have some statistics to show you; but just now I'm looking not so much for the germ as for the germ-carrier."

Maxwell smiled wearily.

"Still sticking to the theory that the blight is imported, are you? It's the only time I've ever known you to be 'yellow,' Calvin. I can imagine some wild-eyed newspaper reporter hatching such an idea, but not you. Think of the absurdity of a bunch of Wall Street stock-jobbers trying to get at us in any such indirect way as that—shipping whiskey in here to demoralize our working force! Pshaw! When these fellows get busy and go to work, they want action—quick action."

The expert put down his knife and fork and sat back in his chair.

"You are so close to the thing that you are continually losing the perspective, Dick," he said earnestly. "You are going on the supposition that those New York looters are trying first one thing and then another. That doesn't follow at all. For all you know, they may be gunning for you in half a dozen different ways this blessed minute—as they probably are. Assume, for the sake of the argument, that this whiskey scheme could be worked; I know you say it can't, but suppose it could: can you conceive of any expedient that would be more certain to kill your traffic, wipe out your earnings, smash your securities, and put you on the toboggan slide generally?"

"Oh, no; if it could be worked." Maxwell's answer this time was less confidently derisive.

"All right; now that you've come that far, I'll say this: it can be worked, and I'm here to tell you that it has been worked. Your railroad is practically an inebriate asylum in the making, right now, Richard. Half of your force has already fallen off the water chariot, and the other half is scared to death at the thought of what the drunken half may do."

Maxwell pushed away his dessert untasted.

"You have the proof of this, Calvin?" he broke out.

"I have some proof, and Tarbell is getting more. You've been blind. You didn't want to admit that your house of discipline was tumbling about your ears, and you've been shutting your eyes to the plain facts. For example: you may or may not be the only man in the service who doesn't know that those two freight engineers—the one who was killed and the other—who overran their orders and smashed into the passenger at Lobo Cut this morning were just plain drunk!"

"What's that? It—it can't be, Calvin!"

"But it *is*," insisted the big man across the table. "It is common talk among your own men; so common that it reached out and hit me—an outsider."

The superintendent drank his small coffee at a single gulp and flung his napkin aside.

"I'll get 'em!" he gritted savagely. "I'll get the last damned booze-fighter in the bunch!" And then: "Good God, Sprague; how could anything like this go on without my knowing it?"

"You would have found it out, sooner or later, of course. But you're a railroad man yourself, and you ought to know railroad men well enough to take into consideration that sort of loyalty among them which keeps them from 'peaching' on one another. Even Tarbell had to be jarred before he would admit that he knew about it. I can imagine that there has been a sort of generous conspiracy among the men to keep you from finding out."

"That's all right; I know now, and I'll sift them out; I'll go through the whole blamed outfit with a club! I'll—"

The man who had called out this upbubbling of righteous wrath was chuckling softly.

"You won't do anything that you say you will," he interrupted good-naturedly. "You stumped me to take the case, and I've taken it; which means that you're under the doctor's orders. When you have cooled down a bit, you'll see very clearly that the worst thing you could do at this particular crisis would be to start a division-wide scrap with the rank and file."

"But, good Lord, Sprague; I've got to do something, haven't I?"

"You surely have; and that something is to help me find the germ-carrier. Somebody has been taking down the bars for your men; who is it?"

"I don't know any more than a goat. I can't yet believe that it is the work of any one man."

"Possibly it isn't; there may be a good many. But I'll chance a guess that some one in authority is setting the pace. Leave that for a moment and we'll take up something else. You have two daily papers here in Brewster: I've noticed that one of them, *The Tribune*, is friendly to your road. How about the other, *The Times-Record*?"

"It is supposed to be independent, with a slant against corporations and 'the system,' whatever that may be."

"Um," said the scientist. "Before I went out on this last trip with Billy, I remarked that this other paper was giving a good bit of space to your road troubles in its news columns, and a good bit of its editorial space to criticisms of the Ford management. It occurred to me then that there might be a reason. How is the paper organized?"

"It is owned by one of our near-millionaires; a retired ranchman named Parker Higginson, who has dabbled in real-estate, in mines, and latterly in politics. His grouch against the railroad is purely personal. He has asked favors that I couldn't legally grant; and on one occasion he took offence because I told him that a newspaper man should be the last person in the world to invite us to become law-breakers."

"And his editor?" queried the expert.

"Is a bird of the same feather; a rather 'yellow' little fice named Healy."

Sprague looked rather dubiously at the two cigars which the waiter was tendering on a server. "No, I think not, George," he said, waving the cigars aside and feeling for his own pocket-case of stronger ones. And then to Maxwell: "This is all very nourishing. It may help out more than you suspect. Later in the evening I may ask you to call with me at the office of *The Times-Record*—though we may not have to go that far up the ladder to find what we are looking for. In the meantime, Tarbell is waiting for us out yonder in the lobby. Suppose we go and see what he wants."

They found the young man, who looked like a younger brother to Starbuck, and who had made his record chasing cattle thieves in Montana, methodically rolling a cigarette in the loggia alcove, and Sprague began on him briskly.

"Spit it out, Archer; what have you found?"

"I didn't make out to find what you sent me after," was the half-evasive reply.

"All right; tell us what you did find."

The young man dropped his cigarette and looked up with a glint of stubbornness in his stone-gray eyes.

"If it's just the same to you, Mr. Sprague, I'd a heap ruther not," he said.

Sprague reached out and turned the lapel of Tarbell's coat, exposing the small silver star of a deputy sheriff.

"You took an oath when you got that, Archer; and Mr. Maxwell pays you for wearing it."

Tarbell threw up his head defiantly. "Deputy or no deputy, I ain't goin' to name no names," he began slowly. "But here's what I found out: I been in twenty-three saloons and dives since you told me to go chase, and I counted thirty-one railroad men in 'em. Not all of 'em was drinkin' or gamblin', but some of 'em was."

Sprague turned to Maxwell.

"You see, I knew what I was talking about."

The superintendent was shaking his head.

"As openly as that!" he exclaimed. "I must have been the blindest fool in all this hill country!"

Tarbell chipped in quickly. "It ain't been that bad for very long. But it's just as Mr. Sprague says; it's spreadin' like murrain on a dry range. I saw men in them places this evenin' that I'd a swore never got off the water-wagon. I ain't namin' no names."

"Mr. Maxwell isn't asking you to give anybody away," the expert qualified. And then: "Had your supper?"

Tarbell nodded. "I had a hand-out in one o' the saloons."

"Good. Then I'll give you another job. Look around town for a man about Mr. Maxwell's build, only about twenty pounds heavier. He is between twenty-five and thirty years old, wears a slouch hat soft gray in color, dresses in pepper-and-salt, is clean-shaven, red-faced, blue-eyed, and walks with a little hitch to his left leg which isn't quite a limp. When you catch up with him, find out who he is and come and tell me. I'll be over at Mr. Maxwell's office."

Tarbell vanished, rolling a fresh cigarette as he went, and Sprague thrust his arm in Maxwell's.

"I'll go over to your shop with you," he said. "I know you're anxious to climb back into the working saddle. I'm not going to bore you; I merely want to have a little talk with that irreproachable chief clerk of yours, Harvey Calmaine."

A little later they climbed the stair to the office floor of the railroad building together, and Maxwell went on down the corridor to the despatcher's room. When he came back to his own office a half-hour later and found Sprague and young Calmaine figuring together at the chief clerk's desk in the outer room, he went on to his own inner sanctum without disturbing them.

It was perhaps another half-hour farther along when the expert, who had been patiently going over a mass of statistics with the alert, well-groomed young fellow who served as the superintendent's right hand, sat back in his chair and relighted the fat black cigar which had been suffered to go out many times during the figuring process.

"It seems that a good many things besides wrecks have been happening in the past few weeks, Mr. Calmaine," he suggested musingly. "In that short interval you have had many changes in the force, especially in the motive-power department. I don't know whether you have remarked it, but fully half of the men in the shops and roundhouses are new men. And that is the department in which the sickness seems to be the worst. Your maintenance costs have increased three hundred percent. over the same period last year."

"I know it," admitted the chief clerk. "It is the more marked because Dawson, our former master mechanic, made such phenomenally good records."

"I remember Dawson," said the big man, slipping easily from the statistics into the humanities. "He was here the first time I came over the road, early in the summer. Has he left the Short Line?"

"He has been promoted. He is superintendent of motive-power on the east end of the Southwestern."

"That is recent, isn't it?"

"Yes; it was only a few weeks ago."

"And you have a new man as department chief?"

"We have—Judson Bascom. You may remember him as the man who ran the special train for you and Mr. Maxwell the day you made the blind trip to Tunnel Number Three. He is a sort of slave-driver and seems to have a good deal of trouble with his men—is continually hiring and firing, you'd say, from the appearance of his pay-rolls."

The big expert's eyes narrowed.

"Was he also promoted from some other place on the system?" he asked.

"No; he is a new man. I don't know where he got his experience; somewhere in the East, I suppose."

"Another question," put in Sprague. "Does Mr. Maxwell have the appointment of his own motive-power chief?"

"No; this appointment was made in New York—by the executive committee, I imagine."

"Somebody's nephew or brother-in-law?" queried the chemist, with a twinkle in his eye.

"I don't know about that. I guess it happens that way, once in a while, on any railroad. But Bascom is all kinds of capable."

Sprague shook his head. "The true test of capability is always in the final result, my son," he said reflectively; adding, "and results nowadays are usually measured in dollars and cents. As an outsider, I should say that this Mr. Bascom is a pretty expensive man to have around, judging from his cost sheets. He drinks some, doesn't he?"

The young chief clerk closed one eye gravely.

"I'm not supposed to know anything about that, Mr. Sprague."

"No, of course not. As you might say, it's nobody's business but Mr. Bascom's. By the way, what is that whistle blowing so persistently for?"

Calmaine leaped out of his chair as if it had been suddenly connected with the grounding wire of a forty-kilowatt generator.

"By George! It's a fire!" he exclaimed; and the sound of hurrying feet in the corridor confirmed the surmise. Maxwell's door opened at the same instant, and the three rushed out to join the crowd which was already streaming across the yard tracks toward the company's shops.

The fire was in the shops, originating in the boiler-room; and, thanks to the timely alarm and the comparative earliness of the hour, it was soon extinguished. Investigation, promptly instituted on the spot by the superintendent, proved that it was the result of pure carelessness. Some of the mechanics had washed their overalls and had hung them too near the sheet-iron stack in the fire-room; that was all.

Sprague lingered at Maxwell's elbow while the investigation was going on, and he appeared to be a more or less perfunctory listener when Bascom, oozing wrathful profanity at every pore, told the superintendent what he would do to the careless clothes-driers when they should show up in the morning. But later, after the return to the head-quarters offices, the man from Washington sat for a long time in Maxwell's easiest chair, smoking steadily and with his gaze fixed upon the disused gas chandelier marking the exact centre of the ceiling.

It was not until after Maxwell had finished his quota of night work and was closing his desk that Tarbell came in to make a whispered report to the big man apparently dreaming in the easy-chair.

Sprague listened, nodded, and rose to join the office-closing retreat.

"That is about what I thought, Archer," he said soberly. "Now I have one more little job for you, and when it is done we'll call it a go for tonight. Come around to my laboratory with me and I'll explain it to you." And when the four of them reached the plaza-fronting street he excused himself to Maxwell and the chief clerk and went, with Tarbell at his elbow, to the little second-floor den in the Kinzie Building where his experiments in soil analysis were conducted.

Reaching the back room which served as the laboratory proper, Sprague provided his follower with half a dozen small bottles, empty and tightly corked.

"There you are," he said, from which it may be inferred that the nature of the remaining "job" had been explained on the way up from the railroad head-quarters. "Do it neatly, Archer, and don't let them catch you at it. Everything will have quieted down by this time, and you shouldn't have any trouble. I'll wait for you here."

Tarbell was gone possibly half an hour, and when he returned the bottles they were filled, two of them with a black-brown liquid, thick and viscous, and four with what appeared to be specimens of more or less dirty water. Each bottle was carefully marked on the blank label pasted upon it. Sprague stood them in a row on the laboratory working-table.

"I shall be busy here for twenty or thirty minutes," he said. "I don't want to ride a willing horse to death, but I'd be glad if you'd go by the hotel and ask Mr. Maxwell to wait up for me. I want to see him before he goes to bed."

Tarbell nodded, but he hesitated about going.

"I got a hunch that we ain't doin' all the shadow work by our little lonesomes, Mr. Sprague," he ventured to say. But before he could go on, Sprague lifted a finger for silence, made a whirling half-turn with a swiftness marvellous in so huge a body, and flung himself through the open door into the unlighted outer office-room to which the laboratory was an inner extension.

There were sounds of a collision, a fall, and a brief struggle before Tarbell could get action. At the end of it Sprague came back into the lighted laboratory, dragging a thick-set, square-shouldered man in pepper-and-salt clothes; a man with a clean-shaven red face down the side of which a thin line of blood was trickling.

"You were eminently correct, Archer," said the expert, slamming his unresisting burden into a corner of the room after he had deftly gone through the pepper-and-salt pockets for weapons with the result of turning out a cheap revolver and a wicked-looking knife. "I'm sorry I can't keep my word and let you go to bed, but the plot has thickened a little too rapidly. Go around to the Topaz and ask Mr. Maxwell to wait. Then come back here and keep this fellow quiet while I do my work."

When Tarbell went out, Sprague quickly stripped his coat and went to work at his laboratory table. For some little time the man in the corner lay as he had been cast, and the worker at the table paid no attention to him. But a few minutes before Tarbell's return, the red-faced man gasped, gurgled, and sat up to hold his head in his hands as one trying to remember what had happened to him. Presently he looked up, and after a long stare at the big figure of the man at the work table, he found his voice.

"Say, guv'ner, wot am I doin' here?" he asked huskily.

Sprague, who was skilfully dropping a fuming yellow liquor from a glass-stoppered bottle into a beaker, replied without turning his head.

"If anybody should ask, I should say you are waiting for an officer to come and take you to jail."

"Who, me? Wot have I been doin'?" queried the husky one, in the anxious rasp of a deeply aggrieved victim of circumstances.

"You've been shoving threatening letters under my door in the Hotel Topaz, for one thing," said Sprague, still busy with his experiment.

"Who, me? My Gawd—just lissen to 'im!" wheezed the red-faced man, as if appealing to some third person invisible.

A silence followed during which the crouching man's feet drew themselves by imperceptible fractions of an inch at a time into position for a tackling spring. Sprague did not look aside, but when the leg muscles of the man began to bulge as if testing themselves for the leap, the worker at the table spoke again.

"I shouldn't try it if I were you. This stuff that I am fooling with is nitric acid, ninety-eight percent. pure. If any of it should happen to get spilled on you, there wouldn't be sweet oil enough in this town to put the fire out."

"My Gawd!" gasped the red-faced one, suddenly sticking his feet out in front of him again; and just then Tarbell came in.

"I'll be through in a minute, Archer," said the experimenter at the work-table, still without looking around. "Did you find your man?"

"Yes; and Starbuck is with him. What do you want me to do with this geezer?"

"Nothing. I'll fix him when we're ready to go."

"I've got a pair of handcuffs," Tarbell suggested.

"They won't be needed—not for this one."

Tarbell dragged out a chair and sat down, tilting comfortably against the wall and staring half-absently at the man in the corner. "Before I'd let any bare-handed man take my arsenal away from me and slam me around like that," he murmured, quite impersonally.

The man on the floor lifted the challenge promptly.

"Lemme git up and gimme half a chanst," he croaked. "I won't hurt you none if you don't git in the way o' that door."

"Not this evenin'," said Tarbell succinctly; and there the matter rested until Sprague put his beakers and test-tubes aside, and, resuming his coat, took a flat black box from a shelf and slipped it into his pocket.

"Now we're ready," he announced; and then he turned to the captured spy. "We're going to leave you here in the dark for a little while, and there will be nothing between you and a get-away but a small matter of fear. After we turn the lights off I shall leave a few bottles of stuff around where they will do the most good. If you should happen to upset one of them in moving about, it's good-bye. If it doesn't burn you to death, you'll stifle."

"My Gawd!" said the captive; and he was still saying it over softly to himself when they switched off the lights, shut the office doors, and went away.

"There is a good example of the power of matter over mind, Archer," said Sprague whimsically, when they reached the street. "If that fellow would use his reason even a little bit he'd know that I hadn't made any very elaborate preparations to hold him; there wasn't time between the turning off of the lights and our leaving. Yet I'll bet a small chicken worth twenty-five dollars that we find him still crouching in his corner and afraid to move when we go back. He saw me using acid in my little experiment; saw the fumes and probably got a whiff of them. That was enough."

They found Maxwell and Starbuck sitting on the hotel porch, smoking. Sprague took the superintendent aside.

"It's rather worse than I thought it was, Dick," he began, when they had drawn their chairs a little apart. "That is my excuse for keeping you up so late. We have one of the conspirators under a sort of mental lock and key over at my place in the Kinzie Building, but he is only a hired striker, and I'd like to flush the big game. Are you good for a watch-meeting—you and Starbuck? It may last all night, and nothing may come of it, but it's worth trying."

Maxwell spread his hands.

"Whatever you say, Calvin," he acquiesced. "After the jolt you've given me tonight, I can only get into the harness and pull when you give the word."

"All right. We'll take Tarbell for a guide. Tarbell, you know your way around in the shops pretty well, don't you?"

"I reckon so," was the young man's reply.

"We want to go to the foundry, or to some place near by where we can keep an eye on the pickle shed. Can you get us there without arousing anybody's curiosity?"

"Sure," said Tarbell.

"Good. Pitch out," was the curt command, and the four of them left the hotel to make a circuit through ill-lighted streets and around the lower end of the eastern railroad yard to come at the long line of shop buildings from the rear.

On the way Maxwell inquired curiously: "What do you know about pickling-sheds, Calvin?"

"I know that every well-regulated foundry has one where castings which are to be machined are treated with acid to take the hard sand-scale off."

"And why, just why, are you anxious to get a near-hand view of ours, at this time of night?"

"I'm hoping we shall find the answer to that in your foundry yard, Dick. If we don't, the joke will be on me."

The approach to the locomotive-repairing section of the railroad plant was made through a river-bank yard littered with slag dumps, piled flasks, and heaps of scrap iron. There was no moon, and when they got among the lumber sheds in the rear of the car-shops the darkness was almost tangible. But Tarbell knew the ground, and when he finally called a halt the twin cupola stacks of the foundry loomed before them in the darkness and the acrid smell of the warm, moist moulding sand was in the air.

When the pickling-shed had been located for him, Sprague chose the waiting-place under a flask shelter directly opposite and the silent watch began. For a weary half-hour nothing happened. Though the month was August, a cool wind crept down from the Timanyoni snow peaks, and the splash and gurgle of the near-by river added its suggestion of chill to the moonless night. Over in the western yards the night crew was making up the midnight freights; but with the buildings of the plant intervening, the noises of the shifter's exhaust and the clankings and crashings of the shunted cars came faintly to the ears of the watchers.

On the even hour of one the watchman made his round. They could see his lantern twinkling through the windows of the shops, and later he made a circuit of the outbuildings. His route led him finally through the foundry, and as he came out the light of his lantern fell upon the piled castings and the pickling-troughs, and on the carboys of vitriol. There were four of the boxed acid-holders standing under the shed. Sprague drew down his left cuff and made pencil marks on it in the darkness when the watchman passed on.

It was possibly fifteen minutes after the watchman had disappeared when Maxwell broke the strained silence with a whisper.

"Duck!" he said to Starbuck, who was standing up. "Dunkell's coming back—without his lantern!"

Sprague spread his arms and crushed the other three back into the shadows. "It isn't the watchman this time—be ready!" he whispered; and as he said it the figure of a man appeared coming down the littered roadway from the blacksmith shop.

Though he walked in darkness there was no incertitude about the man's movements. Turning abruptly out of the material-road he went straight to the foundry shed. A moment later a beam of white light played steadily upon the acid carboys, a sheltered beam which seemed to come from a tiny electric search-light. Plainly they saw a pair of hands place a large bottle on the ground, remove the stopper, and fix a tin funnel in the neck. Then one of the carboys was tilted, presumably by the same pair of hands, though the hands were invisible now, and a thin stream of the yellow acid gurgled through the funnel.

When the bottle was filled the carboy slowly righted itself; the hands came in view again to remove the funnel and to replace the stopper; and then the search-light went out with the faint snap of an electric switch. Almost at the same instant the watchers saw the figure of the man fading away into the inner and darker blackness of the foundry.

"We've got to follow him, Tarbell," said Sprague, hurriedly; "and we lose out if he discovers us. Can you pilot us?"

"I can," asserted Maxwell, and under the superintendent's lead the shadow race was begun.

Happily, there was a noisy diversion to make the secret pursuit feasible. The train-making clamor had come down from the western yards, and for the moment the yard crew was working on the freight-house tracks opposite the shops. Under cover of the out-door clamor the four pursuers were able to close up on the bottle-carrier until they were treading almost in his footsteps. The route led through the foundry floor to the machine shop. On the erecting pits were two locomotives, apparently ready to be hauled out and put into service after their period of back-shop repairs.

Into the cab of one of the engines the bottle-bearer climbed, first placing his burden carefully in the gangway. A little later they heard him climbing over the coal in the tender, heard him remove the cover of the water manhole, and heard the *glug-glug* of liquid issuing from a bottle-neck.

Sprague silently drew a small square object from his pocket, the little flat black box he had caught up as he was leaving his office in the Kinzie Building. Then he whispered to Tarbell: "Cover him, Archer, and don't hesitate to shoot if you need to: ready!" At the word there was a blinding burst of illumination and the report of a flash-light cartridge, followed instantly by the crash of the breaking bottle, silence, and black darkness. Then Sprague's mellow voice boomed into the stillness.

"Come down, Mr. Bascom. We've got your picture, and a man who doesn't often miss what he shoots at is covering you with his gun."

It was a grim little group of five which gathered in the master mechanic's room in the office wing of the machine shop a few minutes after the flash-light photograph had been taken in the erecting shop. Bascom's ruddy flush was gone when he sat down heavily in his desk chair; but his natty brown crush hat was pushed back, and the gleam in his small, lynx-like eyes was not of fear.

"Just name the kind of a hand-spring you'd like to have me turn, gentlemen," he said, half-sardonically, when Tarbell had switched on the second circuit of incandescents. "I'm not much of an acrobat, but I'll do the best I can to amuse you."

It was Sprague who did the talking for the prosecution.

"We want to know first who is with you in this job of inside worm-eating, Mr. Bascom," he said coolly.

"Nobody," came the prompt lie.

Sprague's smile was affable. "I'm sure you'll make one exception," he urged; "a man named Murtagh, who was for a little time one of your shop machinists and who is now a press-repairer on *The Times-Record*."

Bascom sat up and swore a savage oath.

"So that damned scab has welshed, has he?" he grated.

Sprague branched off and began again, this time in the straitly criminal field.

"How many locomotives have you treated with the acid cure, first and last, Mr. Bascom?"

"Enough so you'll still be resetting flues in 'em a year from now."

This time it was Maxwell's turn to swear, and for a minute or two the air of the office was sulphurous. When the atmosphere had cleared again, Sprague went on.

"I presume that your defence in court will be that you were trying an experiment to neutralize the effect of the alkaline water of this region?"

Bascom grinned appreciatively. "You're an expert chemist yourself, Mr. Sprague. The water in this country, outside of the Park, is pretty badly alkali, as you probably know."

"But that defence will scarcely explain why you put acid in the oil which is used for lubricating the internal parts of the engines—cylinders and valves," Sprague cut in quietly.

The master mechanic's chair righted itself with a crash, and the crash punctuated another blast of bad language directed at the man who had been left crouching in the corner in Sprague's uptown laboratory.

"So Murtagh gave you that, too, did he?" Bascom finished. "It's your lead, Mr. Sprague; what do you want me to play?"

"Names," said the expert curtly.

"But if I say I was playing a lone hand?"

"We should know you were lying. This acid business may be all your own; but there are other things. You've had plenty of help in the drink-fest and the demoralization game, Bascom."

The big master mechanic's lips shut like the jaws of a steel trap. But after a time he said: "What do I get if I spout on the others?"

"A chance to get out of the country—eh, Maxwell?"

The superintendent nodded. "Yes; if he can get away before I can find a gun to kill him with."

Bascom reached into his desk, found a scratch-pad and tossed it over to Starbuck. "Take 'em down," he said briefly; and then followed a black-list that was simply heart-breaking to Richard Maxwell, a man who had built his reputation as a railroad executive, and would have staked it instantly, upon the loyalty of his rank and file. Shop foremen, roundhouse bosses, bridge men, yard foremen, section bosses, a travelling engineer, a clerk here and a telegraph operator there—the list seemed endless.

When Bascom paused, Sprague began again.

"What was the plan, Bascom, as it was outlined to these others?"

The master mechanic's smile showed his fine even teeth.

"To make this jerk-water railroad a little easier to work for," he sneered. "When we found the right kind of a man we made him believe that the discipline was keyed up too damned tight and showed him how he could loosen up a little, if he felt like it. Murtagh was barkeep' and handed out the bug-juice. That's all there was to it."

"Not quite all," said Sprague evenly. "You got Murtagh his job on *The Times-Record* in order to have him handy without being too much in the way or too much in evidence. How much do the *Times-Record* people know about the scheme for smashing the Nevada Short Line securities from the inside?"

Bascom laughed hardily.

"You'll never catch a newspaper man," he said. "But I'll tell you this: Parker Higginson is a pretty smooth politician, and he's got a mighty long arm when it comes to reaching for the thing he wants. He was the man who got me my job here, and I'll bet those New York people who appointed me don't know yet why they did it. Another thing: when I'm gone, Higginson will still be here—don't you forget that!"

"We'll try to remember it," Sprague promised. Then he looked at his watch. "The overland passenger, westbound, will be here in a few minutes, and when it goes, you may go with it, Mr. Bascom. But first we want a few more names, the names of the New York people who are behind both you and Mr. Higginson."

Bascom got up, went to a wardrobe in one corner of the office, and dragged out two heavy suitcases.

"I've been fixed for this for some little time," he volunteered. "Send Murtagh to the stone-pile for splitting on us, and I won't make any claim for the half-month's salary that's due me. As to the names of the big fellows, I only wish I knew them, Mr. Sprague. If I did, I'd go east instead of west and make somebody come across with big money. As it is, I guess it's South America for mine. Good-night, all. I wish you luck with the booze-fighters, Mr. Maxwell. You'll have a bully good time loading some of them back onto the water-automobile." And he went out into the night with a suit-case in either hand.

"Talk about cold gall!" said Starbuck, when the door closed behind the retreating figure of the big master mechanic; "Great Cat! That fellow's got enough to swim in." Then he turned to Sprague. "Is the show over?"

The man from Washington laughed genially.

"That is for Maxwell to say. We might go uptown and give those newspaper people a bad quarter of an hour, though I doubt if we'd make any money at it."

Maxwell looked up quickly.

"You think they're in it, Calvin? Bascom wasn't lying about that part of it?"

"Yes; they are in it up to their necks. I suppose it's politics for Higginson. Haven't I heard somewhere that he is one of the State bosses?"

"You might have," drawled Starbuck. "He's It, all right."

Sprague stood up and yawned sleepily.

"Perhaps, a little later on, we can throw a scare into this Mr. Parker Higginson," he suggested. "Just now, I'm for the hotel and a few winks of much-needed sleep. Tarbell, you go up to my office and get Murtagh. Have him locked up on a charge of—oh, any old charge will do; breaking into my office tonight, if you can't think of anything better. If we can manage to hold onto him for a while, we may be able to keep this Mr. Higginson quiet while Maxwell is straightening out his booze-fighters. Let's go."

"Hold on, just a minute," pleaded Maxwell. "There are three of us here who have seen the wheels go round, and I don't forget that I was the one who said there weren't any wheels. How in the name of all that is wonderful have you been able to work this puzzle out in less than twelve hours, Sprague?"

The big chemistry expert sat down again and locked his hands behind his head.

"My gosh!" he said; "have I got to open up a kindergarten for you fellows when I'm so sleepy that I don't know what I'm going to have for breakfast tomorrow morning? It was easy, dead easy. Half an hour with those delayed train crews at Angels this morning showed me that the discipline strings were all off; one of the freight conductors even offered me a nip out of his pocket-flask when I intimated that I was thirsty. With that for a pointer, I had my eyes open at the wreck, and what I saw there you all know. Moreover, I noticed that the pocket-flasks were all alike, as if they'd all been handed out over the same bar. All straight, so far?"

"Go on," said Maxwell.

"I got my first pointer on Bascom at the wreck, too. I saw that the men in the trainmaster's gang didn't drink when the boss was looking, a condition which didn't apply in the other crew. Again, I noticed that Bascom took his track-clearing privilege with a large and handsome disregard for the salvage. He didn't care how much property was destroyed in the process, and once I saw him give the signal to the crane engineer to drop a car loaded with automobiles—which was promptly done and the autos properly smashed."

"The cold-blooded devil!" growled the superintendent.

"When we reached town, Tarbell here promptly confirmed my guess about the whiskey; and in the evening Calmaine helped some more by going with me over the pay-rolls for new names, and over the cost-sheets for increases. Naturally, we dwelt longest upon the motive-power and repair department, with its huge increases, and it so happened that my eye fell upon the various charges for vitriol in carboys. I asked Calmaine what use a railroad shop had for so much sulphuric acid, and he told me it was used to pickle castings. Afterward I sent Tarbell out to bring me samples of water from the tanks of the crippled locomotives on the shop track and of the oil in their cylinder-cups. Analyses of both, which I made on the spot, showed the presence of sulphuric acid in the water, and also in the oil."

"Still, you didn't have any cinch on Bascom," Starbuck put in.

"No, but things were leaning pretty heavily his way. Tarbell had traced Murtagh for me and had found out the one thing that I needed to know; namely, that Murtagh had been 'placed' on *The Times-Record* by Bascom's recommendation. Murtagh was the man who put the threatening note under my door; the note was printed on a scrap of scratch-paper—copy paper—of the sort that you rarely find outside of a newspaper office. Here I simply put two and two together. Bascom had been conferring with Higginson, or his editor, or both of them, and telling them of my rubbernecking at the wreck. They had agreed among themselves that I'd better be warned off the grass, and they took about the stupidest possible way they could think of to do it."

"Still, you didn't have Bascom," reiterated Starbuck.

"No; but he was the man who had been signing the requisitions for the big purchases of acid, and I was far enough along to chance a jump at him. I knew that if he were the man who was poisoning the locomotives, he wasn't trusting anybody else; he was doing it himself, often and by littles. I wasn't at all sure of catching him tonight, of course; but we saw him down here at the fire, and I thought there was an even chance that he might stay and do a little more devilment."

Maxwell stood up and shook himself into his coat.

"I'm onto you now, Sprague," he chuckled, in a brave attempt to jolly himself out of the depressive nightmare which had been weighing him down for weeks. "You're a guesser—a bold, bad four-flusher, with a perfectly miraculous knack of drawing the other card you need when you reach for it. Now, if you could only guess me out some way in which I can straighten up these poor fellows of mine who have been pulled neck and heels off of the water-wagon—"

"Pshaw! That's a cinch," said the big man, yawning sleepily again. "We'll just put our heads together and get out a little circular letter, talking to the boys just as you'd talk to a bunch of them in your office. Tell 'em it's all off, and the bar is closed and padlocked, and you'll have 'em all eating out of your hand again, same as they used to. You don't believe it can be done? You let me write the letter and I'll show you. All you have to do is to apply the scientific principle; surround the whole subject and look at it calmly and dispassionately, and—ye-ow! Say, I'm going to chance another guess—the last in the box. If you don't head me over to the hotel and my room, you'll have to carry me over and put me to bed. And that's no joke, with a man of my size. Let's go."

CHAPTER 5

THE CLOUD-BURSTERS

It was an article in the news columns of *The Brewster Morning Tribune* which first called attention—the attention of the Brewsterites and the inter-mountain world in general—to the plans and purposes of the Mesquite Valley Land and Irrigation Company.

Connabel, a hard-working reporter on *The Tribune*, had been sent over to Angels, the old head-quarters of the Red Butte Western on the other side of the Timanyonis, to get the story of a shooting affray which had local-ized itself in Pete Grim's place, the one remaining Angelic saloon. Finding the bar-room battle of little worth as a news story, and having time to kill between trains, Connabel had strolled off up the gulch beyond the old cop-per mines and had stumbled upon the construction camp of the Mesquite Company.

Being short of "copy" on the fight story, the reporter had written up the irrigation project, taking the general outlines from a foreman on the job whose tongue he loosened with a handful of Brewster cigars. A big earth dam was in process of construction across the mouth of the rather precipi-tous valley of Mesquite Creek; and the mesa below, which, to Connabel's unrural eye, seemed to be a very Sahara of infertile desolation, was to be made to blossom like the rose.

Kendall, managing editor of *The Tribune*, had run the story, partly be-cause real news happened to be scarce at the moment, and partly out of sheer astonishment that an enterprise of the magnitude of the Mesquite project had not already flooded the country with the brass-band publicity literature which is supposed to attract investors.

That a land and irrigation company should actually wait until its dam was three-fourths completed before it began to advertise was a thing suf-ficiently curious to call for editorial comment. Why Editor Kendall did not comment on the news item as a matter of singular interest is a query which had its answer on the loggia porch of the Hotel Topaz in the evening of the day on which Connabel's write-up appeared.

It was Kendall's regular habit to close his desk at seven o'clock and to spend a leisurely hour over his dinner at the Topaz before settling down to his night's work. On the evening in question he had chanced to sit at table with Maxwell, the general superintendent of the railroad, and with Maxwell's friend and college classmate, Sprague. After dinner the three had gone out to the loggia porch to smoke, and it was the big chemistry expert who spoke of the Mesquite news story which had appeared that morning in *The Tribune*.

"Yes," said the editor; "Connabel got on to that yesterday. I sent him over to Angels to write up a shooting scrape, and he had more time on his hands than he knew what to do with. We've all known, in a general way, that an Eastern company was doing something over there, but I had no idea that they'd got their dam pretty nearly done and were about ready to open up for business."

"It's wild-cat, pure and unadulterated!" cut in the railroad man snappily. "What they are going to do to a lot of woolly investors will be good and plenty. That Mesquite Mesa land is just about as fertile as this street pavement here."

Kendall was a dried-up little wisp of a man, with tired eyes and a face the color of old oak-tanned leather.

"That is what you would think—that they are out for the easy money," he agreed. "But there is something a little queer about it. They haven't advertised."

"Not here," supplemented Maxwell. "It would be a trifle too rank. Everybody in the Timanyoni knows what that land is over in the edge of the Red Desert."

"They haven't advertised anywhere, so far as I can ascertain," put in the editor, quietly. "What is more, Jennings, who is the engineer in charge of the dam-building and who seems to be the only man in authority on the ground, came in this afternoon and raised sand with me for printing the news story. He said they were not exploiting the scheme here at all; that their money and their investors were all in the East, and they were asking no odds of the Brewster newspapers."

"Bitter sort of devil, that fellow Jennings," was Maxwell's comment; but it was the big chemist who followed the main thread of the argument.

"What reason did he give for making such an extraordinary break as that, Mr. Kendall?"

"Oh, he had his reason pat enough," rejoined the editor, with his tired smile. "He said he realized that we have irrigated land of our own over here in the Park upon which we are anxious to get settlers, and that public sentiment here would naturally be against the Mesquite project. He asked, as a matter of fairness, that we simply let the desert project alone. He claimed that it had been financed without taking a dollar out of the Timanyoni, so we could not urge that there were local investors to be protected."

"Umph! That argument cuts both ways; it's an admission that the Eastern investors might need protection," scoffed the railroad superintendent. Then he added: "They certainly will if they expect to get any of the money back that they have been spending in Mesquite Valley. Why, Kendall, Mesquite Creek is bone-dry half the year!"

"And the other half?" inquired Sprague.

"It's a cloud-burst proposition, like a good many of the foot-hill arroyos," Maxwell explained. "Once, in a summer storm, I saw a wall of water ten feet high come down that stream-bed, tumbling twenty-ton bowlders in the thick of it as if they had been brook pebbles. Then, for a month, maybe, it would be merely a streak of dry sand."

"Perhaps they are counting upon storing the cloud-burst water," commented Kendall dryly. Then as he rose to go back to his work: "As you say, Maxwell, it has all the ear-marks of the wild-cat. But so long as it doesn't stick its claws out at us, I suppose we haven't much excuse for butting in. Good-night, gentlemen. Drop in on me when you're up my way. Always glad to see you."

The two who remained on the hotel porch after the editor went away smoked in comradely silence for a time. The night was enchantingly fine, with a first-quarter moon swinging low in a vault of velvety blackness, and a gentle breeze, fragrant with the breath of the mountain forests, creeping down upon the city from the backgrounding highlands. Across the plaza, and somewhere in the yards behind the long two-storied railroad headquarters building and station, a night crew was making up trains, and the clank and crash of coupling cars mingled with the rapid-fire exhausts of the switching engine.

The big-bodied chemistry expert was the first to break the companionable silence, asking a question which had reference to the epidemic of disaster and demoralization which had recently swept over Maxwell's railroad.

"Well, how are things coming by this time, Dick? Are the men responding fairly well to that little circular-letter, man-to-man appeal we concocted?"

"They are, for a fact," was the hearty assurance. "I have never seen anything like it in railroading in all my knocking about. They've been coming in squads to 'fess up and take the pledge, and to assure me that it's the water-wagon for theirs from now on. By George, Calvin, it's the most mellowing experience I've ever had! It proves what you have always said, and what I have always wanted to believe: that the good in the mass definitely outweighs the bad, and that it will come to the front if you only know how to appeal to it."

"That's right," averred the chemist. "It is the strong hope of the country that there is justice and fairness and sane common-sense at the American bottom of us, if you can only get at it. I think you can call the booze-fight and demoralization round-up a trouble past and begin to look around you for the signs and symptoms of the next biff you're going to get."

The stockily built little man who stood as the railroad company's chief field-officer on the far-western fighting line moved uneasily in his chair.

"I have been hoping there wasn't going to be any 'next time,'" he said, chewing thoughtfully upon his cigar.

"I should hope with you, Dick, if we had been able, in any of the former scrimmages, to secure good, indubitable court evidence against the men who are backing these buccaneering raids on your securities. The one thing that big money really fears today is the law—the law as the Federal courts are likely to construe and administer it. But to obtain your day in court you've got to have evidence; and thus far we haven't been able to sweat out anything that would implicate the man or men higher up. Therefore, you may continue to sleep on your arms, keeping a sharp eye out for surprises."

"I guess that is pretty good advice," was the ready admission; "but it is rather difficult to put into practice, Calvin. There are five hundred miles of this railroad, and my job of operating them is big enough to keep me busy without doing any detective stunts on the side."

"I know," Sprague nodded reflectively, "and for that reason I've been half-way keeping an eye out for you myself."

"You have? Don't tell me you've been finding more grief!"

Sprague threw away his outburned stub and found and lighted a fresh cigar.

"I don't want to pose as an alarmist," he offered at length, "but I'd like to dig a little deeper into this Mesquite irrigation scheme. How much or little do you know about it?"

"Next to nothing. About two months ago Jennings, the construction engineer, made application for the through handling, from Copah, of a train-load of machinery, tools, and camp outfit. He asked to have the stuff delivered at the end of the old copper-mine spur above Angels. We put the spur in shape for him and delivered the freight."

"Well, what else?"

"That is about all we have had to do with them in a business way. Two weeks ago, when we had that wreck at Lobo, they were asking Benson for an extension of the copper-mine spur to a point nearer their job, chiefly, I think, so they could run a hand-car back and forth between the camp and the saloon at Angels. Benson didn't recommend it, and the matter was dropped."

"Without protest?"

"Oh, yes; Jennings didn't make much of a roar. In fact, I've always felt that he avoided me when he could. He is in town a good bit, but I rarely see him. Somebody told me he tried once to get into the Town and Country Club, and didn't make it. I don't know who would blackball him, or why; but evidently some one did."

The ash grew a full half-inch longer on Sprague's fresh cigar before he said:

"Doesn't it occur to you that there is something a bit mysterious about this dry-land irrigation scheme, Dick?"

"I had never thought of it as being mysterious. It is a palpable swindle, of course; but swindles are like the poor—they're always with us."

"It interests me," said the big man, half-musingly. "A company, formed nobody knows where or how, drops down in the edge of the Red Desert and begins—absolutely without any of the clatter and clamor of advertising that usually go with such enterprises—to build what, from all reports, must be a pretty costly dam. If they have acquired a title to the Mesquite Mesa, no one seems to have heard of it; and if they are hoping to sell the land when the dam is completed, that, too, has been kept dark. Now comes this little newspaper puff this morning, and Mr. Jennings promptly turns up to ask Kendall to drop it."

"It is rather queer, when you come to put the odds and ends of it together," admitted the railroad man.

"Decidedly queer, I should say." So far the Government man went on the line which he himself had opened. Then he switched abruptly. "By the way, where is your brother-in-law, Starbuck? I haven't seen him for three or four days."

"Billy has been in Red Butte, figuring on a little mining deal in which we are both interested. But I am looking for him back tonight."

"Good. If you should happen to see him when the train comes in, ask him to come over here and smoke a pipe with me. Tell him I'm losing my carefully acquired cowboy accent and I'd like to freshen it up a bit."

The superintendent promised; and, since he always had work to do, went across to his office in the second story of the combined head-quarters and station building.

Some hour or so later the evening train came in from the west, and at the outpouring of passengers from it one, a man whose air of prosperous independence was less in the grave, young-old face and the loosely fitting khaki service clothes than in the way in which he carried his shoulders, was met by a boy from the superintendent's office, and the word passed sent him diagonally across the grass-covered plaza to swing himself lightly over the railing of the hotel porch.

"Dick made motions as if you wanted to smoke a peace pipe with me," he said, dropping carelessly into the chair which had been Maxwell's.

"Yes," Sprague assented; and then he went on to explain why. At the end of the explanation Starbuck nodded.

"I reckon we can do it all right; go up on the early-morning train to the canyon head, and take a chance on picking up a couple of bronc's at Wimberley's ranch. But we could hoof it over from Angels in less than a quarter of the time it'll take us to ride up the river from Wimberley's."

"For reasons of my own, Billy, I don't want to 'hoof it,' as you say, from Angels. To mention one of them, I might ask you to remember that I tip the scale at a little over the half of the third hundred, just now, and I'm pretty heavy on my feet." And therewith the matter rested.

At an early hour the following morning, an hour when the sun was just swinging clear over the far-distant blue horizon line of the Crosswater Hills which marks the eastern limit of the great desert, two men dropped from the halted eastbound train at the Timanyoni Canyon water-tank and made their way around the nearest of the hogbacks to the ranch house of one William Wimberley.

As Starbuck had predicted, two horses were obtainable, though the ranchman looked long and dubiously at the big figure of the Government chemist before he was willing to risk even the heaviest of the horses in his small *remuda*.

"I reckon you'll have ter set sort o' light in the saddle, Mister," he said at the mounting; and then, apparently as an after-thought: "By gollies, I wouldn't have you fall over ag'inst me f'r a farm in God's country, stranger! Ef you was to live round here, we'd call you Samson, and take up a c'lection fer the pore, sufferin' Philistines. We shore would."

Sprague laughed good-naturedly as he followed Starbuck's lead toward the river. He was well used to being joked about his size, and there were times when he rather encouraged the joke. Big men are popularly supposed to be more or less helpless, physically, and Sprague was enough of a humorist to enjoy the upsetting, now and then, of the popular tradition. In his college days he had held the record for the heavy lift and the broad jump; there was no man of his class who could stand up to him with the gloves or on the wrestling-mat; and in the foot-ball field he was at once the strongest "back" and the fastest man on the team—a combination rare enough to be miraculous.

"You say you want to follow the river?" said Starbuck, when they had struck in between the precipitous hills among which the green flood of the Timanyoni made its way toward the canyon portal.

"Yes, if it is at all practicable. I'd like to get some idea of the lay of the land between this and the camp on the Mesquite."

"I'm anticipatin' that you'll get the idea, good and plenty," agreed the superintendent's brother-in-law dryly; and during the three-hour jaunt that followed, the prediction was amply confirmed. There was no trail, and for the greater part of the way the river flowed between rocky hogbacks, with only the narrowest of bowlder-strewn margins on either hand.

Time and again they were forced to dismount and to lead the horses around or over the natural obstructions; and once they were obliged to leave the river valley entirely, climbing and descending again by a circuitous route among the rugged hills.

It was late in the forenoon when they came finally into the region of upper basins, and, turning to the eastward, threaded a dry arroyo which brought them out upon the level-bottomed valley known as the Mesquite Mesa. It was not a mesa in the proper meaning of the term; it was rather a vast flat wash brought down from the hills by the sluicing of many floods. Here and there its sun-baked surface was cut and gashed by dry gullies all pointing toward the river, and each bearing silent witness to the manner in which the mesa had been formed.

At a point well within this shut-in moraine, Sprague dismounted, tossed his bridle reins to Starbuck, and went to examine the soil in the various gullies. Each dry ditch afforded a perfect cross-section of the different strata, from the thin layer of sandy top-soil to the underlying beds of coarse sandstone pebbles and gravel. Sprague kicked the edges from a dozen of the little ditches, secured a few handfuls of the soil, and came back shaking his head.

"I don't wonder that these people don't want to advertise their land, Billy," he commented, climbing, with a nimbleness astonishing in so large a man, to the back of his mount. "As they say down in Tennessee, you couldn't raise a fuss on it. Let's amble along and see what they are doing at the head works."

At the head of the wash the valley of Mesquite Creek came in abruptly from the right. On a bench above the mouth of the valley they found the construction camp of the irrigation company, a scattered collection of shack sheds and tents, a corral for the working stock, and the usual filth and litter characterizing the temporary home of the "wop."

Across the valley mouth a huge earthwork was rising. It was the simplest form of construction known to the dam-building engineer: a mere heaping of earth and gravel moved by two-horse scrapers from the slopes of the contiguous hills on either hand. There was no masonry, no concrete, not even the thin core wall which modern engineering practice prescribes for the strengthening member in an earth embankment designed to retain any considerable body of water.

Moreover, there was no spillway. The creek, carrying at this season of the year its minimum flow, had been stopped off without an outlet; and the embankment upon which the force was heaping the scrapings from the hillsides was already retaining a good-sized lake formed by the checked waters of the stream.

Starbuck and Sprague had drawn rein at the outskirts of the construction camp, and they were not molested until Sprague took a flat black box from his pocket, opened it into a camera, and was preparing to take a snapshot of the dam. At that, a man who had been lounging in the door of the camp commissary, a dark-faced, black-bearded giant in brown duck and service leggings, crossed the camp street and threw up a hand in warning.

"Hey, there; hold on—that don't go!" he shouted gruffly, striding up to stand squarely in the way of the camera. "You can't take any pictures on this job."

"Sorry," said Sprague, giving the intruder his most amiable smile, "but you were just a half-second too late," and he closed the camera into its box-like shape and dropped it into his pocket.

The black-bearded man advanced threateningly.

"This is company property, and you are trespassers," he rasped. "Give me that camera!"

Starbuck's right hand went softly under his coat and stayed there, and his steady gray eyes took on the sleepy look that, in his range-riding days, had been a sufficient warning to those who knew him. Sprague lounged easily in his saddle and ignored the hand extended for the camera.

"You are Mr. Jennings, I take it," he said, as one who would temporize and gain time. "Fine dam you are building there."

"Give me that camera!"

Sprague met the angry eyes of the engineer and smiled back into them.

"I'll take it under consideration," he said, half-jocularly. "You'll give me a little time to think about it, won't you?"

Jennings's hand dropped to the butt of the heavy revolver sagging at his hip.

"Not a damned minute!" he barked. "Hand it over!"

Starbuck was closing up slowly on the opposite side of his companion's horse, a movement which he brought about by a steady knee pressure on the bronco's off shoulder. Jennings's fingers were closing around the grip of his pistol when the astounding thing happened. Without so much as a muscle-twitching of warning Sprague's left hand shot out, the fingers grappled an ample breast-hold on the engineer's coat and shirt-bosom, and Jennings was snapped from his feet and flung, back down, across the horn of Sprague's saddle much as if his big body had been a bag of meal. Starbuck reached over, jerked the engineer's weapon from its holster, broke it to eject the cartridges, and flung it away.

"Now you can get down," said Sprague quietly; and when he loosed the terrible clutch, Jennings slid from the saddle-horn and fell, cursing like a maniac.

"Stand still!" ordered Starbuck, when the engineer bounded to his feet and started to run toward the commissary, and the weapon that made the bidding mandatory materialized suddenly from an inner pocket of the ex-cowman's khaki riding-coat.

But the trouble, it seemed, was just fairly getting under way. Up from the embankment where the scrapers were dumping came two or three fore-men armed with pick-handles. The commissary was turning out its quota of rough-looking clerks and time-keepers, and a mob of the foreign labor-ers—the shift off duty—came pouring out of the bunk houses and shacks.

Sprague had unlimbered and focussed his camera again and was calmly taking snap-shot after snap-shot: of the dam, of the impounded lake, of the up-coming mob, and of the black-bearded man held hands-up in the middle of the camp street. When he shut the box on the last of the exposures he turned to Starbuck with a whimsical smile wrinkling at the corners of his eyes.

"They don't seem to be very enthusiastic about keeping us here, Billy," he said, with gentle irony. "Shall we go?"

Starbuck shook the reins over the neck of his mount and the two horses wheeled as one and sprang away down the rough cart-road leading to the end of the copper-mine spur above Angels. At the retreat, some one on the commissary porch began to pump a repeating rifle in the general direction of the pair, but no harm was done.

Starbuck was the first to break the galloping silence when an interven-ing hill shoulder had cut off the backward view of the camp at the dam, and what he said was purely complimentary.

"You sure have got your nerve with you, and the punch to back it up," he chuckled. "I reckon I'm goin' to wake up in the middle of the night laughin' at the way you snatched that rustler out of his tracks and slammed him across the saddle. I'd give a heap to be able to do a thing like that; I sure would."

"Call it a knack," rejoined Sprague modestly. "You pick up a good many of those little tricks when you're training on the squad. Perhaps you've never thought of it, but the human body is easier to handle, weight for weight, than any inanimate object could possibly be. That is one of the first things you learn in tackling on the foot-ball field."

They were jogging along slowly by this time and had passed the cop-per-mine switch on the road leading to the station at Angels. Starbuck was not over-curious, but the experiences of the forenoon were a little puzzling. Why had his companion wished to take the long, hard ride up the valley of the Timanyoni? And why, again, had he taken the chance of a fight for the sake of securing a few snap-shot pictures of the irrigation company's construction camp and dam? A third query hinged itself upon the decidedly inhospitable, not to say hostile, attitude of Jennings, the irrigation company's field-officer. Why should he object so strenuously to the common sight-seer's habit of kodaking anything and everything in sight?

Starbuck was turning these things over in his mind when they reached Angels. As they rode into town Sprague glanced at his watch.

"I have been wondering if we couldn't get this man Dickery at the town corral to take charge of these horses of ours until Wimberley can come and get them?" he said. "That would make it possible for us to catch the eleven-thirty train for Brewster."

Starbuck said it was quite feasible, and by the time they had disposed of the horses the train was whistling for the station. When they boarded the train, Sprague proposed that they postpone the mid-day meal in the diner in order to ride out on the rear platform of the observation-car.

"We'll get to town in time for a late luncheon at the hotel," was the way he put it; "and on as fine a day as this I like to ride out of doors and take in the scenery."

Starbuck acquiesced, and smiled as one well used to the scenery. Truly, the trip through the Timanyoni Canyon was one which usually brought the tourists crowding to the rear platform of the train, but until the morning of this purely sight-seeing jaunt he had been thinking that Maxwell's big friend was altogether superior to the scenic attractions.

Now, however, Sprague seemed greatly interested in the canyon passage. Again and again he called his companion's attention to the engineering difficulties which had been overcome in building the narrow pathway for the rails through the great gorge. Particularly, he dwelt upon the stupendous cost of making the pathway, and upon the temerarious courage of the engineers in adopting a grade so near, in dozens of places, to the level of the foaming torrent at the track-side.

"Yes," Starbuck agreed; "it sure did cost a heap of money. Dick says the thirty-six miles are bonded at one hundred thousand dollars a mile, and even that didn't cover the cost of construction on some of the miles."

"But why did they put the grade so close to the river level?" persisted the expert, when the foam from a mid-stream bowlder breathed a misty breath on them as the train slid past. "Isn't there constant trouble from high water?"

"No, the Timanyoni's a tolerably dependable creek," was Starbuck's answer. "Summer and winter it holds its own, with nothing like the variation you find in the Mississippi Valley rivers. An eight-foot rise is the biggest they've ever recorded at the High Line dam, so J. Montague Smith tells me."

"They are fixed to take care of that much of a rise at the High Line dam, are they?" queried Sprague.

"Oh, yes; I reckon they could take a bigger one than that, if they had to. That dam is built for keeps. Williams, who was the constructing engineer, says that the dam and plant will stand when the water of the river is pouring through the second-story windows of the power-house."

"And that, you would say, would never happen?" put in the expert thoughtfully, adding, "If it should happen, your brother-in-law would have to build him a new railroad through this canyon, wouldn't he?"

"He sure would. That eight-foot rise I spoke of gave them a heap of trouble up here—washouts to burn!"

"What caused that rise—rains?"

"Rains and cloud-bursts, in the season of the melting snows. It was just as Smith was turning heaven and earth upside down to get the dam completed, and for a little spell they sure was anticipatin' trouble a-plenty; thought they were going to be plumb paralyzed."

"I want to meet that man Smith," said the expert, going off at a tangent, as his habit was. "Stillings, your friend the lawyer who has his offices next door to my laboratory, says he's a wonder."

"Smith is all right," was Starbuck's verdict. "He's a first-class fighting man, and he doesn't care much who knows it. He got big rich out of that High Line fight, married old Colonel Baldwin's little peach of a daughter, and is layin' off to live happy ever afterward."

From that on, the rear platform talk had to do chiefly with Mr. J. Montague Smith and his plucky struggle with the hydro-electric trust which had tried, unsuccessfully as the event proved, to steal the High Line dam and water privilege. In due time the train shot out of the gorge, and after a dodging course among the Park hills, came to the skirting of the High Line reservoir lake lying like a silver mirror in its setting of forested buttes and spurs.

At the lower end of the lake, where the white concrete dam stretched its massive rampart across the river gorge, the train halted for a moment in obedience to an interposing block-signal. It was during the momentary stop that a handsome young fellow with the healthy tan of the hill country browning his frank, boyish face, came out of the near-by power-house, ran up the embankment and swung himself over the railing of the observation platform.

"Hello, John!" said Starbuck; and then he introduced the new-comer to his companion.

"Glad to know you, Mr. Sprague," said the young man, whose hearty hand-grip was an instant recommendation to the good graces of the big expert. "I've been hearing of you off and on all summer. It's a saying with us out here that any friend of Dick Maxwell's owns Brewster—or as much of it as he cares to make use of."

"I have certainly been finding it that way, Mr. Smith," Sprague rejoined, in grateful recognition of the Brewster hospitality. And then: "We were just talking about you and your dam as we came along, Starbuck and I. You have a pretty good head of water on, haven't you?"

"An unusually good head for this time of the year. The heavy storms we have been having in the eastern foot-hills account for it. Our power plant is working at normal load, and our ranchmen are all using water liberally in their late irrigating, and yet you see the quantity that is going over the splash-boards."

"Yes, I see," observed Sprague thoughtfully. And when the train began to move onward: "With this big reservoir behind you, I suppose a sudden flood couldn't hurt you, Mr. Smith?"

The young man with the healthy tan on his clean-cut face promptly showed his good business sense.

"We think we have a comfortably safe installation, but we are not specially anxious to try it out merely for the satisfaction of seeing how much it would stand," was the conservative reply.

Sprague looked up curiously from his solid planting in the biggest of the platform folding-chairs.

"And yet, three days ago, Mr. Smith, you said, in the presence of witnesses, that a ten-foot rise wouldn't endanger your dam or your power plant," he put in shrewdly.

Mr. J. Montague Smith, secretary and treasurer of the Timanyoni High Line Company, was plainly taken unawares.

"How the dev—" he began; and then he tried again. "Pardon me, Mr. Sprague; you hit me when I wasn't looking for it. I believe I did say something like that; in fact, I've said similar things a good many times."

"But not in exact feet and inches, I hope," said Sprague, with a show of mild concern. "These exactnesses are what murder us, Mr. Smith. Now, I presume if somebody should come to you today and threaten to turn another ten feet of river on you, you'd object, wouldn't you?"

"We certainly should—object most strenuously!"

"Yet, if that person were so minded, he might quote you as having said that ten additional feet wouldn't hurt you."

The young treasurer laughed a trifle uneasily.

"I can't believe that anybody would make a bit of well-meant boasting like that an excuse for—but it's altogether absurd, you know. Your case is unsupposable. Nobody pushes the button for the rains or the cloud-burst storms. When you introduce me to the fellow who really has the making of the weather in the Timanyoni head-waters, I'll be very careful what I say to him."

"Just so," said the expert quietly; and then a long-continued blast of the locomotive whistle announced the approach to Brewster.

Sprague took leave of his latest acquaintance at the station entrance, where a trim, high-powered motorcar, driven by an exceedingly pretty young woman in leather cap, gauntlets, and driving-coat, was waiting for Smith.

"I am a soil expert, as you may have heard, Mr. Smith," he said at parting, "and I am interested at the moment in alluvial washes—the detritus brought down from the high lands by the rivers. One of these days I may call upon you for a little information and help."

"Command me," said the young financier, with another of the hearty hand-grips; and then he climbed in beside the pretty young woman and was driven away.

Sprague was unusually silent during the tardy luncheon shared with Starbuck in the Topaz café; and Starbuck, who never had much to say unless he was pointedly invited, was correspondingly speechless. Afterward, with a word of caution to his table companion not to mention the morning's adventure to any one, Sprague went to his laboratory, to test the specimens of soil gathered on the Mesquite mesa, Starbuck supposed.

But the supposition was wrong. What Mr. Calvin Sprague busied himself with during the afternoon was the careful developing of the film taken from his pocket camera, and the printing of several sets of pictures therefrom. These prints he placed in his pocket note-book, and the book and its enclosures went with him when, after the evening meal, at which he had somehow missed both Maxwell and Starbuck, he climbed the three flights of stairs in the Tribune Building and presented himself at the door of Editor Kendall's den.

Kendall was glad to see him, or at least he said he was, and, waving him to a chair at the desk end, produced a box of rather dubious-looking, curiously twisted cigars, at which the visitor shook his head despondently.

"You'd say I was the picture of health, wouldn't you, Kendall, and you wouldn't believe me if I were to tell you that I am smoking a great deal too much?" he said, with a quizzical smile that was on the verge of turning into a grin.

The editor was not fooled; as a matter of fact, it was an exceedingly difficult matter to fool the tired-eyed tyrant of *The Tribune* editorial rooms.

"Cut it out," he said, with his mirthless laugh. "You wouldn't expect to find fifty-cent *Rienas* in a newspaper shop—any more than I'd expect you to climb up here with a news story for me. Smoke your own cigars, and be damned to you." And in sheer defiance he lighted one of his own dubious monstrosities, while Sprague was chuckling and passing his pocket-case of fat black *Maduros*.

"You say, any more than you'd expect a news story. Perhaps I have a news story for you. Cast your eye over these," and he threw out the bunch of lately made photographs.

The editor went over the collection carefully, and at the end of the inspection said, "Well, what's the answer?"

"The construction camp of the Mesquite Land and Irrigation Company at about half-past ten this forenoon. The held-up man is Mr. Engineer Jennings, posed by Billy Starbuck, who was kindly holding a gun on him for me. The people running are Jennings's workmen, coming to help him obliterate us. The water is the irrigation lake; the heap of dirt is the dam."

"Still, I don't quite grasp the news value," said Kendall doubtfully. "Why should Jennings wish to obliterate you?"

"Because I was taking pictures on his job. He was unreasonable enough to demand my camera, and to make the sham bad man's break of handling his gun without pulling it on me."

The editor studied the pictures long and thoughtfully.

"You've got something up your sleeve, Mr. Sprague; what is it?" he asked, after the considering pause.

Sprague drew his chair closer; and for five minutes the city editor, who had come in for a word with his superior, forbore to break in upon the low-toned earnest conference which was going on at the managing editor's desk. At the end of it, however, he heard Kendall say, "I'll get Monty Smith on the wire, and if he coincides with you, we'll take a hand in this. I more than half believe you're right, but you'll admit that it sounds rather incredible. *The Tribune's* motto is 'All the news that is news,' but we don't want to be classed among the 'yellows.'"

"You run no risk in the present instance," was Sprague's confident assurance. "Of course, there is no direct evidence; if there were, the case would be promptly taken to the courts. As a matter of fact, I'm hoping that Mr. Smith will take it to the courts as it stands. But in any event, an appeal to the public will do no harm."

"All right; we'll see what Smith says," said Kendall; and then the patient city editor had his inning.

Leaving the Tribune Building, the chemistry expert went to the nearest telephone and called for the house number of Mr. Robert Stillings, the attorney who served locally for the railroad company and was also counsel for the High Line people. Happily, it was the young lawyer himself who answered the 'phone.

"This is Sprague," said the downtown caller. "How busy are you this evening?"

The answer was apparently satisfactory, since the big man went on: "All right; I wish you would arrange to meet me in the lobby of the Topaz. Catch the next car if it won't hurry you too much. You'll do it? Thank you. Good-by."

Fifteen minutes later the Government man, writing a letter at one of the desks in the hotel lobby, looked up to greet his summoned visitor, a keen-eyed, self-contained young man whose reputation as a fearless fighter in just causes was already spreading from the little inter-mountain city of his adoption and becoming State-wide.

"I'm here," said Stillings briefly; and Sprague rose and drew him aside into one of the alcoves.

For some little time after they had drawn their chairs together, Sprague held the floor, talking earnestly and exhibiting a set of the snap-shot pictures. Stillings listened attentively, examining the pictures by the aid of a small pocket magnifier. But when Sprague finished he was shaking his head doubtfully, unconsciously following the example set by *The Tribune* editor.

"We have nothing definite to go on, Mr. Sprague, as you yourself admit. These people are well within their legal rights. As you probably know, there is no statutory provision in this State requiring the builders of a dam to conform to any particular plan of construction; and, as a matter of fact, there are dozens of dams just like this one—mere earth embankments without masonry of any kind."

"Do you mean to say that the safety of the entire Timanyoni Valley can be endangered by a structure like this, and that the property owners who are imperilled have no legal recourse?" demanded the expert.

"Recourse, yes; plenty of it after the fact. If the dam should give way and cause damage, the irrigation company would be liable."

"Humph!" snorted the big-bodied one, half-contemptuously. "Law is one of the few things that I have never dabbled in. What you say amounts to this: if I find a man training a cannon on my house, I have no right to stop him; I can only try to collect damages after the gun has gone off and ripped a hole through my property. I could make a better law than that myself!"

Stillings was staring thoughtfully through the opposite window at the lights in the railroad building across the plaza.

"There are times, Mr. Sprague, when we all feel that way; crises which seem to call for something in the way of extra-judicial proceedings," he admitted. And then: "Have you told Maxwell about this?"

"Not specifically. Dick has troubles of his own just now; he has had enough of them this summer to turn his hair gray, as you know. I have been hoping that this latest move of the enemy could be blocked without dragging him into it."

Stillings turned quickly. "That is the frankest thing you've said this evening. Is it another move of the enemy—the New Yorkers?"

Sprague spread his hands and his big shoulders went up in a shrug.

"You have just as much incriminating evidence as I have. How does it strike you?"

The attorney shook his head in doubtful incredulity, again unconsciously following Editor Kendall's lead.

"It doesn't seem possible!" he protested. "Think of the tremendous consequences involved—outside of the crippling of the railroad. The Short Line wouldn't be the only sufferer in case of a dam-break in the Mesquite. The entire valley would be flood-swept, and our High Line dam—" he stopped abruptly and half-rose to his feet. "Good Lord, Sprague! The breaking of the High Line dam would mean death and destruction without end!"

Sprague had found a cigar in an overlooked pocket and was calmly lighting it. Though he did not tell Stillings so, the argument had finally gotten around into the field toward which he had been pushing it from the first.

"Three days ago, your High Line treasurer, Mr. J. Montague Smith, declared in the presence of witnesses—it was right here in this hotel lobby, and I happened to overhear it—that a ten-foot rise in the river, which, as you know, would submerge and sweep away miles of the railroad track in the canyon, would by no means endanger his dam. There you are, Mr. Stillings. Now fish or cut bait."

"Great Scott! What could Smith have been thinking of!" ejaculated the lawyer.

"It was merely a bit of loyal brag, as he admitted to Starbuck and me on the train this afternoon; and it had been craftily provoked by one of the men who heard it. But he said it, and what is more, he said it to—Jennings!"

This time the attorney's start carried him out of his chair and stood him upon his feet.

"I shall have to see Smith at once," he said hurriedly. "Still, I can't believe that these New York stock pirates would authorize any such murderous thing as this!"

"Authorize murder or violence? Of course not; big business never does that. What it does is to put a man into the field, telling him in general terms the end that is to be accomplished. The head pushers would turn blue under their finger-nails if you'd charge them with murder."

"But that is what this would amount to—cold-blooded murder!"

"Hold on a minute," objected Sprague. "Let's apply a little scientific reasoning. Suppose this thing has been accurately figured out, engineering-wise. Suppose that, by careful computation, it has been found that a certain quantity of water, turned loose at the mouth of Mesquite Valley, would produce a flood of a certain height in the full length of Timanyoni Canyon—say ten or twelve feet—sufficient to obliterate thirty-five or forty miles of the railroad track. Below its path of the greatest destruction it comes out into your High Line reservoir lake, with some miles farther to go, and a greatly enlarged area over which to diffuse itself."

Stillings was nodding intelligence. "I am beginning to see," he said. "Ten feet in the canyon wouldn't necessarily mean ten feet at Smith's dam."

"No; but at the same time Smith is on record as having said that ten feet wouldn't endanger his dam or the power plant. So there you are again."

Stillings walked the length of the alcove twice with his head down and his hands in his pockets before he stopped in front of the expert to say: "You've half-convinced me, Mr. Sprague. If we could get the barest shred of evidence that these people are building a dam which isn't intended to hold—"

"There spoke the lawyer again," laughed Sprague. "If you had the evidence, what would you do?"

"Institute legal proceedings at once."

"And how long would it take you to get action?"

"Oh, that would depend upon the nature of the evidence I had to offer, of course."

Sprague laughed again, derisively this time.

"Yes, I thought so; and while you were getting out your writs and monkeying around—do you know what that piece of canyon track cost, Mr. Stillings? I was told today that three million dollars wouldn't replace it—to say nothing of what it would mean to the railroad company to have its through line put out of business indefinitely. No; if we mean to—"

The interruption was the intrusion into the alcove of a huge-framed, hard-faced man who was fumbling in his pocket for a paper.

"Hello, Harding," said Stillings; and then, jokingly: "What brings the respected sheriff of Timanyoni County charging in upon us at this time of night?"

"It's a warrant," said the sheriff, half in apology. And then to Sprague: "I hate like the mischief to trouble you, Mr. Sprague, but duty's duty."

Sprague smiled up at the big man. "Tell us about it, Mr. Harding. You needn't bother to read the warrant."

"It's that scrap you had with Jennings up at the Mesquite this morning. He's swore out a warrant against you for assault and battery."

"And are you going to lock me up over night? I fancy that is what he would like to have you do."

"Not me," said the sheriff good-naturedly. "I got Judge MacFarland out o' bed and made him come down to his office. I'm goin' to ask you to walk around there with me, just to let me out of it whole. I've fixed it with the judge so you won't have to give bail."

"I'll go with you," Stillings offered; and a few minutes later, in the magistrate's office, the Government man had bound himself on his own recognizance to appear in court the next morning to answer the charge against him.

On the sidewalk in front of the justice shop, Stillings reverted to the more pressing matter.

"I'm going to see Smith before I sleep, if I have to drive out to the Baldwin ranch to find him," he declared. "In the meantime, Mr. Sprague, if you can devise any scheme by which we can get a legal hold on these fellows—anything that will serve as an excuse for our asking that an injunction be issued—"

"That would come before Judge Watson, wouldn't it?" Sprague broke in.

"Yes."

"See Kendall, of *The Tribune*, about that. From what he told me a couple of hours ago, I should say that your petition for an injunction would be only a crude loss of time. We'll try to think of a better way, or at least a more effective way. Good-night; and don't omit to throw the gaff into Smith, good and hard."

On the morning following Sprague's visit to *The Tribune* editorial rooms, the newspaper-reading public of Brewster had a small sensation served, in Starbuck's phrase, "hot from the skillet." A good portion of the front page of *The Tribune* was given to a news story of the work which was under way in the Mesquite Valley, and pictures were printed of the camp, the dam, and the growing lake.

On the editorial page there was a caustic arraignment of the Mesquite Company, which was called upon to show cause why it should not be condemned as a public nuisance of a kind which had already brought much reproach upon the West as a field for legitimate investment, and the suggestion was made that a committee of responsible citizens be sent to investigate the Mesquite project, to the end that the charges made might be either substantiated or set aside.

Specifically, these charges were that there was no arable land within reach of the Mesquite dam, and that the dam itself was unsafe. Throughout his editorial Kendall had judiciously refrained from making any mention of a possible disaster to the railroad; but he hinted broadly at the danger to which the High Line dam—the source of the city's power and lights—would be subjected in the event of a flood catastrophe on the distant project.

Maxwell, who was living at the hotel in the absence of his family, had read the paper before he came down to join Sprague at the breakfast-table, and, like every other newspaper reader in Brewster that morning, he was full of the latest sensation.

"By George, Calvin," he began, "somebody has been stirring up the mud for those people we were talking about night before last. Have you seen *The Tribune*?"

Sprague nodded assent.

"What do you make of it?" asked the railroad man.

"I should say that somebody—possibly the High Line management—is beginning to sit up and take notice, wouldn't you?"

"Y-yes; but see here—any such thing as Kendall hints at would knock the Nevada Short Line out long before it would get to the High Line dam!"

"Naturally," said Sprague coolly.

"Great Jehu! Was that what you meant when you were making me dig this Mesquite project over for you the other day?"

"I didn't want to drag you into it, and don't yet," said Sprague quietly. "You've had grief enough for one summer. But the detective half of me tells me that there is little doubt that this thing is another attempt on the part of the big-money crowd to side-swipe your railroad off the map. It can be done, and you have no preventive recourse; Stillings says you haven't."

"But, Calvin—something's *got* to be done! Are we going to sit still and—"

"One kind of a something is doing itself, right now," interrupted Sprague. "It's your play, this time, to keep out of it, if you can. You'd say that the High Line people, J. Montague Smith and his crowd, inspired that blast in *The Tribune* this morning, wouldn't you?"

"It looks that way, yes."

"Well, let them stir up the mud and make the fight. You sit tight in the boat and say nothing. What kind of an agent or operator have you at Angels?"

"Disbrow?—he's a good man; so good that I'm going to promote him to a better station next week."

"Let that promotion wait a while. Give this good man instructions to watch every move that Jennings makes, and to report at once anything out of the ordinary that may happen. Do you get that?"

"I'll do it. Anything else?"

"No, not at present. Later on, say after the evening edition of *The Times-Record* comes out, I may want to get you on a quick wire. But the chief thing just now is to post the Angels man, and to have him keep in touch with you."

After Maxwell had gone the chemistry expert finished his breakfast with epicurean leisure, smoked a reflective cigar in comfortable solitude in the hotel lobby, and, when the court hour arrived, went around to the office of the justice of the peace to answer to the charge of assault. As was to be expected, Jennings was not present; was not even represented by an attorney. Sprague pleaded guilty and paid his nominal fine, which MacFarland took with a quiet smile.

"I don't know what you did to that black-faced bully, Mr. Sprague, but I hope you got your money's worth," he said. "Every time he turns up here in Brewster he proves himself an undesirable citizen, right from the word go."

"Tough, is he?" queried Sprague.

"As tough as they make them. I wonder he didn't try to get square with you with a gun. That would be more like him."

"Perhaps he will, later on," suggested the fined one, with a good-natured smile; after which he went across to his laboratory and was invisible for the remainder of the morning.

Just before noon Stillings dropped into the laboratory office. He found the chemist working among his retorts and test-tubes.

"I fell in to give you a pointer," was the attorney's excuse for the intrusion. "Jennings is in town. He came over on the ten-o'clock local and went straight to *The Times-Record* office."

Sprague grinned. "You were looking out for him, were you? Somebody got waked up at last?"

"Yes; the High Line people are on, all right," was the reply. "Smith called an emergency meeting of his directors early this morning. Two of them are Red Desert cattle barons, and they know the Mesquite situation like a book. What none of them can understand is the 'why'; why the Mesquite outfit should take ninety-nine chances in a hundred of sending a flood down the Timanyoni when there is no money to be made by it."

"What action did the directors' meeting take?"

"Instructed me to feel Judge Watson on the question of holding things up with an injunction. I did it, and it turned out as you intimated it would; nothing doing. Smith asked me to borrow Maxwell's special officer, Arch Tarbell, suggesting that we ought to keep in touch with Jennings. Archer was going over to Angels on the afternoon train, but Jennings has saved him the trouble by coming to town."

"Well, what next?" Sprague inquired.

"That is just what I'd like to ask you," was the lawyer's frank admission. "We're all looking to you to set the pace. You're the one man with the holy gift of initiative, Mr. Sprague. You haven't admitted it in so many words, but I know as well as I know anything that you are the man who started this newspaper talk."

"Pshaw!" said the expert, in genial raillery; "I'm only a Government chemist, Mr. Stillings."

"That's all right, too; but that isn't why the railroad men call you 'Scientific Sprague.' Four times this summer you've dug Maxwell and his railroad out of a hole when the rest of us didn't know there was any hole. What I'm most afraid of now is that Jennings will put up some sort of a scheme to get you out of the way. He knows well enough by this time that you are the key to his situation."

"I'm a tenderfoot," said the big man, with naïve irony. "What would you suggest?"

"That you go to Sheriff Harding and get him to swear you in as a special deputy. Then you can be prepared to defend yourself."

Sprague's mellow laugh rumbled deep in his big body.

"I guess I can take care of myself, if it comes to that, without 'packing hardware,' as Starbuck would put it," he averred. "There won't be more than three or four of them to tackle me at once, will there? But about your campaign—I have been hoping that the High Line people, backed by public sentiment, would be able to head this thing off. I am still hoping it. It will be altogether better if the railroad doesn't have to take a hand on its own account. The New Yorkers would be sure to make capital out of it, holding the Ford-Maxwell management up to public execration as a corporation which deliberately strangles development propositions in its own territory."

"That's a fact," the attorney agreed.

"Working along that line, we can afford to wait, for a little while at least, to see how the cat is going to jump. Jennings is over here to get into the newspaper fight himself. In Maxwell's demoralization tussle of two weeks ago, it was demonstrated that *The Times-Record* had been subsidized by the enemy. Now we shall see Higginson and his editor jump in and take up the clubs in defence of the Mesquite Company."

"I guess that is pretty good advice—to wait," said Stillings. "But we have an active crowd in the High Line, and its blood is up. Our people will want to be doing something while they wait."

"Let them talk," said Sprague quickly. "Tell them to resolve themselves into committees of one to throw the big scare into the Brewster public which depends upon the safety of the High Line dam for its own safety. Then pick out a few good, dependable men like Smith, his old fighting father-in-law the colonel, and Williams the engineer, who will hold themselves in readiness to start at a moment's notice, night or day, for the firing line—any firing line that may happen to show up."

"That is more like it," rejoined the attorney. "I'm sworn to uphold the majesty of the law, but—"

"But, as you remarked last night, there are extra-judicial crises now and then which have to be met in any old way that offers. Let it rest at that, and see me at the hotel this evening, if you can make it convenient."

With the appearance on the streets of the evening edition of *The Times-Record*, the Brewster public learned that there were two sides to the Mesquite question. In terms of unmeasured scorn Editor Healy attacked the narrow prejudice which would seek to place stumbling-blocks in the way of a great enterprise designed to benefit, not only the region locally concerned, but the entire West.

In the course of a long and vituperative editorial, the High Line company, the Brewster public-service corporations, and the railroad, each came in for its share of accusation, and their joint lack of public spirit was roundly condemned. It was pointed out that the High Line plant, by the admission of its own officials, would be in no danger even in the unsupposable case of the breaking of the Mesquite dam. Also, it was urged that the penny-wise policy of the railroad in adopting the low grade in Timanyoni Canyon was a matter of its own risk. Was the development of the nation to be halted, it was asked, because a niggardly railroad company was unwilling to spend a little money in raising its grade beyond a possible danger line?

But the sting of the editorial for Maxwell was in its tail. Healy concluded by darkly hinting that certain of the railroad officials were interested financially in sundry Timanyoni Park lands owned by the High Line Company, and that they were willing to kill the prospects of the new district for the sake of their own pockets.

Maxwell was furiously hot about this blast in the evening paper, as his demeanor at the dinner-table, where he spoke his mind freely to Sprague, sufficiently proved.

"Why, the miserable liars!" he raged. "There isn't an official on the Short Line from President Ford down who owns a single share of stock in the High Line! We all did help out at first, but Ford made every man of us turn loose the minute the dam was completed and the project was securely on its feet. He insisted that we couldn't afford to work for two dividend accounts!"

"He was quite right," said Sprague calmly. "But that is neither here nor there. It was Jennings's turn at bat and he took it. Let it go, and tell me what you hear from that good and reliable man, Disbrow, at Angels."

"I had him on the wire myself, just a few minutes ago," was the superintendent's answer. "He says something has stirred things up over on the Mesquite. They're working night shifts—began last night."

"Rain?" queried the expert.

"How the devil do you manage to jump at things that way?" demanded Maxwell, half-irritably. "Yes; there have been cloud-bursts in the eastern foot-hills. The river rose two feet today."

"Ah? That may bring on more talk—before the stenographers are ready to take it down. Any more items from Angels?"

"Nothing special. The Mesquite people got half a car-load of dynamite this morning. That shows you how careful Disbrow is; he is spotting every-thing—even the common routine things."

"Um; dynamite, eh? What use has Jennings for so much high explosive as that?"

"I don't know; uses it in excavating, I suppose. The more he uses, the bigger his rake-off from the powder company. Where there's a big graft, there are always a lot of little ones."

Sprague ate in silence for five full minutes before he said, quite with-out preliminary: "How long would it take a light special train to run from Brewster to Angels, with a clear track and regardless orders, Dick?"

"I made it once in my own car in two hours and fifty-five minutes, with two stops for water. Why?"

"Oh, I was just curious to know. Two fifty-five, eh? And how long would it take to get the special train ready?"

"Fifteen or twenty minutes, perhaps, on a rush order."

Sprague sat back and began to fold his napkin carefully in the original creases.

"As I have said before, I don't want to pose as an alarmist, Maxwell; but if I were you, I'd have that special train hooked up and ready to pull out—and I'd keep it that way, on tap, so to speak."

The railroad man rose to the occasion promptly.

"Beginning tonight?" he asked.

"Yes, beginning tonight."

"Has Jennings gone back?"

"He has. He went over on the evening train. Your man Tarbell kept cases on him while he was here. He spent most of the day with Higginson and Healy in *The Times-Record* office."

Maxwell refused his dessert and ordered a second cup of black coffee.

"This suspense is something fierce, Calvin," he said, when the waiter left them. "Have we got to sit still and do nothing?"

"That is your part in it," was the quiet reply. "If a party of prominent citizens should call upon you for a special train at some odd hour of the day or night, you want to be ready to supply it suddenly. Aside from that, you are to keep hands off."

For forty-eight hours beyond this evening dinner in the Topaz café—two days during which the railroad agent at Angels reported increased ac-tivities at the Mesquite dam—the newspaper wrangle over the merits and demerits of the irrigation project in the edge of the Red Desert went on with growing acrimony on both sides. But by the end of the second day it was apparent that *The Tribune* had public sentiment with it almost unanimously.

It was also on this second day that further bitterness was engendered by a street report that Judge Watson had enjoined the High Line Company from interfering in any way with the operations on the Mesquite. This was the last straw, and public indignation found expression that night in a monster mass meeting of protest, in which the speakers, with J. Montague Smith to set them the example, criticised the court sharply in free Western phrase.

After the meeting, adopting all sorts of resolutions condemnatory of everything in sight, adjourned—which was between nine and ten o'clock— there was a street rumor to the effect that Judge Watson would declare some of the speakers in contempt, and cinch them accordingly.

Maxwell and Starbuck brought this report to Sprague, who was smoking one of his big, black cigars on the porch of the hotel.

"Going to institute contempt proceedings, is he?" said the expert, with interest apparently only half-aroused.

"Wouldn't that jar you?" commented Starbuck. "I was telling Dick just now that Judge Watson has about outlived his usefulness in this little old shack town. This injunction of his is about the rawest thing that ever came over the range."

"Smith is red-hot," Maxwell put in; "hot enough to get out and scrap somebody. And his directors are all with him."

Still the big-bodied expert seemed only mildly interested.

"If anybody should happen to get mixed up legally with the Mesquite folks on this job of theirs, it would be pretty hard to get a jury in Brewster which would lean the way the judge does, wouldn't it?" he asked.

Maxwell's verdict was unqualified. "It would be practically impossible." He had found his pipe and was filling it when Sprague pointed to the spur track at the end of the railroad building opposite.

"Is that your special train over there, Dick?"

"Yes. You see I've obeyed orders. That train has been standing there for two days, with three shifts of men dividing up the watch in the engine cab."

"And the committee of prominent citizens hasn't yet materialized, eh? Never mind; you've done your part. What is the latest from Angels?"

"More cloud-bursts in the hills, and more activity up on the Mesquite. Disbrow says that Jennings has been offering all sorts of big pay to the scattered ranchmen to get them to come on the job with scraper-teams."

"That's bad," said the chemistry man briefly; adding, "I don't like that."

Starbuck got up to stand with his back to a porch pillar. From the new position he could look through the windows into the thronged hotel lobby.

"This town's stirred up some hotter than I've ever seen it before," he drawled. "Look at that mob inside—and every blame' man of it chewing the rag over this water proposition."

"I don't like that," Sprague repeated, thus proving that he had entirely missed Starbuck's comment on the excitement. Then he sat up suddenly. "There's a boy just coming down from your offices, Maxwell; it's the night watchman's boy, isn't it? Run across and head him, Starbuck; I believe that's a telegram he has in his hand."

Starbuck swung himself over the railing and caught the lad before he could disappear in the street throngs.

"You were plumb right," he said, when he came back to take his place on the porch. "He did have a message; it's for Dick. Here you are."

Maxwell tore the envelope across and held the telegram up to the ceiling light.

"Here's news," he announced. "It's from our man at Angels. He says: 'Jennings's force disbanded, and most of it gone east on Limited. Been shipping teams and outfit all afternoon. Too busy to wire sooner.'" The superintendent crumpled the telegram and smote fist into palm. "Bully for you, Sprague!" he exulted. "You pushed the right button just right! Jennings couldn't stand the pressure; he's given up the job and quit!"

There was no answering enthusiasm on the part of the big man who rose suddenly out of his chair and reached for the telegram. Quite the contrary, the hand which took the crumpled bit of paper was trembling a little.

"Dick," he began, in his deepest chest tone, "you hike over to the despatcher's office on the dead run and have Connolly clear for that special train. Don't lose a minute! Starbuck, it's up to you to find Smith, Tarbell, Williams, Colonel Baldwin, and two or three more good men whom you can trust—trust absolutely, mind you. Herd your crowd at the station in the quickest possible time; and you, Maxwell, make it your first business to tell the agent at Angels that there is a special train coming over the road. Don't tell him its destination; just say it will leave Brewster, going east, in a few minutes. Don't slip up on that—it may mean a dozen human lives! Get busy, both of you!"

After he was left alone, Sprague shouldered a path through the crowd in the lobby and had himself lifted to his rooms. When he came down a few minutes later he had changed his business clothes for the field rig which he wore on his soil-collecting expeditions. He had scarcely worked his way through the throng to the comparative freedom of the porch when Maxwell came hurrying across from the railroad building.

"Bad luck," said the superintendent, with brittle emphasis. "There's a freight-train off the steel half-way between Corona and Timanyoni, this side of the canyon, and the track is blocked."

"And we can't get by? There is nothing on the other side of the wreck that you could order down to meet us at the block?"

"Nothing nearer than Angels. There is an eastbound freight held there, loading the last of Jennings's outfit. To order the engine back from that would add at least an hour and a half to the two-hour-and-fifty-minute running schedule I gave you the other day."

Sprague swore out of a full heart, which, since he was the least profane of men, was an accurate measure of his growing disquietude.

"That's on me!" he grated. "I had it all figured out to the tenth decimal place, *and I didn't put in the factor of chance*! Dick, I want the biggest automobile in this town, and the one man among all your thousands who is least afraid to drive it."

Maxwell was able to answer without hesitation. "The car will be Colonel Baldwin's big 'six,' with Starbuck for your reckless chauffeur. But I doubt if you can get over the range in anything that goes on wheels." Then he added: "What is it, Calvin? What have you figured out?"

Sprague ignored the anxious query and spoke only to the fact.

"Can't get over the range? I tell you, we've got to get over the range! Good Lord! Why in Heaven's name doesn't Starbuck hurry?"

Starbuck had hurried. He had looked to find most, if not all, of the men he had been told to summon, closeted in conference with Stillings, and his guess had gone true to the mark. Only Tarbell was missing, and him they picked up in front of *The Tribune* office as they were hurrying to the rendezvous in the colonel's big touring-car.

Maxwell saw the car as it came under the corner electrics. "There's a little luck, anyway!" he exclaimed. "That is the Colonel's car, now, and Billy is driving it."

"Tools and arms; half a dozen picks and shovels, and anything you can find that will shoot," commanded Sprague, vaulting the porch railing to the sidewalk as easily as Starbuck had vaulted it a little while before. "See to that part of the outfit yourself, Dick, while I'm looking after the human end of it."

One minute afterward the big man was standing beside the touring-car which had been drawn up at the town-side platform of the railroad building. Sprague shot the emergency at the five men in the car in bullet-like sentences.

"Gentlemen, we've got to get over to the Mesquite as quick as the Lord'll let us. The railroad is blocked, and it's an auto or nothing. Maxwell says we can't do it. I say we've got to do it. What do you say?"

"I reckon we can do it," drawled Starbuck, speaking for all. Then he turned to Smith, who was in the tonneau. "How about the tanks, Monty?"

"I filled them tonight, before we left the ranch," said the High Line treasurer. "Also, there is an extra gallon of oil aboard—we always carry it."

"How about it, colonel?" Sprague demanded of the erect, white-mustached old man in the back seat.

"Sure!" was the quick reply. "You haven't told us yet whether it's a fight or a frolic, but we're all with you, either way, Mr. Sprague. Hop in, and we'll be jogging along."

It was at this moment that Maxwell, followed by a couple of yard men, came up. The men were carrying the picks and shovels, which were hastily stowed in the car, and the superintendent handed over a small arsenal of weapons, three of them being sawed-off Winchesters.

"I had to raid the express office," he explained, "and I took what I could find." Then to Sprague, who had mounted to the seat beside Starbuck. "Don't you want me along?"

"No; you can do a great deal more good right here. Listen, now, and follow my directions to the letter. Go upstairs to the wire and get in touch with your man at Angels. It will be your job to keep him in doubt as to what is on the road *between his station and the lower end of the canyon*. Lie to him if you have to; tell him a part of the wrecked freight is on its way up the canyon, or something of that sort, and keep him believing it as long as you possibly can. Don't fall down on it! Everything depends now upon the length of time you can keep some such story as that going over the wires."

Starbuck had adjusted a pair of goggles to his eyes, and had his foot on the clutch-pedal. "All set?" he asked.

"Go!" said Sprague; and at the word the big car shot away from the platform, rounded the end of the plaza, and bore away through a cross street to the eastward, gathering headway until, when the city limits were passed, its cutout exhausts were blending in a deafening roar.

Sprague was the only member of the party who had not at some time in the past had experience with Starbuck's driving. But before the first ten-mile lap on the mesa road had been covered he, too, had had his initiation. There was a little lamp on the dash which poured its tiny ray on the dial of the speedometer. Sprague saw the index pointer go up to thirty-five, jump to forty, crawl steadily onward until it had passed the forty-five and was mounting to the fifty. After that he saw no more, for the simple reason that he was obliged to close his unprotected eyes against the hurricane speed blast. The big man from Washington had asked for the fastest car in Brewster and for a man who was not afraid to drive it. He had got both.

At the same time, alarming as the pace might seem, Starbuck was not taking any needless chances. He knew his road, and knew also that there were many miles of it among the mountains that would have to be taken at slower speed. None the less, when the long mesa stretch was covered, and the big car was making zigzags up the precipitous slopes of Mount Cornell to reach the gap called Navajo Notch, the pace was still terrific, and the sober-faced driver was leaning over his wheel and pushing the motor like a true speed-maniac.

There was an hour of this risky zigzagging, and then the pass, lying cold and grim in the half moon-light at altitude ten thousand feet, was reached and threaded. Following the summit-gaining came the down-mountain rush on the eastern slope, and again Sprague closed his eyes, confessing inwardly that the steadiest nerve may have its limitations. With precipices shooting skyward on the right, and plunging sheer to unknown depths on the left, and with a man at the wheel who had apparently hypnotized himself until he had become a mere machine driving a machine—

When Sprague opened his eyes the great car was once more on an even keel and its wheels were spurning the hard red sand of the desert. In the far distance ahead a light was twinkling, the lamp in the station office at Angels. Sprague spoke to the iron-nerved driver at his side.

"Hold on, Billy; can you make the remainder of the run without the lamps?"

Starbuck brought the big machine to a stand, and leaned over and extinguished the lights. A little later, under Sprague's directions, he was making a silent circuit of the town, with the muffler in and the engine speeded at its quietest.

Since it was far past midnight, the better part of Angels was abed and asleep, with lights showing only at the railroad station and in Pete Grim's dance-hall, where, arguing from the row of hitched horses, a round-up of Red Desert cowboys made merry. Sprague stopped the car by a sign to Starbuck and turned to Tarbell.

"Get out, Archer, and make a quick run over to the station. I want to know what's going on in Disbrow's office."

Tarbell made the reconnaissance and was back in a few minutes.

"Disbrow is at his wire, with a man walkin' the floor behind him; and there's a piebald bronc' hitched out beyond the freight shed," was the brief report.

"Who is the floor-walker?" asked Sprague.

"I couldn't get a fair squint at him, but he looked mightily like the fellow I been keepin' cases on for the last two or three days."

"Gentlemen, we're in luck, for once," Sprague said impressively. "That's Jennings, without doubt; and he is waiting for a wire—the right kind of a wire—to come from Brewster. You remember what I told Maxwell, as we were leaving? That was one time when a guess was as good as a prophecy. Go on, Billy, and head straight for the Mesquite. And you gentlemen back there, get your weapons ready. If there happens to be a guard at the dam, we'll have to rush it."

Singularly enough, when the short run was accomplished they found that there was no guard. The shack camp was deserted, with all the disorder of a hasty evacuation strewn broadcast. But in the valley itself there was a startling change. The lake, which, three days earlier, had reached only half-way up the earth embankment, was now lapping within a foot of the dam top, the result of the continued storms and cloud-bursts reported by the Brewster weather station.

Starbuck eased the big car up to the dam head, and Williams and Tarbell made a quick quartering of the deserted camp. "Nobody here," the engineer reported, when they came back to the car; and then Sprague asked Starbuck to relight the head-lamps.

With the acetylenes flinging their broad white beam across the earthwork, another change was made apparent. In the centre of the dam a square pit, plank-lined like the shaft of a mine, had been either sunk or left in the building. Over this pit stood a three-legged hoist, with the block-and-tackle still hanging from its apex.

"What is that thing out there?" queried the colonel, shading his eyes with his hand.

"Jennings would probably tell you that it is a new kind of spillway, by which, in case of need, the reservoir lake can be emptied," suggested Sprague. "But we haven't time to investigate it just now. Our job at the present moment is to take the law into our hands and empty this lake, and to do it, if we can, without bringing on the catastrophe it was designed to accomplish."

"Heavens!" ejaculated Colonel Baldwin. "That's a criminal offence, isn't it?—and in the face of Judge Watson's injunction, at that!"

"It is criminal," was the calm reply; "unless we shall find sufficient justification for it as we go along. There is one chance in a dozen that we may find it first. Tarbell, take this little flash-light of mine and skip out there and look into that pit."

Tarbell paused scarcely a moment at the mouth of the mid-dam shaft. "It's filled up to within a few feet of the top with dirt," he said, when he returned.

"That is what I expected. We might find another warrant for what we are about to do, but we haven't time to search for it. Jennings may come back at any minute, and if he suspects anything wrong, he'll bring that bunch of dance-hall cowmen with him. If you'd like to hide the car and stand aside to see what he will do when he comes—"

"By Jove! I'm with you, injunction or no injunction!" cried Smith, and he began to take the picks and shovels out of the car.

"Go to it," said the colonel; and Sprague turned to Williams.

"Mr. Williams, you're an engineer. Our problem is to drain this lake in the shortest possible time in which it can be done without raising a dangerous flood-level in the Timanyoni River. We're under your orders."

Williams took the job as a dog snaps at a fly, barking out his directions with the curt precision of a man who knew his business. Planks were brought from the dismantled shacks to be thrust down on the inward face of the dam as a protection, and these were weighted in place with a make shift buttressing built out of the bags of sand which had been used as temporary coffer-dams in the construction work. When all was ready, a small ditch was opened across the protected end of the dam and the water began to pour through.

Immediately the wisdom of Williams's precaution became evident. Instantly the rushing stream began to eat into the loosely built dam, threatening to turn the ditch into a gully and the gully into a chasm, and quick work was necessary with more planks and sand-bags to check the rapid widening of the spillway. Even at that, the ditch grew swiftly deeper and more cavernous as the torrent emptied itself through it, and the roar of the artificial cataract filled the air with a note of sustained thunder.

"Jennings'll be deaf if he doesn't hear this plumb down at the railroad!" shouted Tarbell. But there was no time to consider the consequences Jennings-wise. Every man of the six, including the colonel, was constrained to work like mad to prevent the catastrophe they were trying to avert.

It was when the flood was pouring through the gap in a solid six-foot stream that shot itself far out to fall in a thunderous deluge upon the barren Mesquite mesa, and the planking and sand-bagging was sufficing to hold it measurably within bounds, that Sprague took steps looking toward a defensive battle should the need arise. Under his direction the auto was drawn out to one side and the lamps were extinguished. Then a hasty breastwork was made of the remaining bags of sand, and Tarbell and Starbuck were sent out as skirmishers to keep watch on the Angels road while the others renewed their efforts to hold the pouring torrent within safe limits.

A toiling half-hour, during which the spillway flood had slowly grown in volume until it threatened to become a destroying crevasse, slipped away, and at the end of it the two scouts came hurrying in.

"They're coming!" yelled Starbuck; and once again the big man from the East took the command.

"Down behind the sand-bags!" he shouted. "If Jennings gets near enough to strike a match on this hill-side, we'll all go to glory!"

Sprague had predicted that if Jennings suspected trouble he would not return to the dam alone. The prediction was verified when a squad of mounted men came in view at the turn in the road leading around the hill shoulder. The moon, declining to its setting behind the Timanyonis, flung ghostly shadows across the valley, and the watchers behind the sand-bag breastwork saw only the dark blot of blacker shadow sweeping up the road.

"Give 'em a volley over their heads!" Sprague ordered, and the three sawed-off Winchesters barked spitefully.

"That means war," said the colonel, when the charging cavalcade stopped abruptly and a dropping fusillade of revolver-shots spatted into the sand breastwork and whined overhead. "We're strictly in for it, now."

"If those fool cowpunch's only knew what they're fightin' for, they'd turn their artillery the other way," growled Starbuck. "I reckon they're the 'Lazy X' outfit, and Cummings, their owner, is one of the High Line directors."

"It's a pity we can't get word to them some way," said Smith. "We're not out to kill anybody if we can help it."

"No, but they're out to kill us," grunted Williams, as a second shower of bullets thudded into the breastwork and tore up the gravel on either hand. Then: "What are they doing now?"

The defenders of the breastwork were not left long in doubt as to what was doing. The horsemen in front were deploying in a thin line which rapidly bent itself into a semi-circle across the hill slope. To let any one of these skilled marksmen gain the rear meant death for somebody, and again Sprague gave the word of command.

"Better kill horses than men," he said. "We've got to stop that manœuvre," and again the Winchesters spoke, this time to deadlier purpose. At the third volley two of the horses were down, and the scattering line was drawing together again and galloping out of range.

In the lull which succeeded, Williams dropped his weapon and crawled quickly away to the edge of the spillway torrent. When he came back there was a new note of alarm in his voice.

"That spillway of ours is eating away the dam at the rate of a foot a minute!" he announced. "If we can't get to work on it again, the whole business will go out with a rush!"

It was a cruel dilemma, and it was quickly made worse by a new movement on the part of the attackers. Jennings's party was closing in again, and flashes of red fire were appearing here and there on the hill-side to herald a dropping hail of pistol bullets. Under cover of the irregular firing, a man was worming his way down toward the edge of the ravine through which the wasting torrent was rushing out upon the mesa. It was Sprague who first saw the crawling man and divined his purpose.

"That's Jennings!" he exclaimed, "and if he reaches the edge of that gully, we're all dead men! Stop him, Starbuck! Don't kill him if you can help it, but stop him!"

Starbuck levelled his short rifle over the top of the breastwork and took careful aim. The light was bad and he could scarcely see the sights. At the trigger-pulling, those who were watching saw a little cloud of dust and gravel spring up directly in front of the crawling man; saw this, and heard above the roaring of the torrent his yell of pain as he doubled up and clapped his hands to his face.

"Good shot, Billy!" gritted the white-haired colonel. "You've blinded him! Now if we could only choke those crazy range-riders off.... Tarbell, can't you—where's Tarbell gone?"

Tarbell's place at the end of the breastwork was empty, and Smith, who was next in the line, accounted for him.

"Archer dropped out a minute or two ago. I think he's trying to make a dodge-around to get at those cow-punchers."

The firing had ceased for the moment, and the man who had tried to creep down to the ravine was stumbling back up the hill. Williams nervously thrust in his plea again.

"I tell you, we've got to get to work on this thing behind us and do it quick!" he urged. "There is still water enough in the lake to tear the heart out of Timanyoni Canyon if it all goes at once!"

Sprague set the temerarious example by springing to his feet, and the others followed him. There was no answering volley from the hill-side. On the contrary, the black blot of things animate on the slope was melting away, and a minute later Tarbell came running back.

"The boys have got their hunch!" he cried. "A couple of them are taking Jennings back to Angels, and the rest of 'em'll be here in a minute to help us. They didn't know what was up."

As one man the half-dozen flung themselves upon the task of keeping the roaring crevasse under control; and a little later eight of the cowmen came racing down to swell the working force. But even for the augmented numbers, it proved to be a fiercely fought battle, with the issue hanging perilously in the balance for a long time.

Hour by hour they toiled, making plank bulk-heads out of the shack lumber, piling sand-bags against the crumbling embankment, and fighting inch by inch with the gnawing flood as the night wore away.

And it was thus that the graying dawn found them; soaked, muddied, gasping, and haggard with fatigue, but with the victory fairly won. The flood was still pouring through the gap which had by now widened to the cutting away of a full half of the dam; but the great body of water had already passed out and there was no longer any danger.

When the sun was just beginning to redden on the higher peaks of the western mountains, a shout from the hill-side road broke upon the morning stillness. A moment later Maxwell and Stillings came running to the brink of hazard.

Sprague stumbled up out of the crevasse chasm and pointed down to the washed-out heart of the dam. There, piled in the bottom of what had once been the plank-lined pit with the hoisting-tackle over it, and laid bare now by the scouring flood, was a great pile of dynamite stacked solidly in its shipping-boxes. And, half-buried in the sand and detritus of the outflow, lay the iron pipe through which the firing fuse had been carried to the gully edge Jennings had tried to reach.

"There is the warrant for what we've been doing, gentlemen," said the big expert wearily. "Take a good look at it, all of you, so that if the courts have anything to say about this night's work—"

Maxwell cut in quickly.

"There's nobody left to make the fight. Jennings went east from Angels on the first train that got through. He was badly blinded, so Disbrow says; got a fall from his horse, was the story he told. We'll fix this lay-out so it will stand just as it is until everybody who wants to has seen it!"

"You couldn't stay away, could you?" said the white-haired colonel, grinning up from his seat on the last of the sand-bags. "I told the boys here you'd be turning up as soon as your railroad track was open."

"We've had a mighty anxious night," Stillings put in. "The river is up five feet, and we couldn't tell what was happening over here. Great Jonah! But you men must have had your hands full!"

"We did," said Smith; "but it's all over now."

"All but the shouting," said Maxwell. "But post your guards and let's get back to town. My car is at Angels, and we came up special. When we left Brewster the plaza was black with people waiting for news."

It was on the way down the flood-swollen canyon that the chemistry expert explained to the private-car company at the breakfast-table how he had been able to diagnose the case of the cloud-bursters.

"It was merely a bit of what you might call constructive reasoning," he said modestly. "I knew by personal investigation in the line of my proper work—soil-testing—that there was no arable land within reach of the Mesquite project. The other steps followed, as a matter of course. Starbuck, here, is wondering why I risked his life and mine to get a few photographs for *The Tribune*, but if any of you will examine the snap-shots carefully under a magnifier, you will see that they prove the existence of the central pit in the dam, and that one of them shows the pipe-line through which the fuse was to run. For the possible legal purpose I was anxious to have this evidence in indisputable form. That's all, I believe."

"Not quite all," Maxwell broke in. "How did you know that Jennings would be hanging over the wire at Angels while you people were making your flying trip across the mountain in the auto?"

Sprague laughed good-naturedly.

"Call it a guess," he said. "It was evident that Jennings wasn't anxious to kill a lot of innocent people. His inquiries about the strength of the High Line dam proved that. It ran in my mind that he wouldn't touch off his earthquake until he could be reasonably sure that the flood wouldn't catch a train in transit in the canyon. That would have been a little too horrible, even for him. Now you've got it all, I guess."

"But you haven't got yours yet," laughed Stillings. "When this thing gets out in Brewster the whole town will mob you and want to make you the next mayor, or send you to Congress, or something of that sort."

"Not this year," said the big man, with another mellow laugh. "And I'll tell you why. Just before this train reaches town it's going to stop and let us law-breakers get off, scatter and drop into town as best we can without calling attention to ourselves. And tomorrow morning you'll read in *The Tribune* how the Mesquite dam, weakened by the recent storms and cloud-bursts, went out by littles during the night, watched over and kept from going as a disastrous whole by a brave little bunch of"—he looked around the table and winked solemnly—"by a brave little bunch of cowboys from the 'Lazy X.'" Then, with sudden soberness: "Promise me that you won't give it away, gentlemen all. It's the only fee I shall exact for my small part in the affair."

And the promise was given while the locomotive whistle was sounding for the Brewster yard-limits, and Maxwell was pulling the air-cord for the out-of-town stop.

CHAPTER 6

THE HIGH KIBOSH

Since it is a Western boast that the West does nothing by halves, the Brewster Town and Country Club owns two houses; a handsome pink-lava home on one of the quieter business streets of the city, and a rambling, overgrown bungalow at the golf-links on the north shore of the High Line reservoir lake, rechristened, in honor of Colonel Baldwin's pretty daughter, "Lake Corona."

On Saturday afternoons, which are bank holidays in the progressive little inter-mountain city, the links at Lake Corona are well patronized; and on a certain Saturday in early September, in the year written down in the annals of the inter-mountain region as "the year of the great railroad war," one of the players was the big-muscled athlete who figured for the Brewsterites as an expert soil-tester in the Government service, and whose nickname in the Timanyoni country was "Scientific Sprague."

Sprague's opponent on the links on this particular Saturday afternoon was Stillings, the railroad lawyer; and at the conclusion of the game, which had been a rather easy walk-over for the big athlete, Stillings offered the winner a seat in his runabout for the return to Brewster.

"Sorry, but I can't go with you this time, Robert," said the heavy-weight, when he had tipped his caddie and struggled into his coat. "Maxwell is coming out to dinner and I promised to wait for him. He thinks he is up for another match game with the big-leaguers."

Stillings paused with his hand on the dash of the runabout. "That so?" he queried. "More piracy?"

"Nothing actually in sight, as yet. But Dick has been getting fresh tips from the New York head-quarters. The big-money people who want your railroad have been keeping pretty quiet since the Mesquite fizzle; possibly they were afraid you folks might have the evidence on them. But now the air seems to be full of lightning again, and nobody, not even President Ford himself, appears to know just where it is going to strike."

The lawyer reached over and retarded the spark on the racing engines of the little car.

"It's a queer fight," he commented. "I never heard of anything just like it before. Of course, we all know what it means: the Transcontinental needs our five-hundred-odd miles of Nevada Short Line to put in with its Jack's Canyon branch for a short cut to the southern coast. Ordinarily, those things are fought out on the floor of the Stock Exchange, and the people who are operating the railroad never know what hits them until they're safely dead. If the big fellows want the Short Line so bad, why the dickens don't they go in and buy it up decently?"

The large man who had played such a successful game of golf winked one eye solemnly.

"You wouldn't expect a Government chemist to find you the answer to any such conundrum as that, would you?" he asked, in cheerful irony.

"I'll bet you know, just the same," asserted Stillings confidently.

"I do happen to know, Robert," was the even-toned reply. "A financial transaction entered into in the early summer by the Ford management—a transaction having nothing whatever to do with the fight—makes a break in prices absolutely necessary before the control can be acquired. What the Ford people did was to build a solid wall of protection around themselves without knowing it or intending to. They deposited something like sixty percent of the Short Line stock with a syndicate of New York and Boston banks as collateral for a loan to be used in double-tracking."

"Still, I don't see," objected the lawyer.

"Don't you? That sixty percent of the stock—which is the control—can't be touched by any fireworks business on the Exchange. The big-money people have played the market up and down with the forty percent which is not pooled, and nothing has happened. The loaning banks have merely sat tight in the boat, knowing that they held the joint control of a good paying property, and that no amount of sky-rocketing on the Street could make any difference, any real difference, in the value of their collateral so long as the property itself was earning dividends."

"That is good as far as it goes," said Stillings, with a frown of perplexity. "But it doesn't explain why the big-money crowd, or somebody, has been turning heaven and earth upside down all summer to wreck, not the stock, but the property itself. You know that is what has been done. No stone has been left unturned, from demoralizing Maxwell's force to dynamiting tunnels and planning forty-mile washouts. If big business wants the road, why is it trying to wreck it physically?"

The big man who was fond of insisting that he was first, last, and all the time a Government chemist grinned amiably.

"It doesn't agree with your mentality to get beaten at golf, does it, Robert?" he said jokingly. "It is plain enough, when you get hold of the right end of it. Big money's play is to throw a real scare, not into the stockholders, but into these loaning bankers, don't you see? If the road's earnings fall off and it has bad luck enough to make these creditor-bankers really nervous about the value of their collateral, the trick will be turned. The Ford people will immediately be asked to make good or pay up; and there you are."

"Why, sure!" said the attorney, in a tone which sufficiently emphasized his complete understanding. Then he climbed slowly into the driving-seat of the runabout. "I don't see why some of the rest of us haven't caught on long ago," he went on. "I suppose any of us might have had the simple facts if we had taken the trouble to dig for them." Then, abruptly: "You're look-ing for more trouble, Sprague?"

"Maxwell is; and so is Ford, apparently," was the evasive reply.

"Never mind Maxwell or Ford; you're the man," snapped the lawyer.

"No, I'm not," was the decisive denial. "It's true, I have been willing to help out and take a hand in standing off a few of the attempted smash-ings; but that was only because Dick Maxwell is my friend, and it suited my humor to ride my little reasoning hobby in his behalf. I'm not a sleuth, Stillings; I'm a Government chemist, and I am out here for the ostensible purpose of making a technical report on the soils of this charming valley of yours. You forget that every now and then."

"Pardon me, old man; I did forget it," was the hearty apology. "Just the same, you mustn't throw us down while the fight is still on. Maxwell put it about right the other day when he said that the Nevada Short Line would have been dead and buried two months ago if it hadn't been for you."

"Nevertheless, I can't help out this time, Stillings. That is why I am staying here this evening—to meet Maxwell and tell him that he'll have to fight for his own hand if the New Yorkers come after him again."

"Good goodness, Sprague! What's happened?"

"A thing which nobody could have foreseen, and for which nobody is to blame. At the same time, it lets me out. I've got to quit you."

The attorney adjusted the spark and throttle and cut the wheels of the little car preparatory to the start.

"I can't very well argue with you—not having any grounds," he said. "But I hope you won't decide finally until after you've had another talk with Maxwell. Think it over between now and dinner-time, and weigh the consequences to Dick, Sprague. If there's another earthquake on the way, and you throw him down, he's a ruined man. I know what you will say: that he is well fixed and doesn't have to be a railroad superintendent. That's all right, but his job means more to him than it might to a poor man; it's his ambition. If there is anything I can do—"

The big chemistry expert shook his head. "There isn't anything that anybody can do, Robert," he said soberly; and at that, Stillings eased the clutch in and drove away.

Two hours later Maxwell was sitting out the after-dinner interval with his friend and classmate on the broad lake-fronting veranda of the bungalow club-house. It was a fine night, and the Saturday evening crowd was larger than usual. There was a dotting of canoes on the reservoir lake, and the verandas were filling slowly as the great dining-room emptied itself. For a time the two men had let the talk drift into college reminiscences; but it took a more strictly personal turn when the superintendent said:

"Do you know, Calvin, I've often wondered how you came to be assigned to this job of soil-testing—this particular job, I mean—for the Department. It has been a sort of special providence to me; but things don't often happen that way, unhelped."

"This thing didn't happen that way—unhelped," was the big expert's quiet rejoinder. "I asked for the job."

"I've wondered if you didn't. It was mighty good of you to maroon yourself out here in the tall hills for the sake of helping me fight the money pirates, Calvin."

Sprague was silent for a full minute before he said: "I wish I could claim a motive as disinterested as that, Dick; but if I should, it wouldn't be honest. I had quite another reason for wishing to return to the Timanyoni after my flying trip through it last July on my way back from California. I can't tell you what it was; it's too idiotic for a grown man to own up to."

The superintendent's curling mustaches took a grinning uptilt, and he laughed joyously.

"When you talk that way you don't need to tell me," he chuckled. "It was a girl."

"It was," admitted the self-confessed simpleton, matching his accuser's grin. "Since you've guessed that much, I'll tell you a little more. I saw her first on your eastbound train, the train that took on the sham dead man at Little Butte and afterward picked up your office-car. You'll remember you asked me to stay over a day or two with you in Brewster, and I did. As a matter of fact, your persuasion wasn't needed. I would have stopped off anyway, because the girl stopped off."

"Heavens and earth!" ejaculated Maxwell, in ecstatic appreciation; "how are the mighty fallen! Lord of love! I never expected to see the day when Cal Sprague, the idol of the foot-ball rooters, would fall for a pretty face just seen, as you might say, in passing! Oh, gosh!"

"Have your laugh, you old married hyena!" grunted the late-comer in the sentimental field. "I can't get back at you because I didn't happen to be around when you were making seventeen different kinds of a donkey of yourself over old Hiram Fairbain's daughter—as I have no doubt you did. But that's neither here nor there; the young woman I'm speaking of tagged me, and I'm It; I've been It ever since that first day on the eastbound train."

"And you say she stopped off in Brewster?"

"Yes."

"But you didn't meet her?"

"No. You've been calling me an amateur detective, Dick; I'm a fake! That girl and the people she was with just vanished into thin air the minute they hit the platform at the Brewster station. I lost them as completely as if they had stepped off into space."

"So you came back, later, to hunt her up?"

"I did; or to try to get some trace of her—just that."

"Of course, it says itself that you have found her."

Sprague's mellow laugh rumbled deep in his chest.

"Richard, I have been here seven weeks, and I found her—just three days ago! In all my knocking around with you and Starbuck and Stillings and the rest of you, not one man in the bunch has thought it worth his while to tell me that there is a cottage settlement of Eastern summer people up in the mountains on Lake Topaz. I had to blunder around and find out for myself, as I did last Wednesday, when Starbuck took me up to your mine on Mount Geechy."

"Great guns!" exclaimed the superintendent; "how in the name of common-sense was anybody going to suspect that you needed to know? That summer colony is as old as Brewster. But go ahead and tell me more. I'm interested, if I don't look it."

"There isn't much to tell. I found her; met her. She is stopping with an aunt of hers, and by chance—good luck you'd say—I have something a little better than a speaking acquaintance with the aunt—through some common friends in New York. There's nothing to it, Richard. The girl can have her pick—she has already turned down a couple of English titles—and she isn't going to pick any such overgrown slob of a man as your humble. Let's talk about something else."

"If I branch off, it will be into my own grief," said Maxwell half-reluctantly. "I had another wire from Ford this afternoon. The big-money people are getting ready to swat us again, and Ford admits that he can't find out where it is to come from, or what it is to be. If it wasn't for the name of the thing, and what I owe Ford, I'd be about ready to throw up my job, Calvin. I have money enough to live on, and this business of dragging along from day to day with the feeling that any minute you may get the knife between your ribs isn't very exhilarating."

"You say Ford can't give you any hint of what is coming next?"

"Not the slightest. But there is something in the wind. You know Kinzie, the president of the Brewster National Bank? He cornered me last night at the club and asked a lot of queer questions that didn't seem to have any particular bearing on anything."

"What kind of questions?" inquired the expert.

"Oh, about our right-of-way through the town of Copah, and about our outstanding floating debts, and finally about a ridiculous damage suit that has been dragging its way through the courts."

Sprague sat up and relighted his fat, black cigar.

"What about the damage suit?" he asked.

"It's a piker's graft," was the half-impatient rejoinder. "We have a little branch line over to the bauxite mines in the western edge of the county. The telegraph company doesn't maintain an office, and our agent is authorized to handle what few commercial telegrams there are. It seems that one came for a man named Hixon, a prospector whose exact whereabouts could not be ascertained at the moment. The message was three days old when it was delivered, and Hixon sued for ten thousand dollars damages; said he'd lost the sale of a mine by the delay."

"You are fighting the suit?"

"Of course—it's point-blank robbery! Stillings has had the case postponed two or three times in the hope of wearing Hixon out. It comes up again next week, I believe."

"And you say Kinzie was curious about this lawsuit?"

"Yes. It seems that Hixon is, or has been, a customer of the bank; and Kinzie suggested that we ought to compromise."

"Um," said the big-bodied man thoughtfully. "In whose court does the case come up?"

"In Judge Watson's."

"Has Hixon a good lawyer?"

"He has the Kentucky colonel, suh," laughed Maxwell; "our one original, dyed-in-the-wool, fire-eating spellbinder from the Blue-grass. When Colonel Bletchford gets upon his feet and turns loose, you can hear the bird of freedom scream all the way across Timanyoni Park."

The big chemistry expert with the athletic slant was moving uneasily in his chair. After a little interval of silence he said: "I can't be with you in any more of these little two-steps with the money trust, Richard. I'm going back to Washington tomorrow."

Maxwell's start carried him half-way out of his chair, and he dropped his short pipe and broke the stem of it.

"Great Scott, Calvin—don't say that!" he implored. "You can't throw us down that way! Why, good Lord, man, if it hadn't been for you and your brains.... But, pshaw! There's no use in talking about it; you simply *can't* go and leave us hanging over the ragged edge!"

"I can; and I guess I must," insisted Sprague gently. "And the worst of it is, Dick, I can't tell you or anybody else the why. It's just up to me, and I've got it to do."

Maxwell's perturbation had cleared his brain like a bucketing of cold water. "Tell me, Calvin," he broke out; "is the girl mixed up in it?"

"She is," was the brief admission.

"Is she gone, or going—back East, I mean?"

"N-no; not immediately, I believe."

Maxwell sat back in his chair and began to twist nervously at the charm on his watch-fob.

"I suppose I haven't any kick coming," he said at length. "What you have done for me this summer couldn't be measured in money, and I have no right to ask you to go on giving your time and your brains on the score of friendship."

"There isn't any bigger score in this little old round world of ours, Dick," said the other gravely. "I'm a cold-blooded fish, and I know it. I ought to stand by you; every decent thing in me but one urges me to stand by you. But that one exception queers me. I hope you'll win out; I hope to God you'll win out, Dick; but I can't be the man to put the club into your hands this time."

The snappy little superintendent took his defeat hard. For some further time he used every argument he could devise to persuade Sprague to change his mind. But at the end the big man was shaking his head regretfully.

"It's no use, Richard," he said finally. "If you were in my place, you'd do just as I'm doing—and for the same reason. Let's go back to town. It's too cheerful here to fit either one of us just now."

Maxwell had driven out to the club-house on the shore of Lake Corona in his small car, and when he returned to town Sprague occupied the mechanician's seat beside him. It was a run of only a few miles, over the best driving road in the county, and there was neither time nor the occasion for much talk.

When the car had trundled across the Timanyoni bridge and the viaduct over the railroad tracks, Maxwell would have set Sprague down at his hotel across the plaza from the station; but Sprague himself objected. "You are going over to your office? I'll go with you, if you don't mind. It's my last evening, and I'm not in the humor to sit it out alone. I won't interfere, if you want to work," was the way he put it.

It was thus it happened that they climbed the stair to the second story of the railroad building together, and together walked down the corridor to the door of the despatcher's room. Connolly, the fat night despatcher, was at his glass-topped table behind the counter railing, and when he saw the superintendent he held up a pudgy hand.

"Benson's been trying to get you on the wire from Copah for an hour or more, Mr. Maxwell," he said. "I didn't know where to raise you."

"Is he on the wire now?" asked Maxwell, letting himself and his companion through the wicket in the counter rail.

"No; but I'll call him for you." Followed a sharp rattling of the key and a few broken snippings from the sounder, and then the despatcher got up out of his chair. "Here he is," he said. "He wants to talk to you, personally."

Maxwell took the vacated chair and key, and Connolly stood aside with the big expert. "Seems right good to have you dropping in every now and then, Mr. Sprague," said the fat one. "You'd ought to belong to us out here. We'd sure make it warm for you in the Short Line family."

Sprague looked the dumpling-like despatcher over in mild and altogether friendly criticism.

"Speaking of families: you got married yourself a little while ago, didn't you, Dan?" he asked.

"You bet I did!" was the enthusiastic reply. "Sadie ain't got done talking yet about that set of knives and forks you sent her from Philadelphia."

Again the big-muscled man was looking the despatcher over critically, this time with a quizzical twinkle in his gray eyes.

"Tell me how you did it, Dan," he urged soberly. "You're fatter than I ever dared to be. How did you manage to make a girl believe that there might be a man inside of a big body as well as in a medium-sized one?"

The night despatcher laughed until his moon-like face was purple; until the car-record clerk in the distant corner of the room looked up from his type-writer to see if he, too, might not share the joke.

"Gi-give me a little time," wheezed Connolly; and he was presumably going to tell how it had been done when Maxwell got up from the glass-topped table and broke in.

"Twenty-six is asking for orders, Dan," he said; and when Connolly had resumed his chair and his key: "That's all, Calvin. We'll go across to my office, if you like."

It was behind the closed door of the superintendent's room, after Sprague had chosen the easiest of the three chairs and settled himself for a smoke, that Maxwell said:

"I'm going to miss you like the devil, Calvin; I'm missing you right now."

Sprague blew a series of smoke rings toward the disused gas-fixture hanging from the centre of the ceiling.

"Something that Chief Engineer Benson has been telling you over the wire from Copah?" he suggested.

"Yes."

Another series of the smoke rings, and then: "Well, I didn't tell you you couldn't talk, did I?"

Maxwell did not haggle over the inverted terms of the permission to talk. The necessity was too pressing.

"Benson has struck something that he can't account for. For a week or more the Transcontinental people have been gathering a working camp at the Copah end of the bridge on which their Jack's Canyon branch crosses the Pannikin. Nobody seems to know what they are going to do, or where they are going to do it. At Leckhard's suggestion, I sent Benson over to pry around a little."

"And he hasn't found out what the T-C. folks have in mind?"

"No, he hasn't. But it is plainly some sort of a track-building job. He says they have a hundred or more scraper-teams in camp, a train-load of new steel, and forty car-loads of cross-ties. And this afternoon they brought down a mechanical rail-layer—a machine much used nowadays for rushing a job of track-laying."

The big guest smoked reflectively for a full minute or more before he said: "No jangle with the Copah city authorities about any trackage rights in the town, or street crossings, or anything of that sort?"

"Not that I have ever heard of. The T-C. has its own Copah yard, and has a switching connection with the Pacific Southwestern yard tracks; though, naturally, there is little exchange of business between the two competitive systems."

"Do they connect with you?" asked Sprague.

"Not directly. Our yard was originally an independent lay-out, lying a mile to the west of town. When the Short Line became a grand division of the Pacific Southwestern, the two yards, ours and the P. S-W., were operated as one, though they are still separate lay-outs."

"I see. What else does Benson say?"

"He has been asking questions and chewing the rag with anybody who would talk, he says; but we all know Jack. He is too downright and bluff to be much of a detective."

Maxwell turned to his desk and began on the ever-present pile of waiting work; and the big expert settled himself more deeply into his chair and smoked on with his gaze fixed upon the ceiling gas-pendant. After the lapse of many minutes he said: "Have you a blue-print of the Copah yards, Dick?"

Maxwell rose and went to a filing-case in the corner of the office. After a little search he found the required blue-print and gave it to Sprague, explaining the locations and the relative positions of the three railroad yards.

The expert studied the map thoughtfully, even going so far as to scrutinize the fine lettering on it with the help of a small pocket magnifying-glass.

"And right over here by the river is where you say the new camp has been pitched?" he asked, indicating the spot with the handle of the magnifier.

"Yes; Benson says it's at the south end of the bridge, and just west of the T-C. bridge siding."

Sprague looked up quickly. "Did Benson say they had an electric-light outfit for night work?"

"Why, no; I don't remember that he did."

"Go and ask him," said Sprague shortly; and the superintendent, who had learned to take the expert's suggestions without question, left the office to do it.

He was back in a few minutes, with the light of a newly kindled excitement in his eyes.

"By Jove, Calvin, you're a wizard!" he exclaimed. "Your guess is better than another man's eyesight. They've not only got the light outfit—they've strung it up and gone to work! Benson says they are laying a track out across the valley of the Pannikin like this," and he traced a curving line on the blue-print, which Sprague was still holding spread out on his knees.

Sprague nodded slowly. "That is move Number One," he said. "Dick, you're in for a fight to a finish, this time. They've got you foul in some way, and they are so sure of it that they are already beginning to take possession. Don't you see what this new track means?"

"No, I don't," Maxwell confessed, with a frown of perplexity.

"You will see before tomorrow night. Pull yourself together, old man, and do a little clear-headed reasoning. Why are these people starting out to build a railroad at ten o'clock Saturday night? Surely you've had experience enough in crossing fights to know what that means!"

Maxwell straightened up and swore out of a full heart.

"You mean that they are going to cut a crossing through the Southwestern main line, and do it on Sunday, when our people can't stop them with a court injunction?"

"You've surrounded at least half of it," said the expert. "The other half will come later. If I wasn't going away tomorrow—"

Maxwell walked to the window and stared across at the flaming arc light hanging in front of the Hotel Topaz on the opposite side of the plaza. When he turned again, Sprague had rolled the blue-print into a tube and was laying it on the desk.

"Calvin, you've had time to think it over," said the man at the window. "You haven't made it very plain for me, but I can understand that it's friendship against—against the girl. I'm human enough to know what that means, but—"

Sprague was holding up one of his big square-fingered hands in protest.

"I have been thinking it over, Dick," he admitted gently. "I'll stay—for the line-up, anyway. But it's only fair to warn you that I may drop out at any minute; perhaps when the game is going dead against you. Now we'll get action. You go back to the wire and keep in touch with Benson. We want to know at the earliest possible moment exactly what it is that the T-C. people are trying to do. While you're wiring, I'll go out and try to find Stillings."

This was the situation at ten o'clock on Saturday night. At the nine-o'clock Sunday morning breakfast in the Topaz café, when Maxwell, hollow-eyed and haggard from his night's vigil at the wires, next had speech with Sprague, the news from the seat of war at Copah was sufficiently exciting.

As Maxwell had predicted, the Transcontinental track-layers had built up to the Southwestern main line, and had finally succeeded in cutting a crossing through it, though not without a fight. The Southwestern force, with Leckhard, the division superintendent, at its head, had resisted as it could. Since it was past midnight, with no hope of obtaining legal help until Monday morning, Leckhard had "spotted" a locomotive on the crossing, and when the men in charge of it were overborne by numbers, the engine had been derailed and "killed" before it was abandoned.

The stubborn resistance had purchased nothing more than a short delay. The marauders had a wrecking-crane as part of their equipment; and half an hour after its abandonment the derailed Southwestern engine had been toppled over into the ditch, and the track-layers were at work installing the crossing frogs.

"And after that?" queried Sprague, when Maxwell had told of the losing fight at the main line crossing.

"After that they went on building across the valley and heading for the western end of our yard. At the last report, which came about eight o'clock, they had less than a mile of steel to lay before they would be on our right-of-way. Benson is crazy. He is yelling at me now to petition the governor for the militia."

"You haven't done anything?"

"There isn't anything to do. They are on neutral ground, now, and will be until they reach our right-of-way—if that is what they are heading for. We have no manner of right to interfere with them until they become actual trespassers; and as for that, no physical force we could muster would stop them. Benson says there are between four and five hundred men in that track gang, and many of them are armed."

Sprague nodded. "It is a fight to a finish, as I told you last night. And they have the advantage because we don't know yet where or how they are going to hit us. Have you communicated with Ford?"

"I have tried to; but I don't get any reply."

"Tally!" said the big man on the opposite side of the table. "I've been having the same kind of bad luck. I can't locate Stillings."

"Did you try his house?"

"I did that first. His family is out of town, and he has been stopping at the club. But nobody there seems to know anything about him. A little after midnight I found your division detective, young Tarbell, and put him on the job. We're needing Stillings, and needing him badly."

"Tarbell hasn't reported back yet?"

"Not yet; it is beginning to look as if he had dropped out, too. But the day is still young. You'd better go upstairs and get a little sleep. I'll stay on deck and call you if you are needed."

Maxwell had finished his simple breakfast and he took the good advice. It was nine hours later, and the electrics were twinkling yellow in the sunset pinks and grays flooding the quiet Sunday evening streets and the railroad plaza, when he came down and found Sprague just ready to go in to dinner.

"News!" demanded the superintendent eagerly. "I had no idea of wasting the day this way."

Sprague made him wait until they were seated at a table for two in the corner of the café.

"The Copah fight is over, and the T-C. people have broken into your yards with their new track," the expert announced briefly. "Benson had to give up and go to bed about noon, but Leckhard has kept us posted. The track is in, and frogged to a connection with your main line; and the entire attacking force has camped down at the two points of trespass; presumably to keep you and Leckhard from interfering and tearing up their job. Move Number One, whatever it may mean, is a move accomplished."

"I can't understand; I can't begin to understand!" said Maxwell, in despair. And then: "No word yet from Ford?"

"No; and what is more to the point, there is none from Stillings—nor from Tarbell. I'm beginning to think that this is a bigger game than any we've played yet, Dick. I dug up Editor Kendall, of *The Tribune*, this afternoon, and had a little heart-to-heart talk with him. There is big trouble of some sort in the air; he has smelled it, but he can't tell what it is. He has his young men out everywhere, 'on suspicion,' and he has promised to keep in touch with us up to the time his paper goes to press."

"That ought to help us to get at the facts," said the superintendent. "Kendall is our friend, and he has some mighty keen young fellows on his staff. By the way, there's one of them now—just coming in at the door. He's looking for somebody, too."

The young incomer was not long in finding his man. With a nod to the head-waiter, he came across to Sprague's table. "A note for you, Mr. Sprague—from Mr. Kendall," he said. "There's no answer, I believe," and he went on to another table and began to chat with two other young men, strangers to Maxwell, who had come in on the evening train.

Sprague glanced at his note and passed it across the table. Maxwell read it and found that it merely added to the mysteries without offering anything in the way of enlightenment.

Dear Sprague:

Have followed your suggestion, and our young men have spotted at least a score of the strangers at the different hotels. Nobody seems to know any of them, and they won't talk. You will find a list of names, copied from the hotel registers, on enclosed slip. It has occurred to me that Maxwell might know some of them, if your suspicions are well founded.

Kendall.

Maxwell frowned over the list for a moment before handing it back.

"A few of them are familiar," he said. "Tom Carmody is a division superintendent on the west end of the T-C., and this man Hunniwell used to be in their legal department. Vance Jackson is, or used to be, Carmody's chief despatcher; and—why, say! This is a T-C. crowd; here's Andy Cochran, their Canyon Division trainmaster."

"Any more?" asked Sprague quietly.

"No; the other names are all strange to me."

Sprague took the list and pointed with a square-ended forefinger to one of the names.

"This man Dimmock; you don't know him?" he queried.

"No."

"Well, I don't know him, either; but I happen to know something about him. Two years ago I was doing a little soil work down in Oklahoma. It was during the time they were having the scrap with the oil companies. Mr. Dimmock was there, ostensibly as an independent capitalist from the East looking for bargains in oil-wells, but really as a representative of the trust."

"Is this the same man?"

The expert held his fork pointing diagonally across his plate. "Follow the line of this fork," he directed in low tones, "and you'll see him—at the farther table by the door."

Maxwell looked and saw a generously built, smooth-shaven, cold-featured man who looked like big money, dining at a table alone. The big-money look was not obtrusive; but it was sufficiently apparent in the city cut of the Sunday broadcloth, in the spotless linen, and not less in the attitude of the obsequious waiter who hovered around the great man's chair.

"I took the trouble to look up Mr. Dimmock in the Oklahoma period," Sprague went on. "I found that he was pretty well known in New York as the right hand of a certain great money lord whose name we needn't mention here. That being the case, it is hardly necessary to add that his presence in Brewster at this particular crisis is a bit ominous."

"Have you told Kendall this about Dimmock?" asked the superintendent.

"No; but he'll be pretty sure to trace the gentleman for himself. Where a question of pure news is involved, Kendall is apt to be found running well ahead of the field."

"But that doesn't help us out any," Maxwell objected.

"No. We seem to be forced to await developments; and that, Richard, is always a mark of the losing side. I wish to goodness Stillings would turn up."

"It's odd about Bob. He doesn't often drop out without leaving a trail behind him. Have you finished? Then let's go over to the office and see if there is any further word from Benson or Leckhard."

It was when they were leaving the dining-room together that they came upon Tarbell, the ex-terror of Montana cattle thieves. The young man was way-worn and dusty, and his eyes were red for want of sleep. Sprague's question was shot-like.

"You've found him, Archer?"

"Yep; as good as," was the short rejoinder.

"Turn it loose," commanded Sprague.

"He's at the bottom of an old prospect hole up on Mount Baldwin; him and Mr. Maxwell's brother-in-law, Billy Starbuck. I had to come back to town to get a rope to pull 'em out."

"What?" said Maxwell. "How did they get there?"

The young special deputy shook his head.

"I don't know the whys an' wherefores any more 'n a goat," he said simply. "I got onto it through the barkeep' at the road-house out on the Topaz pike. He said a bunch o' fellas came along in an auto late last night and stopped for drinks. They come in two at a time, and two of 'em didn't come in at all. Just as they was startin' off, there was a scrap o' some sort in the auto, and the barkeep', who was lookin' out o' the window, swore to me he got a glimpse o' Mr. Stillings. I found the auto tracks and followed 'em.

They left the road this side o' the lake, crossed the Gloria on the bridge, and shoved that machine up an old wood trail on Baldwin."

"Well, go on," said Maxwell, impatiently.

"I found where they'd stopped and took Mr. Stillings and Billy out o' the car; and it sure looked as if there'd been another scrap, the way the bushes was tore up. About a quarter back from the trail I found the hole. Starbuck hollered up at me when I peeked in. I couldn't see 'em none, but Billy he said they was both there, and wasn't hurt none to speak of—only in their feelin's. He told me to chase back and get a rope."

Maxwell looked at his watch. "How deep is this hole, Archer?"

"'Bout a hundred foot, or maybe more."

"We'll get a car and go after them," was the superintendent's instant decision. "You say this was last night; have they had anything to eat?"

"Yep; Billy said a basket o' grub had been lowered down to 'em a little spell after they was chucked in."

"All right. Go over to the shops and get a coil of rope out of the wrecking-car, and I'll get an auto. Want to go along, Calvin?"

"Sure," was the prompt reply.

Maxwell, being a reasonably wealthy mine owner, as well as the superintendent of the railroad, kept two cars; a runabout and a big touring-machine which, in the absence of his family, were both housed in a downtown garage. In the big car the twenty-mile drive over the Topaz Lake pike was quickly made.

Just before they came to the bridge over the Gloria, they passed an auto with two men in it going toward town. Oddly enough, as it seemed, the in-bound car gave them a wide berth, steering almost into the ditch at the passing, and speeding up to a racing clip as soon as the ditched machine had been yanked back into the roadway. Tarbell, who was driving the Maxwell car, stopped, jumped out, and examined the tracks of the other car by the help of a lighted match.

"That's them," he said laconically, when he resumed the steering-wheel. "That was the same car. It's got a set o' them new-fangled tires with creepers on 'em."

"Hurry!" snapped Maxwell. "We don't know what they've been doing to Stillings and Billy, this time."

Happily they soon found that the evening visit of the two unknown men to the abandoned prospect shaft had been charitable rather than malevolent. Stillings, who was the first of the two captives to be hauled out of the dark pit on the mountain side, told them that another basket of food had just been lowered by a string into the shaft. And when Starbuck came up he brought the basket with him.

Singularly enough, the two rescued ones had no explanation to offer; or, at least, none that served to explain anything. It transpired that they had dined together in the town house of the club the evening before, and had afterward gone to the theatre together. After the play they had taken a taxi to go to Stillings's house in the suburbs to sleep. An auto had followed them, and when they had dismissed the taxi they had been set upon by a number of masked men who tumbled out of the pursuing car. Since they had no weapons, they were quickly overpowered, thrown into the car, carried off to the mountains, and dumped into the prospect hole, the rope by which they had been lowered being thrown in after them. That was all.

"And you don't know what it was for?" asked Sprague, when they were rolling evenly back to the city with Starbuck at the steering-wheel.

"No more than you do," was the lawyer's answer. "Billy and I have speculated over it all day—having no other way of amusing ourselves—and it's a perfectly blind trail. Billy says he knows I must have been the one they were after, and I say he must have been the one. You can take your choice."

At the club town house the two rescued ones were set down, and Tarbell was released to go and get his well-earned rest after the twenty-four-hour task of shadow work.

"Get yourself in shape to go on an advisory committee with us as soon as you can, Robert," was Sprague's injunction to the attorney; and then Maxwell drove down to the railroad building, and the expert was with him when he went up to the despatcher's office.

There was no more news from the Copah seat of war, two hundred miles to the eastward, or, at most, nothing different. The huge alien track-laying force was still guarding the crossing through the Southwestern main line and the new junction with the Nevada Short Line in the western yards. Leckhard reported that Benson was sleeping off his fatigues of the previous night, and said that all was quiet on the late battle-ground.

"And still no word from Ford!" said Maxwell, as he and Sprague, having put the car up at the garage, walked back to the hotel. "By and large, Calvin, that is the most mysterious thing in the bunch. I can't understand it."

"Unless I am much mistaken, we shall all understand many things to-morrow that we can't appreciate tonight," was Sprague's prediction; and long after Maxwell had gone back to his office to put in a make-up period at his desk, the big-bodied man from Washington sat out on the loggia porch of the hotel smoking in thoughtful solitude and staring absently at the unwinking eyes of the mast-head electrics in the railroad yard diagonally opposite.

The Monday morning dawned bright and fair, as a vast majority of the mornings do in the favored inter-mountain paradise known as Timanyoni Park. Notwithstanding his long Sunday sleep, Maxwell came down late to his breakfast, and the café waiter told him that Sprague had eaten at his usually early hour and was gone.

While he was waiting to be served, the superintendent glanced through the morning *Tribune*. There was a rather exciting first-page news story of the track-laying fight at Copah. The story was evidently an Associated Press despatch, and was carefully non-committal in its reference to the Transcontinental's purpose in rushing the new trackage through to a connection with the Nevada Short Line yards. None the less, the impression was given that the Southwestern's opposition to the move had been only perfunctory and for public effect. Also, the impression was conveyed that the Copah public, at least, believed that there was a secret understanding between the two railroad corporations.

Turning to the inside pages, Maxwell found no editorial comment on the news story, and he was still wondering why Editor Kendall had missed his chance when Stillings came in and took the chair at the end of the table.

"They told me I'd find you here," said the lawyer, "and I wanted to have a word with you before the wheels begin to go round. This is our day in court on the Hixon damage suit, and we'll have to fish or cut bait this time. In all probability, we sha'n't be able to get another postponement, and if we let the case come to trial, it's all off. The jury will give Hixon his verdict, if only for the reason that he is one man fighting a corporation. The only question is, shall I try to compromise before it is too late?"

"Is there any chance for a compromise?" asked Maxwell.

"I don't know positively. Bletchford was willing a few weeks ago, but his figure was so high that I refused to talk to him."

"It's a hold-up!" snapped the superintendent shortly. "I haven't changed my mind."

"All right," said the attorney, rising to go. "I thought I'd give you one last chance at it. The case is called for ten o'clock in Judge Watson's court. If you're foot-loose, you might come up and see us lose ten thousand dollars. I guess that is what it will come to." And then, as he was turning to go: "By the way, that was a mighty cold-blooded thing the T-C. people did yesterday, wasn't it? What does it mean?"

"If Sprague hasn't told you, I'm sure I can't."

"I haven't seen Sprague. He left a note at the office this morning, saying he'd be around later; but he hasn't shown up yet. Will you come over to the court-house and see the jury sand-bag us?"

Quite naturally, the hard-working superintendent had no notion of wasting his forenoon in a court-room, and he said so tersely. And beyond

Stillings's departure and the finishing of the late breakfast, he went across to his office and plunged into the day's tasks.

There was an unusual quantity of the work that morning, it seemed, and no sooner was he through with one file of referred papers than Calmaine, the chief clerk, was ready with another. Only once during the forenoon was the steady office grind lightened by an interruption from the outside world. At ten o'clock Benson wired from Copah, saying that the T-C. track-layers were at work again, carefully surfacing and ballasting the new track as if it were to be a permanency. Also, the chief engineer asked if any legal steps had been taken looking to the prevention of further trespass.

Maxwell broke the routine pace long enough to dictate to Calmaine the reply to Benson's asking. It stated the facts briefly. No legal steps had as yet been taken. A full report of the intrusion had gone to the Pacific Southwestern head-quarters in New York, and no action would be taken until New York had spoken.

It was a little before noon when Calmaine carried away the final files of claim correspondence with the superintendent's notations on them, and Maxwell sat back in his chair and relighted his cigar, which had gone out many times during the stressful morning. In the act the door of the private office suddenly opened and the heavy-set, neatly groomed gentleman whom Sprague had pointed out at the hotel dinner-table the previous evening walked in and took the chair at the desk end, removing his hat and wiping his brow with a handkerchief filmy enough to have figured as the *mouchoir* of a fine lady.

"Mr. Maxwell, I believe?" he said, dropping a card bearing the single line, "C. P. Dimmock," on the desk.

"That is my name," returned Maxwell, bristling with a wholly unaccountable prickling of antagonism.

"I have come, as an officer of Judge Watson's court, to take over your railroad," announced the cold-featured man calmly, and as he said it, the telephone buzzer under Maxwell's desk went off as though a general fire-alarm had been sounded from the central office.

Maxwell reached for the telephone and put the receiver to his ear. It was Stillings who was at the other end of the wire, and he was frantically incoherent. But out of the attorney's coruscating babblement the superintendent picked enough to enable him to surround the principal fact. In the face of all precedent, in defiance of all its legal rights, the Nevada Short Line had been practically declared bankrupt and a receiver had been appointed.

Notwithstanding his nerve, which was ordinarily very good, the snappy little superintendent's hand trembled when he replaced the ear-piece on its hook and turned to his visitor.

"So you've got us at last, have you, Mr. Dimmock?" he said, constraining himself to speak calmly. "It was on the Hixon case, our attorney tells me."

The visitor nodded blandly.

"You should have compromised that case, Mr. Maxwell—if you will allow me the privilege of criticising, after the fact. But we needn't come to blows over the purely academic question. Judge Watson has appointed me receiver—temporary, of course—for the railroad property. I am here to take charge in the interest of all concerned, and I am assuming that you won't put yourself in contempt of court by any ill-considered resistance. Here is the court order." And he tossed a folded paper across to the desk.

For the moment Maxwell was speechless. Then he slowly straightened up and took a few packets of papers out of the desk pigeon-holes marked "R. Maxwell, Private," putting them into his pocket. That done, he removed the desk and door keys from his pocket ring and laid them upon the desk.

"I think that is about as far as I have to go, personally," he said, rising and reaching for his hat. "And, of course, I have nothing to ask for myself. But for the staff and the rank and file, Mr. Dimmock—I hope you're not going to make a clean sweep. We have a mighty good working organization, and it will cause a great deal of hardship if you take the usual course of discharging and replacing all heads of departments."

The new head of all departments smiled, and in the smile much of the cold hardness of his face disappeared.

"That is a matter with which I shall have very little to do, Mr. Maxwell," he returned. "Mr. Carmody, lately in charge of the Transcontinental's Pacific Division, will be my operating chief, and I am sure that you yourself, as a practical railroad man, would counsel me to give him a free hand."

Maxwell took the additional bitter dose of the medicine of defeat like a man, but he made one more attempt—an attempt to save Calmaine's head.

"My chief clerk—the young man who admitted you here—I hope you can provide for him, Mr. Dimmock. Apart from any personal relations, I have found him the most faithful, the most painstaking—"

The new receiver lifted a faultlessly manicured hand in genial protest.

"You know I couldn't do that, Mr. Maxwell," he objected. "Your young man has probably been much too close to you to make it possible or prudent. You are a rich man yourself, and you can very easily provide for your secretary, as I make no doubt you will. Must you go? Don't be in a hurry. We needn't make this a personal fight, I'm sure."

The ex-superintendent looked at his watch and told a lie for the sake of keeping the peace.

"It is my luncheon hour," he said. "If there are any routine matters upon which you may wish to consult me, you will find me over at the hotel." And he went out with his hat pulled over his eyes and his blood boiling. To have stayed another minute would have been to risk an explosion.

It was a small but exceedingly fervent indignation meeting which gathered in Attorney Stillings's office in the Kinzie Building a little after twelve o'clock on this day of cataclysms. When Maxwell entered, Stillings was trying to explain to Starbuck and Sprague and Editor Kendall—who had been hauled out of bed to lend his presence to the conference—just how it had come about.

As it appeared in the wrathful summing up, it had happened very easily; so easily as to present every indication of careful prearrangement. When the Hixon case had been called in court, Stillings had risen and asked for a further postponement, having, as it chanced, a very good excuse in the fact that the witness by whom he expected to prove that Hixon's claim of a lost mining sale was a pure invention was absent. Instantly the Kentucky colonel counsel for the plaintiff had jumped up, not to protest against the further delay, but to introduce his colleague in the cause—the stranger whose name on the Hophra House register was Mr. Peter Hunniwell.

Before Stillings could get his breath, Hunniwell was on his feet, making an impassioned plea for justice. Rapidly rehearsing the course of the defendant railroad company, which he charged with maliciously striving to defeat the ends of justice, he summed up with a still more serious charge, namely, that the railroad was not only unwilling to pay the just claims upon it, but was unable to do so; was, in effect, practically bankrupt, as the thick packet of affidavits, which he here passed up to the judge, would sufficiently prove.

"After that," Stillings went on, "it was *biff! bang!* and the fight was over. Judge Watson merely glanced through the affidavits—which may or may not be purely faked—while Hunniwell, in a voice like a steam calliope, was demanding that the court appoint a receiver. It was so ridiculous, so absolutely beyond all precedent, that it didn't seem worth while to try to call him down. When Hunniwell finally quit, the judge was looking over his spectacles at us in that mild, half-vacant way of his, and saying, 'I think your point is very well taken. It is time that something was done to bring these defendant corporations to a sense of their responsibilities to the plain people. I shall appoint, as temporary receiver, Mr. C. F. Dimmock, the appointment to take effect this day at noon.' At noon, mind you!" choked Stillings. "And it was at that moment half-past eleven!"

"Of course, you tried to break in," said Maxwell.

"Sure! But I might as well have gone out on the court-house steps and shouted at the scenery! Watson told me, in the same half-absent way, that the receivership was only temporary, and that we should have ample opportunity to show cause, if we could, why the receiver should be discharged at the regular hearing, which he there and then set for the twelfth of the month, naming his chambers as the place. Before I could wedge in another word, court was adjourned and Watson was leaving the bench."

Sprague was nodding slowly.

"Now we know the meaning of the Sunday track-laying, and the sudden influx of strangers—most of whom will doubtless turn out to be T-C. officials and employees—and the mysterious kidnapping of the Short Line's attorney night before last," he said. And then to Maxwell: "I suppose the thing is definitely done, and you have been properly kicked out of your office, Dick?"

Maxwell briefed the short interview with Dimmock for the benefit of the others.

"Dimmock and Carmody are in charge," he concluded, "and before night they will have tried and executed everybody in the service whose head sticks up far enough to give them an excuse for cutting it off. They are going to make a clean sweep. Dimmock practically admitted it. By this time tomorrow the Nevada Short Line will be part and parcel of the Transcontinental System, with only T-C. men in charge."

"Holy Smoke!" said Kendall, and the ejaculation from him meant more than the most frenzied outburst of the average man: and then again he said, "*Holy Smoke!*"

It was Starbuck, himself a small stockholder in the confiscated railroad, who first got his feet upon the solid earth again.

"I reckon we-all are just going to sit around and bite our thumbs and let these hold-ups put it all over us," he said, in his slow drawl; adding, after the proper pause: "I don't think!"

Maxwell sprang out of his chair.

"I must go to the commercial office and wire Ford!" he broke out. "He'll know what to do, if there is anything that can be done. Stillings, you get in touch with our general counsel in Chicago. We're an interstate road, and this thing can't be settled in a Timanyoni county court!"

"Hold on," said Stillings. "That is where we're lame. We allowed ourselves to be sued in this cause, as we have in a good many others, under the old corporate name—The Red Butte Western. That, as you know, was a purely intrastate corporation. Our newer lines are only 'extensions.'"

"Then we can't carry it up to the Federal courts?" gasped Maxwell.

"We can try it, and, of course, we shall try it. But the presumptive facts are against us. What I am hoping is that our Pacific Southwestern backers will be able to help us make a killing and dump these pirates at the regular hearing."

"Then you needn't hope any more," said Sprague quietly. "Apart from the fact that they've put the high kibosh on you today, the element of time comes in to cut the largest figure. For the stock-smashing purpose in this particular instance, a short receivership will prove as efficacious as a long one. You've had one experience with the steam-roller today, and you'll have as many more of them as may seem necessary. It wouldn't make any difference if you should import a train-load of eastern lawyers; the thing's done, and it is going to stay done until it has accomplished the end in view—which is to transfer the stock control of the Short Line to the T-C. Your only chance is to strike back, and strike quickly—before the mischief is done in New York."

"But how?" pleaded Stillings. "Tell us how!"

"By proving clearly, what I presume we all accept as the undoubted fact, that Judge Watson has been bribed."

True to his calling, Stillings was the first to object to so sweeping a charge.

"Oh, hold on!" he exclaimed. "I wouldn't go so far as that. That is a pretty serious charge, Sprague."

"I know it is. But when I say bribery, it doesn't necessarily mean the grosser form of buying with cash money. Let us say that Judge Watson has been 'influenced.' If you can't make that charge and sustain it, you may as well call the incident closed."

Maxwell was leaning against the door-jamb. His eyes were fiery and his breath was coming quickly.

"If you say there has been crooked work, Calvin, that settles it; I believe it. Now tell us what to do, and we'll do it."

Kendall's lean, leathery jaw was set hard, and he was furtively watching the big expert. That a fierce struggle of some kind was going on behind the mask of the ruddy, half-boyish face, he made no doubt. And Sprague's answer quickly confirmed the editor's conclusion.

"You don't know what you're asking, Dick," said the big man slowly.

"I do!" said Maxwell hotly. "I'm asking you to help us send a bunch of criminals—just low-down, ordinary thieving criminals—to jail! Sprague, if you can do it, and *won't* do it—"

There was a strained silence in the shabby little law office that seemed as if it would never be broken. Kendall turned his face away, and Starbuck slid noiselessly out of his chair and went to stand at the window with his back to the others. At length the reply to Maxwell's demand came, wrung out, as it seemed, from the very heart of reluctance.

"It can be done. Every chain that was ever forged has its weak link. For reasons which are purely personal to me, I'd rather be shot than go into this thing with you. I'd refuse, if I could in common decency; and, in any event, I may fall down on you when it comes to the pinch. But I'll go as far as I can. Will that do?"

"Say it!" snapped the ex-superintendent eagerly.

"All right. Stillings, you may come to my room in the hotel at two o'clock, and bring Mr. David Kinzie, our downstairs bank president, with you if you have to club him to do it. Kendall, I'm going to ask you to make just as little as possible of this railroad grab in your news columns for the present, taking my word for it that you shall have the biggest story of the year if we win out. Starbuck, you'll come over to the hotel with me now, and I'll give you your stunt. That's all; the meeting's adjourned."

To say that the little inter-mountain city was stirred to the depths by the news which quickly spread from lip to lip is putting it mildly. In its beginnings, Brewster had been a railroad town in the strictest sense, owing its location and its phenomenal after-growth largely to the fostering policy of the railroad. Under Maxwell's wise and just management the Nevada Short Line had identified itself very closely with the growth and prosperity of the entire inter-mountain region, and it had stood as a shining example of a "good" corporation. To have the popular management swept ruthlessly aside and the rule of another company, operating under the thin mask of a receivership, set up in its place, provoked a storm of indignant protest.

Moreover, many of the well-to-do citizens of the Timanyoni were stockholders in the Short Line, and upon these the blow fell as a disaster. Prominent among these local stockholders stood the owner of the Kinzie Building, Brewster's one multi-millionaire and the president of the Brewster National Bank. At precisely two o'clock David Kinzie, gray and pale, and with his small ferret-like eyes peering shrewdly from under the rim of the soft, gray hat which he always wore, stepped into the Hotel Topaz elevator with Stillings. It had not been necessary for the attorney to bludgeon him to induce him to come to the conference with Sprague.

What went on behind the locked door of Room 403 after the two had been admitted was a secret that was not shared with any fourth party, though one of Editor Kendall's young men promptly waylaid Stillings at the close of the conference.

"Tell Mr. Kendall he shall have the news, and have it first, when there is any," was all the lawyer would say; but Connabel, the star reporter who had done the waylaying, died hard.

"Give me a hint, Mr. Stillings—just the barest shadow of a hint," he begged. "Will the case be taken to the Federal courts?"

"Not for publication, Fred," laughed the lawyer, who was evidently in better spirits. Then he added: "There's a big story in this, my boy, and you shall have it when it's ripe; I'll promise you that—I'll ask Kendall to detail you. And that is positively all you'll get out of me now."

Fifteen minutes after the lawyer and Mr. Kinzie had left Room 403 the door opened again, this time to admit Starbuck.

"Well?" said the big-bodied expert, when Maxwell's brother-in-law had taken the chair recently vacated by the banker.

"The judge is sick, or playing sick," was the answer. "Doc Mangum has just gone out to the house, and the servants have their orders to admit nobody."

"What is the nature of his sickness? Does anybody know that?"

"Oh, yes; it's heart trouble and too much altitude. He's had it before."

Sprague's eyes narrowed and his big hands closed in a vice-like grip on the arms of his chair.

"Billy, does it occur to you that this is a most opportune time for him to be taken sick again? What do they do for patients with heart trouble in this country?"

"Order 'em down to a lower altitude," said the mine owner.

"Exactly. And we shall find that this is what Doctor Mangum will advise in the present case. When he does so, Judge Watson will go."

Starbuck was deftly rolling a cigarette of dry tobacco. "And then what?" he queried.

"Then the regular hearing, which is set for the twelfth of the month, can't be held, and the temporary receivership will hold over until it is either confirmed or set aside by the higher courts. In the meantime the delay will have accomplished its purpose. The New York bank pool of the stock will be broken, the T-C. people will buy it in, and the nail will be driven and clinched."

Starbuck winked gravely.

"You're not going to let Judge Watson get out of town," he predicted. "I can ride up the trail that far without falling off."

"No," said Sprague, "we are not going to let him get away until we are through with him. Did you make the other arrangement I spoke of?"

"I sure did. If anybody's fool enough to let the cat out o' the bag, we'll get the cat. Tarbell's on that part of the job."

Sprague went to the wardrobe at the other end of the room and got out his hat and a light top-coat.

"Yes, we'll get the cat, Billy. The only thing I'm afraid of is that we may get the kitten, too. If that should happen, your Uncle Calvin might fly the track. Let's go. I have an appointment to meet Judge Walsh, of the United States District Court, at half-past three, and I'm going to ask you to borrow Maxwell's car and drive me out to the judge's house."

Before nightfall of the Monday it became plainly evident that the new management of the Short Line had climbed fairly into the executive saddle and was making due preparations to stay there. As Maxwell had prophesied, Receiver Dimmock made a clean sweep, and before the first through train came in over the new routing a score of minor department heads had been let out and their places filled by T-C. men. Even the train-despatchers were discharged; and after dinner Maxwell held a "consolation" meeting in the hotel club-rooms with his fired staff, and listened patiently to the bad language which the wholesale hardship evoked.

To one and all of the losers he said the same thing, however; they were to sit tight and say nothing for the present. It was a long lane that had no turning, and the next turn in the Short Line lane might not be very far distant.

"Just one thing, Mr. Maxwell," Connolly, the fat despatcher, put in, as the meeting was about to break up. "If you'll tell us that Mr. Scientific Sprague is with us I guess we'll all sleep better tonight."

"He is," said Maxwell. "That's all for the present. Just sit tight and don't talk. Go home and take your lay-off. If we win out, you're all under pay, just the same as if you were on the job."

It was late that night, after Maxwell had gone to his room, that the long-delayed word came from New York. Maxwell read the telegram from President Ford, and, late as it was, took it immediately to Sprague's room, which was on the floor below. The expert got out of bed to admit him, and read the few type-written lines thoughtfully.

"He puts it up to you good and hard, doesn't he?" was his comment. "But that is about what I expected. He is up to his neck in the fight to keep those lending bankers from dumping the majority stock and running around in circles. Go to the wire and tell him to keep a stiff upper lip; that you're not dead yet. Also, you might add that Kinzie's backing him with those bankers."

"By Jove!" said Maxwell. "Was that what you wanted Kinzie for to-day?"

"It was one of the things. Get your message in so that Ford will have it in the morning. Good-night."

With the opening of the second day the Brewster excitement had died down to some extent, and the new railroad routine was getting itself shaken into the working rut. On every hand it was evident that the coup had been carefully planned long in advance. Almost without a break the through service was established over the new routing, and a hard-and-fast law was laid down for the Short Line rank and file employees, the vast majority of whom were retained under the receivership. The law briefly exacted loyalty to the new management. There would be no more removals except for cause; but anything less than a hearty acceptance of the court order would be considered sufficient cause for prompt dismissal.

Copies of the receiver's circulars and general orders found their way quickly to Maxwell, and the firm, strong hand of authority appeared in every line of them. How Sprague would go about it to break down the wall of possession which every hour was building higher and stronger, was a puzzle as yet unsolved; and it was not until the forenoon of the Wednesday that the various burrowings which the expert had set afoot began to yield results.

Tarbell brought the first of the results to the lobby of the Topaz at eleven o'clock on this third day in the shape of a note from Banker Kinzie. Hixon, the suing bauxite miner, had received his ten thousand dollars from somebody, and had deposited it in the bank.

Sprague passed the note to Maxwell, who came in just as Tarbell was leaving.

"That's good news, in a way," said the expert. "It tells us that the paymaster has begun to get busy. Any further word from Starbuck?"

"I saw him about half an hour ago. He says that Judge Watson's condition remains the same, and Doctor Mangum makes no secret of the fact that he has ordered him to a lower altitude. I had another message from Ford this morning. He says we are dying by inches at the New York end, and the final smash may come at any minute."

"We've got to have a little time," was the quiet rejoinder. "The trap is baited and set, Dick, but we can't very well spring it ourselves. Any word from Mr. Dimmock?"

"Not to me, no."

Sprague's smile was mirthless. "I haven't escaped so easily," he asserted. "Mr. Dimmock came over to my rooms this morning after breakfast and read me a carefully expurgated edition of the riot act. Translated into plain English, what he said was to the effect that my Government job wouldn't be worth much to me if I meddled in this railroad jangle."

"Then he knows you?"

"He knows of two or three things that I have done in the reasoning line, and—well, I'm inclined to think that he is a little nervous about something. He went so far as to hint that he had reason to believe that his mail had been tampered with."

"What? He didn't charge you with anything like that, did he?" demanded Maxwell, in generous indignation.

"Oh, no; not personally, of course. He merely intimated that, as an officer of the court, he wouldn't stand for any interference."

Maxwell was silent for a time. Then he said: "What are you waiting for, Calvin?—more evidence?"

"No; I'm waiting for the click of the trap, and a word from the man who is watching it."

"Will the trap be sprung?"

"It will. Twice since yesterday there have been nibbles at the bait, and both times the nibbler has been afraid."

"Watson, you mean?"

"Yes."

"What is he afraid of?"

"A man with heart trouble is afraid of many things."

Maxwell put an unlighted cigar in his mouth and began to chew on it absently.

"Dimmock's daughter is here. Did you know that?"

The big-bodied chemistry expert was staring fixedly at the revolving street door which was whirling slowly to admit a group of passengers from the lately arrived Red Butte accommodation.

"I didn't know that he had a daughter; or rather I do know that he hasn't one. He was married only three or four years ago," he returned half-absently.

"That's where you're off wrong," retorted the railroad man. "He certainly has one, and she is here; she was at breakfast with him when I came down this morning. She is so distractingly pretty that I couldn't believe she was the daughter of that hard-featured piece of financial machinery which is running our railroad. So I asked the head-waiter. He said she was Mr. Dimmock's daughter."

"It's a mistake," insisted Sprague. Then he changed the subject abruptly, rising and buttoning his coat. "I have an appointment that I've got to keep, and I may not get away for a couple of hours. Meet me here for a one o'clock luncheon. If I make the point I'm going to try to make, you'll be needed."

When he was left alone, Maxwell did his best to kill time easily and to possess his soul in patience. The inaction of the past two days had been a keen agony, unrelieved by any glimpse into the mysterious depths in which Sprague, after his usual fashion, was groping alone.

Was it possible that Sprague could reason out a way of escape for the captured Short Line? For the hundredth time Maxwell went over the well-intrenched position of the enemy, searching vainly for the weak point in the lines which had been so swiftly and surely drawn about the confiscated property. Every legal requirement had been astutely met, and the law itself seemed to bar the way to any attempt at recovery. True, Judge Watson had grossly misused the authority given him by his high office, but the equity of his act could be questioned only in the courts; questioned, and set aside, it might be, but too late to save the bewildered and panic-stricken stockholders.

Lighting the dry cigar, Maxwell got up to stroll to the clerk's desk. The register lay open on the counter, and he absently read the later signatures. Among them there was a woman's name, written in a firm, bold hand, and lacking the identifying "Miss" or "Mrs." "Diana Carswell" was the name, and in the place-column was written, "New York."

Maxwell's teeth met in the centre of the newly lighted cigar when he saw the signature. He did not know Miss Carswell, truly, but all the world knew of her, and the masculine half of it, at least, was wont to wax eloquent over her beauty, her accomplishments, and her vast wealth. Maxwell remembered vaguely of hearing that her father was dead, and that the Carswell many-millions had been left to the mother and daughter; also that Miss Carswell was the niece of a still larger fortune—namely, that of the great captain of finance whom he and Ford had all along credited with the planning of the raids made on the Nevada Short Line.

Here was food for reflection, plenty of it. What was Miss Diana Carswell doing in Brewster, which was as far apart from her world as if it had been the smallest village on an alien planet? Curiously Maxwell scanned the register for other names which might answer the query. There were none. Miss Carswell was alone, or at least she was not accompanied by any other New Yorkers. It was another mystery, and the ex-superintendent was growing sensitive in his mystery nerve. Possibly Sprague—

Sprague came in a few minutes before one o'clock, and there was a grim set to his big jaw that Maxwell had seen there more than once on the foot-ball field when the game was desperate.

"We'll eat first," was the incomer's crisp dictum. "Shall we go in now?"

Together they went to the café, taking their accustomed table in the far corner of the many-pillared room. At the serving of the bouillon, Maxwell broke out.

"Up to a certain point, Calvin, I can blunder along in the dark with my eyes shut, and do it more or less cheerfully. But past that point—"

"I know; it has been rather hard on you, Dick. But the suspense is nearly over. At two o'clock we are due in Judge Walsh's chambers in the Federal Building, and you will then learn all you need to know—and possibly a good bit more. You'll have to forgive me for fogging you up as I went along. I guess that is part of the detective slant in me; to want to go my own way, and to go it alone. The minute I begin to talk over the reasoning process with somebody else I begin to lose the keen sense of values. Writer people have told me that the same thing is true of plotting and novelling."

Maxwell smiled grimly. "Speaking of novel plots, I hit upon the start for a good one this forenoon—just after you went away. I was glancing over the hotel register and I saw a name there that was full of all sorts of mysteries and plotting suggestions."

"Whose name?" queried the expert.

"I'm going to devil you for a while now, and let you find out for yourself," laughed the railroad man. "I don't know the owner of the name, and

I don't suppose you do; but I'll bet a piebald pinto worth fifty dollars that, when you see what I saw, you'll sit up and take notice and do a little stunt of wondering that will make mine look like a cheap imitation."

The big man grinned good-naturedly.

"Rub it in," he said. "I don't wonder that you are getting a bit collar-sore. But don't forget to eat. Two o'clock is the time, you know. And, by the way, I hope you haven't failed to keep in touch with the various members of your staff—the men whom Dimmock was in such an indecent hurry to discharge. We may need their help a little later."

Maxwell told circumstantially what had been done, and from that the table-talk slipped easily into a discussion of human loyalty in the abstract, and so continued until the waiter brought the cigars. Sprague was looking at his watch as they made their way among the well-filled tables toward the door, and it was in the midst of a sentence pointing to the need for haste to keep the two o'clock appointment that he found Maxwell halting him.

Now it may say itself that a man may be a very Solon among reason-ers and a modern Vidocq in the fine art of unravelling mysteries, without in the least approaching the type which is so aptly described by the slang phrase, "Johnnie-on-the-spot." When Sprague dropped his watch back into its pocket he found himself halted beside a table at which were seated the cold-featured, accurately groomed chief raider of the captured railroad, and a young woman whose radiant beauty was bedazzling more eyes than those of the interested on-lookers at the surrounding tables.

Sprague looked, lost himself, and then came slowly back to earth in the realization that Dimmock was speaking.

"Excuse me, Mr. Maxwell," he was saying: "I wanted you to meet my daughter. Diana, this is Mr. Richard Maxwell, whose wife is one of the Fairbairn girls, you know, and Mr. Maxwell's friend, Mr. Sprague, of the Department of Agriculture."

It was the young woman herself who broke in.

"Oh, yes; Mr. Sprague and I have met before; haven't we, Mr. Sprague?" with a mocking smile for Sprague's benefit. And then: "We've been miss-ing you at Topaz Tepees. Have you been finding it too far to ride?"

What the athletic chemistry expert managed to stammer out in reply, what he went on saying to Miss Carswell during the fraction of a minute or so that Dimmock was holding Maxwell in talk, he could not remember a single second after the swinging together of the glass doors which shut them out of the dining-room. That was because the astounding discovery was still crippling him to blot out all the intermediate details.

But one large fact stood clear in the confusing medley. Clutching Max-well's arm he shoved him headlong into the near-by writing-room, which was opportunely deserted.

"Richard, I'm out of it!" he gasped hoarsely. "Dimmock knew what card to play, and he has played it. My Lord! Why didn't I guess that the Mrs. Carswell he married four years ago was Diana's mother? I didn't guess it; it never entered my mind! I knew Diana was a niece of the chief wrecker—the man we've been after all summer; I found that out last week, and that was why I told you I couldn't stay with you. And now: oh, dammit, dammit, *dammit*!"

"Take it easy, old man," said Maxwell soothingly; "and remember that as yet I'm only groping around the edges. What is it that Dimmock has done to you?"

"Heavens and earth! Don't you see? For Diana's sake I've monkeyed and schemed and side-stepped on this receivership business until I've got it in shape to pull you out without pulling her uncle in. But to do that, I've put Dimmock, her step-father, so deep in the hole that a yoke of oxen couldn't haul him out! He knows it, too; and that was the reason for that bit of by-play just now at the luncheon-table. He was saying to me in just so many words, 'Now you know who you're hitting; go ahead, if you dare!'"

"And, naturally, since Miss Carswell is the one altogether lovely, you don't dare. I can't blame you, Calvin. Drop it, and we'll do the best we can without you."

Sprague was walking the floor of the little writing-room with his big hands jammed deep in the pockets of his short business coat. Suddenly he stopped and smacked a huge fist into a hollowed palm.

"By George, Dick, we'll do it yet!" he broke out. "I'll beat him at his own game—come on!" And again seizing the railroad man's arm, he dragged him out of the hotel and almost flung him into the nearest waiting taxicab.

The order to the cab-driver ran to the Brewster National Bank; and two minutes later Sprague, with Maxwell at his heels, shouldered his way through a group of waiting customers to the president's room. Gray old David Kinzie was at his desk, and he nodded toward a door in the opposite wall of the business office leading to the isolated directors' room. "Stillings and Hunniwell are in there," he said, "and Starbuck has gone after the culprit."

"And the other man?" queried Sprague sharply.

"He didn't want to come, but he will. He thinks it is a conference to discuss the bank's attitude, and he doesn't want to commit himself. I convinced him that he'd better come."

Again Sprague led the way, pausing at the inner door, however, to push Maxwell in ahead of him. The two lawyers were sitting opposite each other at the far end of the long committee table which filled the centre of the room; and their greetings to the new-comers were wordless. Maxwell had scarcely taken the chair next to Stillings when the door opened again, this time to admit a stoop-shouldered, thin-haired man whose face was even grayer than Banker Kinzie's. This last arrival was Judge Watson, and when he saw Sprague and Maxwell he would have withdrawn, only Starbuck was behind him to make it impossible.

As before, the greetings were merely nodded; and a silence that could be felt settled down upon the room. It was the judge who broke it first.

"I think I have made a mistake, gentlemen," he began. "I was expecting to meet Mr.—ah—er—a gentleman who is not here."

The words were hardly out of his mouth before the door was opened for the third time, and Dimmock, closely followed by Kinzie, entered. Like the judge, the receiver would have withdrawn when he saw the group around the table; but again Starbuck intervened, this time to shut the door and to stand with his back against it.

At the click of the latch, Sprague rose ponderously in his place at the head of the table.

"Sit down, Mr. Dimmock," he directed. "This is a little business meeting preliminary to another and more important one, and our time is exceedingly limited."

The receiver looked sharply at the speaker. "My time is much more limited than yours, Mr. Sprague," he retorted crisply. "I shall have to ask you to excuse me."

"Certainly," said Sprague suavely, "if you wish it. But in that case, I must tell you that Mr. Starbuck, who is standing just behind you, has been properly sworn in as a United States deputy marshal, and he will promptly take you into custody on a charge of conspiracy."

If the chemistry expert had suddenly rolled a bomb, with the fuse lighted, down the length of the long table, the sensation could scarcely have been greater or more startling. Dimmock took a backward step and put up his hands as if to ward off a blow; and Hunniwell, the imported attorney, sprang to his feet as if his chair had been suddenly electrified.

"What's this?" he stormed. "This is not a court of law! I demand that that door be opened! We cannot be held in duress!"

"Sit down!" said Sprague shortly. "Mr. Dimmock is your client, and you are here, not to defend him, but to advise him. As to the duress you're so much afraid of, I'll say this: I am going to make one short statement of facts. After you have heard it, if you and your client wish to withdraw, the door will be opened."

"I—I am ill," said the judge weakly, and he made a motion to rise from his chair. Kinzie grimly poured out a glass of water from the pitcher on the table and gave it to him without comment, while Dimmock took the chair Starbuck was offering him and sat down.

"I'll be very brief, gentlemen," Sprague went on, taking out his watch and laying it on the table. "The facts are these. There has been a conspiracy entered into for the purpose of depriving the stockholders of the railroad known as the Nevada Short Line of their property under a form of law. That purpose has apparently succeeded, but I have here"—taking a packet of papers from his pocket—"documentary evidence inculpating various and sundry persons who figure as the conspirators. Three of these persons are here in this room. In another room, namely, in Judge Walsh's chambers in the Federal Building, there is waiting another and quite informal gathering: it is composed of the leading members of the Bar Association of the Timanyoni District, and it is presided over by Judge Walsh. It is assembled to prevent, if possible, one of the greatest scandals that has ever threatened the fair name of the courts of this State."

"I object!" shouted Hunniwell, struggling to his feet again; and this time Sprague pushed him back into his chair without ceremony.

"To this statement of fact," the self-appointed chairman continued, quite as if there had been no interruption, "we will add a demand and impose an alternative. The demand is that the railroad be turned over to its rightful owners at once. If it is not complied with, you, Judge Watson, and you, Mr. Dimmock, and you, Mr. Hunniwell"—indicating each in turn with a squarely pointed forefinger—"may choose your alternative: which is to go with me to Judge Walsh's chambers, where I shall lay before the gentlemen there assembled this packet of evidence."

"It's a bluff!" yelled the attorney for the defence. "Do you think we're going to be taken in by any such flim-flam as that? We'll call your bluff, you damned amateur! You don't dare to show up that evidence here!"

Sprague looked down with a good-natured grin upon the red-headed lawyer. Then he dropped the packet of papers on the table in front of Hunniwell.

"I'll stay with you," he said quietly. "Read for yourself. Those are only copies, however. The originals are locked up in Judge Walsh's safe."

Hunniwell ran through the papers hurriedly and the color came and went in his florid face. Dimmock was staring straight ahead of him at nothing, and his shapely fingers were beating a nervous tattoo on the arm of his chair. The judge had sunk into a shapeless heap in the easy chair he had chosen and his face was ashen.

At the end of his hasty examination of the papers, Hunniwell looked up, and Stillings, who sat opposite, saw defeat in his eyes.

"If I could speak to Mr. Dimmock and Judge Watson in private—" he suggested; and Sprague nodded. There was a small ante-room at the right of the larger directors' room, and the three withdrew, the attorney lending the judge a much-needed arm.

Almost immediately the conferees returned, and Hunniwell acted as spokesman.

"You've turned the trick, Mr. Sprague, for this one time," he said briefly, "but only because one man—a sick man—cannot stand the pressure—which is doubtless what you figured on. Judge Watson will rescind his order at once, and the road will be turned over to its former management—on one condition; that you surrender the original papers which you say are locked up in Judge Walsh's safe."

"No," said Sprague instantly. "The condition does not stand. Stillings, get Judge Walsh on the 'phone, will you?"

That was enough. Hunniwell quickly withdrew the condition; or, rather, he modified it, lawyer-wise.

"Never mind," he cut in hastily. "We'll waive that, with this proviso—that you'll put the papers into Mr. Kinzie's hands, to be destroyed in the presence of such witnesses as we each may choose, after we shall have proved that we have acted in good faith. Do you agree to that?"

Sprague nodded, and Starbuck stepped aside and opened the door leading out through the banker's office. At the upper end of the table, Maxwell and Stillings and the gray-faced bank president were all trying to shake hands with Sprague at one and the same moment; and when Hunniwell had led the tremulous judge away, Dimmock walked the length of the table and took his turn. Stillings, being Western-bred, anticipated violence; but instead of falling upon the big-bodied ex-athlete, Dimmock, too, held out his hand.

"Mr. Sprague, you've outgeneraled us," he said, with more frankness than his hard-lined face and austere manner promised, even as a possibility. "Diana tells me that you are wedded to your Government position, and if that is so, you are simply throwing yourself away. Come to New York, and we'll put you in the way of doing something worth while." Then he added, with the charming smile he seemed to be able to summon at will: "You played a finer game than I thought you would; in fact, I thought I had trumped your ace today at the luncheon-table."

"You did—mighty nearly," laughed the big one. And then to Stillings: "Robert, will you go over to Judge Walsh's chambers and tell the gentlemen who are waiting there—well, tell them what is necessary. You'll know how."

But Dimmock was not to be so easily turned aside.

"I say you played it fine," he repeated, still amiable. "You knew that, under the circumstances, the—er—sentimental circumstances, we may call them—you couldn't afford to go before that larger committee with your evidence, Mr. Sprague."

Sprague's mellow laugh rang in the empty room.

"Just now I am the prisoner at the bar, Mr. Dimmock, and I'm not obliged to incriminate myself," he retorted jokingly. And at that the three who remained went out through the banker's office together. On the sidewalk Dimmock paused for one other word; the word which had been at the bottom of his friendly approach to Sprague.

"Diana knows nothing of this?" he said.

"Nothing more than you have told her," said Sprague.

"And that is less than nothing," was the prompt return. After which they separated, Dimmock going up the street toward Hunniwell's hotel, Maxwell hurrying off to the telegraph office to wire the good news to Ford, and Sprague sauntering slowly back to the Hotel Topaz, wondering if, by any hook or crook of good fortune, he should be lucky enough to find Miss Diana Carswell disengaged and willing to accord him an hour or so of an afternoon which was still young.

It was in the evening of the same day, after Maxwell had been reinstalled in his office by order of the court, and the summarily discharged staff had been reinstated, that the superintendent turned upon Sprague, who was sitting, as his evening custom was, in the easiest of the office chairs, puffing at a black cigar, and with his gaze fixed upon the disused gas chandelier marking the exact centre of the ceiling.

"How did you do it, Calvin?" came the abrupt demand from Maxwell's corner. "Did you really have any evidence against Miss Diana's step-father and her uncle?"

The big-bodied man from Washington chuckled softly.

"Oh, yes; I had the evidence. There was a hitch between Watson and Dimmock, and they were both of them injudicious enough to send notes back and forth; notes which, by the help of two good friends of yours and mine, were intercepted, carefully copied, the originals preserved, and the copies forwarded. It was a little off-color, but when you are fighting the devil you can't always stop to pick your weapons. Watson was to have a Federal judgeship, and Big Money was to see that he got it. The hitch came in reference to Watson's leaving town. He was afraid to go; afraid of public sentiment; and Dimmock was holding him on the rack. I don't know whether the evidence of the letters would have held in an ordinary court, but I do know that I had Judge Walsh on my side."

Maxwell whirled around in his chair.

"Sprague, did those letters incriminate Dimmock and Miss Diana's uncle?"

"Oh, don't let's say 'incriminate'; let's use the milder word, 'inculpate'. Yes, I guess they did, Dick."

"Now I've got you!" snapped the square-shouldered one at the desk. "You would never—never in this wide world—have let that evidence get out. You know you wouldn't!"

The big man was grinning affably. "You're only half right," he rejoined. "Up to luncheon-time today I meant to do it; I had it framed up so that the uncle, who is really the high spellbinder of the entire push, could slip out and the whole load would come down on Mr. Dimmock's shoulders. But that luncheon play queered me, and I had to think quick to invent a new way out. It worked, and that's all there is to it; all but one little item—Miss Diana let me drive her out to Lake Topaz this afternoon, and I stole your car to do it."

"No; there is one other little item," said Maxwell, rising and closing his desk upon the evening's work. "I wired Ford, as you know, and I gave you the credit that belonged to you—which you may not know. Our New York crowd is properly grateful, and they promptly wired Kinzie. I don't know how you're fixed, Calvin, but I guess this won't come amiss if you're going to try to marry Diana Carswell," and he handed Sprague a slip of paper which bore Banker Kinzie's promise to pay ten thousand dollars to the order of one Calvin Sprague.

Sprague took the draft, glanced at the figure of it, and handed it back with another of his deep-chested laughs.

"Where on top of earth did you get the idea that I needed money, Dick?" he asked. "Why, Lord love you! Didn't you know that my California uncle, Uncle William, died five years ago and left me more money than I know what to do with? It's the solemn fact, and I'm working on the Government job purely and simply because I don't know how to loaf comfortably—never did. Of course, I can't quite match up with the Carswell millions; but if that were the only thing in the way—"

"What is the other thing?" demanded Maxwell, in mock solicitude.

Sprague had risen and was stretching his arms over his head and yawning sleepily.

"If you'd see me step on the scales, you wouldn't ask. I'm such a whale of a man, Dick! And, say: did you notice her at table today? 'Pretty,' you'd say, but that isn't the word; it's 'dainty', dainty in every look and move and touch. Imagine a girl like that saying, 'Yes, honey,' to a great big overgrown stale foot-ball artist like me! Let's go over to the house and smoke a bedtime. Nobody loves me, and I'm going out in the garden to eat—"

"That is what makes you so frightfully fat—you eat too many of the fuzzy kind," laughed the snappy little superintendent unsympathetically. And then he flicked the switch of the office lights and they went out together into the calm September night.

www.ingramcontent.com/pod-product-compliance
Lightning Source LLC
Chambersburg PA
CBHW011445170626
46816CB00008B/2521